NEW YORK REVIEW BOOKS
CLASSICS

THE JUDGES OF THE SECRET COURT

DAVID STACTON (1923–1968) was born Lionel Kingsley Evans in San Francisco. He attended Stanford University before serving in the Civilian Public Service as a conscientious objector during World War II, eventually graduating from the University of California at Berkeley in 1951. Stacton went to Europe after college and ended up staying, in his words, "because I liked it and because I could not get my books in print in America." His first novel, *Dolores*, was published in England in 1954. Among the wide-ranging historical and biographical novels for which he would become best known are *On a Balcony*, about Nefertiti and Pharaoh Akhenaten; *Segaki*, set in feudal Japan; *A Signal Victory*, about the Spanish conquest of the Yucatán; *Old Acquaintance*, set at a film festival and telling of the loves of a star resembling Marlene Dietrich; and *People of the Book*, set during the Thirty Years' War. Under various pseudonyms, Stacton also published Westerns, mass-market murder mysteries, and a soft-core gay novel. Twice the recipient of a Guggenheim Fellowship, he also received a Literature Fellowship from the National Endowment for the Arts. In 1968 he moved to Fredensborg, Denmark, to work on a book to be called *Restless Sleep*, about Charles II and the diarist Samuel Pepys; ten days later he was found dead in his new home; he was forty-four years old.

JOHN CROWLEY is the author of a dozen novels and works of fiction, among them *Little, Big*, the Ægypt Cycle, and, most recently, *Four Freedoms*. He is a three-time winner of the World Fantasy Award and a winner of the Award in Literature of the American Academy and Institute of Arts and Letters. Crowley teaches creative writing at Yale University. His reviews and critical essays have appeared in the *Boston Review*, *The Yale Review*, and *The Washington Post*.

THE JUDGES OF THE SECRET COURT

DAVID STACTON

Introduction by
JOHN CROWLEY

NEW YORK REVIEW BOOKS

New York

THIS IS A NEW YORK REVIEW BOOK
PUBLISHED BY THE NEW YORK REVIEW OF BOOKS
435 Hudson Street, New York, NY 10014
www.nyrb.com

Library of Congress Cataloging-in-Publication Data
Stacton, David, 1925–1968.
 The judges of the secret court : a novel about John Wilkes Booth / by David
Stacton ; introduction by John Crowley.
    p. cm. — (New York Review Books classics)
ISBN 978-1-59017-452-4 (alk. paper)
1. Booth, John Wilkes, 1838–1865—Fiction. I. Title.
PS3537.T1178J83 2011
813'.54—dc22

                        2011009961

ISBN 978-1-59017-452-4

Printed in the United States of America on acid-free paper.
10 9 8 7 6 5 4 3 2 1

Introduction

David Stacton's Evidences

The Judges of the Secret Court tells the story of the assassination of Abraham Lincoln by John Wilkes Booth; the subsequent flight, capture, and death of Booth; the roundup of anyone connected with him and his plot by the secretary of war Edwin Stanton; and the prosecution and hanging of a number of these as conspirators.

The book begins, however, many years after those events. Edwin Booth, the greatest American actor of his age and John Wilkes's elder brother, in retirement now, has received the manuscript of a five-act tragedy by a Mrs. Henry Lee, a woman he doesn't know. "The heroine, except, no doubt, in the dressing-table mirror of Mrs. Henry Ferguson Lee, could scarcely be said to live at all... He had only been turning the pages. But the title she had given it haunted him. She had called it *The Judges of the Secret Court*."

It *is* a haunting title. Where did Stacton get it? Not from Mrs. Lee or her play, which are apparently imaginary. I find an unfinished opera by Berlioz, *Les francs-juges*, which title the lutenist Howard Posner translates as "the judges of the secret court"—the opera was to deal with medieval German courts whose judges met in secret and never revealed their decisions (though those they condemned to execution were later seen hung up in public places, an object lesson). Was that Stacton's source? The phrase appears in an early poem of his; perhaps the coinage is his own.

It was something all the Booths were aware of, those judges
... If we are too selfless to believe in God, and yet remain

vii

somehow devout, we are very much aware of the Judges of the Secret Court. We cannot see them, nor do we know who they are. But they are there: the whole world is a courtroom, every life is a trial; if we are guilty, we stand there condemned; if we are innocent...we have to prove it. But who can prove it? For in fact no man is innocent at that bar. He is always accessory, willynilly, before or after some fact.

All that happens in the novel proceeds from this awful sentence (*awful*, in the older sense; *sentence*, in both senses). The fairness or justice of the judges is not at issue, they too are guilty and they are to be judged as well as everyone else. It's the author who places his characters, their world, and in a sense himself before that bar, where all their improvisings, their playacting, their loyalties, their belief in their innocence cannot win them reprieve. To know this is the only mitigation; and almost no one in this brief, harrowing novel is willing to face that knowledge, or has the means to grasp it.

In February of 1963, two years after *The Judges of the Secret Court* appeared, *Time* magazine named what its editors* considered to be the best American novelists to appear in the preceding decade. The list included Joseph Heller, John Updike, Philip Roth, Bernard Malamud, Ralph Ellison, along with a couple of less perspicacious guesses (if enduring fame is the measure) like John Knowles (*A Separate Peace*) and H. L. Humes; but the oddest name to find on the list is David Stacton. The author at that time of nine novels under his own name (except that it wasn't) and some crime and Western paperbacks under other names, Stacton had gained a little praise but sold few copies. His inclusion with

---

*Time reviews and articles were at that time unsigned.

other certified luminaries was perhaps the high-water mark of his literary reputation. I don't remember reading that issue of *Time*, but I had been an admirer of Stacton since fortuitously discovering his 1958 novel *On a Balcony*, about the pharaoh Akhenaten and his sister Nefertiti. I knew only one other person in my generally literate set in college who had ever heard of him, and together we read *The Judges of the Secret Court* on its publication with a sense of exclusive privilege.

Stacton's appearance in *Time*'s approved list helped induce G. P. Putnam's Sons to do an American edition of *Sir William*, his novel about the love of Horatio Nelson and Lady Hamilton, which had been published by Faber in London. Romance, glamour, the Regency, and the precedent of a grade-A movie (*That Hamilton Woman* with Laurence Olivier and Vivien Leigh) should have added up to a solid seller, but *Sir William* sold only some five thousand copies in the Putnam hardback. None of Stacton's novels ever did much better.

In a sense—and as we will see perhaps not inappropriately—Stacton's historical novels were passing, or in disguise, not really members of the genre. Historical novels come generally in three kinds: the ones that tell stories of fictitious characters against a general historical background (*Gone with the Wind*, for example); those that follow the adventures of invented characters who become involved with actual historical characters and events; and those that fictionalize real people of the past, or use the techniques of fiction to reveal or exhibit more of their insides. In all of them, richness of period detail is expected; characters are bold in outline, their conflicts vivid; the page count tends to be high. When Stacton's historicals began to appear in the late 1950s the genre was dominated by such best-selling authors as Thomas Costain (*The Black Rose*), Samuel Shellabarger (*Captain from Castile*), and Lawrence Schoonover (*The Burnished Blade*). "Colorful" was the indispensable adjective. Stacton, in a literal sense, is often quite colorless: his is a world of grays and sables and pallid dimness.

Instead of acting, many of his characters only pretend to act; they brood or are brooded on by the author.

Stacton's novel of Akhenaten (he uses the rarer form Ikhnaton) came only a few years after Mika Waltari's *The Egyptian*, a huge international best seller that dealt with the same historical events—the attempt of Akhenaten (Waltari prefers Akhnaton) to establish a new monotheistic religion, and the consequent fall of his dynasty. The two books couldn't be more different (I wonder if Stacton's book might actually have been conceived in opposition to Waltari's big one). Here's Waltari's description of Akhenaten's new temple-city:

> Thus Akhetaton rose from the wilderness in a single year; palm trees waved proudly along its splendid streets, pomegranates ripened and reddened in the gardens, and in the fish pools floated the rosy flowers of the lotus...Tame gazelles wandered in the gardens, while in the streets the lightest of carriages were drawn by fiery horses with ostrich plumes...[W]hen autumn returned and the swallows emerged to dart in restless flocks above the rising waters, Pharaoh Akhnaton consecrated the city and the land to Aton.

And Stacton's:

> Aketaten was really delightful. Even the servants were new ...there was no one to remind him of the past. He had finally found a solution to the awful boredom of rank, or so he thought. One made the rank higher still. He was not the first nor would he be the last monarch to become a god out of ennui. For the gods must have some amusements...He looked at the city with animated eyes. It was simply wonderful to have so much to do.

All of Stacton's historicals are centered on actual personages and stick closely to the known facts of their public lives (their secret souls are for Stacton to unfold, but even there he doesn't contradict the standard sources). *The Judges of the Secret Court* amounts almost to a documentary novel: the events, down to the smallest, are all in the historical accounts, and Stacton hardly adds to them. He examines them, surrounds them in thought, tries to break into them in imagination. The plot is simply what happened, and Stacton accepts the constraints: he takes the almost perverse chance that readers will go along with him even though the central figure of the book, John Wilkes Booth, dies with a third of the pages remaining.

The assassination and death of Lincoln are narrated with a gripping cold attentiveness, from several points of view, amalgamated as though a prosecutor was assembling evidence, yet with an odd noticing of inconsequential detail. A certain Dr. Leale manages to get into the president's box:

> Leale sent for a lamp, got the body on the floor, and while men stood in a circle around him striking innumerable matches, he searched, by that dim flicker, for the wound... In a few minutes the floor was littered with charred sticks. The sound of scratching, as new ones were lit, was the sound of a nail drawn down a blackboard...The eye glistened in the light, but it was out of focus and the evidence of brain injury was plain enough. The matches smelled abominably of sulfur.

Soldiers try to clear the box of spectators. The dead matches "crunched under their boot heels as they moved about." It may be that, like the other details Stacton relates, those eerie metonymic matches are in the record somewhere, but if so I haven't found them.

Though Booth is its vagrant center, the novel moves among

a half dozen major and several minor characters, seeing events from within their variously limited points of view. This is the "distributed third-person-limited" narration that is, effectively, the default mode of contemporary popular fiction: a few pages of X, switch to Y's point of view, then to Z's, and back to X's. Yet Stacton's deployment of it is quite different from the workaday writer's "show, don't tell." Always, on every page, a ruling consciousness is analyzing, weighing, telling truths, naming virtues and (more often) shortcomings. About the tragically ineffectual Mrs. Surratt when we first meet her:

> In the mirror she saw the face of a woman of forty-five, which was not fair, for she was not forty-five. The body may grow older, but alas, we do not. So we have to corset ourselves in. We have to be staid. We have to remember to control what was once charmingly instinctive, and the ageing body does something to our habitual gestures, it twists and confines them, so that we cannot make them with the same grace any more.

It could be that it is Mrs. Surratt who is pondering in this way, though it would seem beyond her. It is more likely the narration itself thinking, brooding over her case. When that narration considers Booth, its task is more complex; it acts like a recording angel—like a judge—installed in his heart. Without comment the angel records Booth's opinion of Lincoln: "And though the niggers may have followed that tall, shambling, plug-hatted nemesis, no one else had but his own troops." It records Booth's feelings on that assassination Good Friday:

> So far the day had not pleased him. His boots squeaked, and that was annoying. It is impossible to get the squeak out of a pair of boots once it has gotten in, and these were new and expensive ones. He was conscious of himself all over in that

way, down to the last handkerchief or disconcertingly renascent pimple.

But then the same analyzing voice shifts a distance away:

> That was because he was an actor. He had no repose. He did
> not exist, unless he kept moving, and the nature of his own
> existence was something he had never been able to face, even
> in sleep.

Then it passes judgment:

> People like that can be dangerous, for though they are bad at
> planning, who can tell what they are apt to do on the spur of
> the moment? They do not know themselves. They are dan-
> dies. For them life is immediate. They have no time for
> thought. And yet they think they think.

Throughout the novel, and in others of Stacton's, this is the
movement: from the interior of a consciousness to an exterior
judgment, cast in what is termed the *gnomic present*: "Everyone is
ambivalent about his profession, if he has practiced it long enough."
"An actor is limited. He has no right to make the world his stage,
for then he reminds us of what we do not want to know, that we
are merely players." "When a corrupt man becomes incorrupt,
that merely means that he uses the forces of corruption for incorrupt ends. Unlike a man born good, he is hard to dislodge." *Time*
in its 1963 article described Stacton's work as "masses of epigrams
marinated in a stinging mixture of metaphysics and blood." But
unlike true epigrams, these judgments arise in connection with a
certain person, a specific soul (Vice President Johnson is the corrupt man become incorrupt, though "as yet nobody had had the
chance to find that out"). They reach from particularity to generality, a generality that is sometimes withdrawn or brought down

to earth again or even contradicted, as though a fluid situation is changing before the author's gaze.

Many of these authorial judgments are cast in terms of acting, actors, and the stage. The entire novel is concerned with performance—acting a part, changing parts, not being who you seem to be. The Booth family is central to it (John Wilkes's brothers Edwin and Junius Brutus, his sister, and her husband are all suspected in the assassination plot and only reluctantly exonerated). To picture a fictional John Wilkes Booth as acting a part—Southern hero, Byronic avenger—would be a natural tack to take; what's more interesting is how everyone in the story is seen as acting a part. The narration is at once observing the performances and looking out through the performers' eyes at the intended audience—which is sometimes only the performer himself, or herself, the audience that needs to be convinced, from whom the real self must be hidden. The failed conspirator Atzerodt—whom the narration has already labeled a "miserable troll"—has funked, pawned his unused revolvers, and is on a five-day drunken spree, going by the name of Atwood. "That was the name he always took on his drinking expeditions, when he impersonated a normal man." The climactic moment of Booth's role-playing, a moment at once appalling and horribly comic, is his last:

> An officer bent over Booth. Booth could see him plainly. He could also see Mary Ann [Booth, his mother]. "Tell my mother I died for my country," he whispered.
>
> "Is that what you say?" asked Conger [the officer]. He was aware of himself, was Conger, kneeling there. He felt sorry for the poor fool.
>
> "Yes," said Booth. It was only play acting, after all.

The officer is capable of a moment of self-perception, but Booth, even after dreadful suffering and the approach of death, can only exist in the terms of popular melodrama.

One figure—he is at once more and less than a character—is impersonating no one: Abraham Lincoln. "As he lay dying, under the dry shimmering jet of the gasolier, the tact drained out of [his face], and one could see, what usually that tact concealed, the awful marks of knowledge." In physical and moral stature Lincoln bestrides the narrow earth like a colossus, as Caesar is said to do in the Booths' warhorse play; fallen, borne on his funeral train, he is like a great dead god, in whose passing all moral reality is evacuated from the world. There are judgments and judges galore in this book, but only one man fitted for the work: "About Lincoln there was always the reserve of a kindly judge who, kind or not, still sits up there, fingering the dossiers of both sides of the case, whether he admits to doing so or not."

A kindly judge, who, whether kind or not, will know both sides, whom we could hope would judge with charity for all and malice toward none. With him gone, the open court becomes a secret one, driven by the only other character in the book who is not pretending, though he lies often: the secretary of war, Edwin Stanton. Both literally and figuratively a midget compared to Lincoln, the paranoid bully Stanton instantly assumes a huge conspiracy and has the power—martial law is still in force—to arrest, incarcerate, and try in a military court anyone he likes. The great disaster that has suddenly come upon the nation is at once his duty to meet with overwhelming force and an opportunity he won't let slip. He considers legal restraints cowardly. He hated Lincoln. He holds Johnson in contempt. Whatever his actual official status, he is in charge.

It's irrelevant to a proper understanding of a novel written in 1961, and yet it's inescapable that we in 2011 will respond to Stanton and his role in the story in the light of recent events. The ruthless search for hidden enemies; the men and one woman gathered into Stanton's net, kept hooded and shackled in their cells in what we might call "stress positions"; a rapidly assembled military court set up to try them, some guilty to a degree, some not, but all of them—given the national mood and Stanton's ceaseless drive for vengeance and power—without a hope of understanding or effective defense; and in the end the country altered forever. "The Civil War had made it an Imperium." Is it possible for fictions to become retrospectively allegorical?

Even if you are generally well read in American fiction of the last century, it is very likely that this is the first book of Stacton's you have opened; you may well never have heard of him. Even as *Time* included him in its list, the article noted that he was "as nearly unknown as it is possible for a writer to be who has written, and received critical praise for, thirteen novels."

He is "a Nevadan who wears cowboy boots, is fond of both Zen and bourbon," the article said—but he was not a Nevadan, and his outfit was not exactly a working cowboy's. (The only photograph I remember seeing of him when I was first reading his books was taken in London, and shows a handsome young man in all-white cowboy rig, sitting in a chair turned around Western-style, with a rugged smile and teasing eyes: I suddenly understood something about him, and perhaps about the books I'd read.)

Stacton's self-description for *Contemporary Authors* does say he was born in Minden, Nevada, to a couple he names Dorothy and David Stacton, but in fact he was born Lionel Kingsley Evans, or possibly Arthur Lionel Kingsley Evans, or later Lyonel, on May 27, 1923, in San Francisco, where he went to high school and, until World War II intervened, to Stanford.* In the war he was a conscientious objector, though on just what grounds I don't know. In 1942 he began using the invented name "David Stacton"—he told a friend that a writer ought to have a two-syllable name with a staccato rhythm. It wasn't a pen name—he changed his name le-

---

*I first learned what I know of Stacton's life, his career, and the reception his books received from Robert Nedelkoff, an independent researcher and Stacton devotee.

gally. His first book (after a slim volume of verse) was a biography of an eccentric Victorian traveler; his first novel, *Dolores*, was published in London in 1954—British publishers regarded him as a more salable commodity than the Americans. His characteristic historical novels begin with *Remember Me*, a novel about Ludwig II of Bavaria, like Akhenaten a still being within an elaborate self-made prison-palace. The range of his others is remarkable: sixteenth-century Japan (*Segaki*, 1958); Renaissance Rome (*A Dancer in Darkness*, based on the same lurid story as John Webster's play *The Duchess of Malfi*, and similarly nightmarish); the career of Wendell Willkie, of all people (*Tom Fool*, 1962); the Thirty Years' War (*People of the Book*, 1965, his last published novel). Despite slight sales, he did attract a small but devoted readership—in Italy he was introduced to the critic and aesthete Mario Praz (*The Romantic Agony*), who was thrilled by his novels; he compared Stacton to Walter Pater, a high compliment in some circles, but wondered why Stacton, so tall and handsome, needed to play a role with his cowboy boots and ten-gallon hat.

A man, then, who knew something about performance and pretending, but who had either little taste or little ability for the standard ways American novelists have of making the money needed to keep writing. The poet and translator David Slavitt, in the most substantial critical study of Stacton's work I know of,* repeats the Minden, Nevada, story and retails a piquant anecdote about Stacton's arriving by plane to be a visiting professor at Washington and Lee University, in complete though apparently not entirely convincing drag, and departing (prematurely and after a row, it seems, which Slavitt doesn't report) in his white cowboy suit, with chaps and eye shadow. Between coming and going, he seems to have worn standard preppy attire for this his only such appointment. Instead he eked out his income with pulp fiction, written under pseudonyms. Though books like *Muscle Boy*, as

---

*"David Stacton," *Hollins Critic* (December, 2002).

Slavitt notes, "have had an odd *Nachtleben* among Queer Read fans and collectors of kitsch," he finds it sad that Stacton, "a writer of signal refinement," had to "grind out" such stuff.

I wonder if this isn't somewhat backward. Stacton wrote his potboilers and the books that he wished to be remembered by not only at the same time but with the same hand, and his literary novels exhibit methods and techniques that he, and many other pulp writers, commonly used.

Let Him Go Hang, by "Bud Clifton," was published in 1961, the same year as *The Judges of the Secret Court*. Like the last third of *Judges* it's a courtroom drama; like *Judges* it uses an omniscient narration that visits in turn many consciousnesses both major and minor in the story. And like *Judges* it is about the cruelty of justice in the hands of power. Here the jury is being seated; Jan, one of the panel, is called:

> She swore. The others swore. Then they sat down. The judge told the clerk to call a jury of fourteen. Since there were thirty-six on the panel, that meant that twenty-two would have to go home without seeing justice done, or satisfying their curiosity, or whatever they were there for. Jan almost wished she was one of the ones who could go home. This was too much like a game, and a vicious one at that.
>
> But hers was the first name called.

Compare a moment in the courtroom in *Judges*. Spangler, the man Booth asked to hold his horse while he was in Ford's Theatre, is listening to the testimony against him:

> He began to see how easily a man could be hanged for trying to help a friend. He didn't see that it was his fault. You don't usually ask a friend if he's done anything criminal, before you help him.
>
> Now they were talking about whether he wore a mous-

tache. He didn't bother to listen. He'd never worn a moustache in his life.

That was what would save his life.

Robert Nedelkoff has calculated (using the timelines that Stacton, in James Joyce fashion, appended to his literary novels) that
most of Stacton's books were written quickly—some in three
months, none in more than nine. That's pulp-fiction speed. Of
those that I have read, most are uncomplicated as narratives: they
move steadily forward in time order, as though the writer himself
also moved forward page by page without looking back. This is
not solely the method of the paperback writer—the esteemed
Spanish novelist Javier Marías makes a point of never looking
back, never altering what he first laid down—but it seems to connect these two threads of Stacton's work.

Likewise the cold-eyed epigram, the summary judgment, the
revealing aside to the reader, that in pulp novels make for rapid
storytelling. "She was a tough nut to crack, chiefly because there
wasn't much inside her," writes Bud Clifton. The reader turning
the pages of a Western or crime novel can be expected not to take
notice of these common tricks, but Stacton refines them in his
other novels into a highly individual and supple method impossible *not* to notice. In *Judges* the aphorisms eventually come to seem
just as much a part of the material and sensory fabric of the story,
just as *physical*, as the crush of spent matches underfoot, or the
smell of violet pomade in Edwin Stanton's beard, or the bells rung
for Lincoln, "solemn, insistent, and unnecessary." Because the
story shaped by them is a true one, they have a different role than
in the crime fiction. Are they just? Are they *so*, in the light of these
actual events? They make us restive; we shy away from the bleakest
ones. Reflective, contingent, hidden from the characters themselves, it is these summations, not Stanton's certainties or the
thoughts of Lincoln or even the perspectives of history, that are
the judgments of the secret court.

At most they could hope for mercy or reprieve. But of what use was mercy? What use was reprieve? The soul has no reprieve. The best one can hope for there is an extended sentence.

David Stacton died at the age of forty-four, in a small town in Denmark. The Danish medical examiner first named the cause as a heart attack, then later as "unknown." If Stacton ever gains or regains the stature as a writer I think he deserves, his brief life in all its disguises and ambiguities will be a biographer's torment and delight. His oeuvre, unlike his foreshortened life, is necessarily complete: as with Mozart's or Keats's, the work can be seen to have a shape, a progress, a youth, and a maturity that the creator himself doesn't. Not until Stacton's work is easily available as a whole can that shape be discerned, the influences on it sorted out, and Stacton given a place in the American canon. It could be guessed now that that place will be as outlier, his books seen as an intersection of certain modes of popular fiction with a unique sensibility, appearing from the first fully formed and unchanging over time. (Compare, say, Thomas Love Peacock, or—Slavitt's hint—Ronald Firbank.) Perhaps—as undoubtedly queer (in the original sense) as they are—their fanship will always be narrow, though intense. But that judgment is not for us to make; the court of literary fame and obscurity is secret, and though there is pardon there is no appeal.

—JOHN CROWLEY

THE JUDGES OF THE SECRET COURT

for Philip Bagby,
gentleman, scholar, Virginian,
and the best of good friends
Obit 1958
to remember him

I have been studying how I may compare
This prison where I live unto the world:
And for because the world is populous,
And here is not a creature but myself,
I cannot do it.

Richard II

Prologue

Gramercy Park is the most wistful and the gentlest of the New York squares, and the Players Club is one of the handsomest buildings in it. But the man who once lived in that house had the face of an exalted Punch. Not even he knew quite how he had come to look like that. Yet, since he recognized the resemblance, he spent his life these days not in the present, but the past, trying to define to himself—though never to others, for he had great dignity—that moment when fear had become resignation, and resignation the patience and the will to die. Except for his daughter, Edwina, he wanted no more Booths.

Down the corridor, outside the room of his now dead friend Barrett, with whom he had quarrelled, consoled, and acted for so long, there was an aeolian harp. He refused to have it removed.

At unexpected times, when a gust of wind blew through the top floor corridor, the harp would hum to life. Then he would say: "Listen, Barrett's coming." People would think that remark part of his premature senility. But it wasn't. It wasn't even irony, for though he was a gentle man, he had not the education or the character to take refuge in irony. It was just a fantasy. He was not unduly given to a belief in God; he was willing to accept death as final; but he found it a little warming on a cold day to think that there might be someone waiting for him, and Barrett, at least, had always been fond of him, despite their quarrels.

For everything had been taken away from him. Even more as a man than as an actor, he had been forced to lead too many lives.

Yet despite the watchful sadness of that face, Edwin Booth was an amiable man, the doyen of his profession, respected and well liked. It was not, the world felt, his fault. The world

13

had forgotten all about it. Neither did he feel it was; but he had not forgotten all about it, so there were some things he preferred to remain silent about, some things he could not find a name for, and so could not dismiss.

In 1892 he found a name for them.

That was a year before his death. For several years he had lived at the Players Club, on the top floor. Now his daughter was married, the members of the club were all the family he had. The club itself gave him somewhere to go. That was one reason why he had founded it.

He was only fifty-eight, but life had left him feeble. He dined downstairs in the club restaurant. Once or twice a year he went to the theatre, as though he were visiting an unfamiliar country. Occasionally, very occasionally, he went for a short stroll about the square, an almost transparent figure, a little hesitant about the next step, but with nothing hesitant about the eyes.

Sometimes, alone, he looked in the mirror and saw nothing but that pair of eyes. Like poor Johnny, who had abused his voice, and so could not use it, he could no longer speak with ease. But he could see.

The Sargent portrait, which by illusion showed him in his prime, hung over the mantelpiece in the common room downstairs. At nine o'clock he sailed upstairs, in the invalid lift they had installed for him, to the top floor. Up there, in the empty room overlooking the park, were the real memorabilia of life as he had had to live it, even more elusive, if anything, than the tactful epitome Mr. Sargent had created downstairs. There was even a portrait of Johnny, tucked away in the alcove beside his bed.

On this particular night he could not sleep, and neither could he settle on anything to read. He found the room overcrowded and oppressive, and even the reassuring presence of someone, at least, in the house, for it could not be called a home, downstairs in the public rooms, did not help, as he had designed it to do.

He did not want to think. He did not even want to look at all these cluttered images of his own past on the walls. So he settled down to the works of Miss Althea Lathrop Lee.

14

It was about midnight. Miss Althea Lathrop Lee (Mrs. Henry Ferguson Lee, as her covering letter explained), who had known his sister Asia in London (not very well, he imagined. Nobody had known Asia well), had sent him a verse drama in five acts.

Goodness only knew why. He was retired and he had no influence. Nor did he enjoy the thought of reading it, for he was a tragedian by profession. He had played all the standard Shakespearian parts and a good many melodramatic ones besides, for bread and butter. Richelieu, for instance, or Sir Giles Overreach in *A New Way to Pay Old Debts*. He knew very well what to make of a verse drama in five acts.

Essentially the play was the story of a beautiful Protestant girl who defied Torquemada. The hero, since it was a tragedy, died in act five. The heroine, except, no doubt, in the dressing table mirror of Mrs. Henry Ferguson Lee, could scarcely be said to live at all.

He had not been concentrating on her unrhymed pish-tush for an hour, he realized. He had only been turning the pages. But the title she had given it haunted him. She had called it *The Judges of the Secret Court*.

Why had he never thought of that before? For that was what had given him that look of a terrified Punch, and now the resignation of a scarecrow worn out and thrown away: he had seen the Judges of the Secret Court.

Yet no one sees them. Rather he had become aware of them.

He had always been aware of them, even before Johnny; even before he had had to give up everything to become the keeper of that untrained bear, his father. It was something all the Booths were aware of, those judges.

They made everything so simple. For if we are too selfless to believe in God, and yet remain somehow devout, we are very much aware of the Judges of the Secret Court. We cannot see them, nor do we know who or what they are. But they are there: the whole world is a courtroom, every life is a trial; if we are guilty, we stand there condemned; if we are innocent, for the *procès* is French, we have to prove it. But who can prove it? for in fact no man is innocent at that bar.

15

He is always accessory, willynilly, before or after some fact.

Nor is the guilt apparent, even afterwards, in our sense, for no sentence is ever passed, no jury sits, no judgment is handed down. It is merely that we plead, we plead, we plead. Because, compared to our factual crimes, the rape of the soul seems to us no more than petty theft, there is no jury to appeal to. There is not even a Supreme Court, to set a precedent by means of any single case it may judge apt to define the law. For there is no law. There are only the judges, cold, remote, and indifferent, though not without a certain pawky humour, who sift papers, peer down at us, yawn with boredom, cannot even hear us, and no doubt reach an exact, impartial decision of which we never learn, but which we suspect seldom if ever agrees with our own or the world's view of the case.

He had spent his whole life in that courtroom, with his family, with his acquaintance, and with himself, which was worst of all. His walls were hung with exhibitions for the prosecution, except that there is no prosecution, just as there is no defence. They were all guilty. They were guilty of being themselves. So they would have been pulled down in any case.

The actual count did not matter, for the debate before that Presidium turns not upon what one does, but what one is. Yet, though no one ever mentioned the matter in his presence, he knew that for convenience, to himself and to the world, if not perhaps to the Secret Judges, the evidence was focused upon that one day, 14th April 1865. And upon Johnny, who would be a gentleman, but was only a Randy Dan.

For even now he could not bear to think of Johnny, portrait by his bed or no.

16

Part One

I

He could see it now: they were a little mad, the Booths, though each in a different way. For like the Sephardic Jews, in the London their father had fled from, and their father was the maddest of the lot, they would be gentry when they were not, and therefore they lived apart, in a world of their own, where the pretence was actual, and made forays into the other world, the unreal one the rest of us live in, only to fetch supplies, going down into the world as the rest of us go to the village, to do their shopping, and perhaps to prove to the tenants that the master was still alive.

It was Junius Brutus the Elder who had begun all that. He was mad as a hatter, but just as lovable, and what in another man would have been called insanity, the children and their mother conspired to call "your father's indisposition".

"Your father is not himself today," Mary Ann would tell them, and for that matter tell the world, except that the world knew it already, and that Mary Ann seldom ventured any farther from home than Baltimore.

They had a great deal to forget, the Booths, but they never forgot their roles, any more than their father did, and for three generations they always played the same parts. Shakespeare was where they belonged; to them those plays were a corridor of mirrors, redecorated by Cibber and Garrick, and for "your father is not himself today", they automatically supplied the two apposite definitions of "Richard is himself again", and "I am myself alone".

And they could all remember their Grandfather Richard, a pretentious drunk, cowered by expatriation and the excesses of his own son, stalking them down. The longer he was dead, the stronger became their one residuary image of him, tall and crapulous, stalking them through the dark house, in the clothes of a gentleman of thirty years ago, musty and foodstained, but for some reason without shoes, his untrimmed toenails clacking against the rough boards of the flooring, so they always knew when he was coming to accuse them in the dark, but had no way to stop him, even after his death, for in their nightmares they could still hear him approach.

He had had such burning eyes. They all had burning eyes.

Even as a child Edwin, and only Edwin, had guessed what they would come to. The knowledge gave him the most haunted eyes of the lot. For, being the sanest, he was the worse concerned with their insanity; the most detached, he could best see what it was that happened on a stage. He had watched his father often enough from the wings to know, even as a child, that the stage is a naked parable. It does not make us, but it shows us, what we are. From *Julius Caesar* and *Richard III*, his father had come soon enough to the madness of *King Lear*. In the repertoire there is a part waiting for everyone, his own part, from which, once he has reached it, he can never escape. He did not want to see those parts discovered. He certainly did not want to see his own.

Yet on the stage or off, they played their parts. His sister Asia was already Cordelia, and always would be. His mother, though she meant well, and he was fond of her, was already as ominous as Queen Margaret in *Richard III*, and as unreal to him. And he had been thrust on the stage, whether he would or no, first through the drunkenness of his father, and then, in the Gold Fields of California, because there was no other trade he knew.

Among them they had had the gall to divide America into three parts. Junius Brutus junior held the Far West, himself the East, and John Wilkes the South. A few months before they had been in the same play, for a benefit. That had filled him with dread. He had already grown into his own role, despite himself, and it was not the inevitable bustle of *Julius Caesar*. It was *Hamlet*, the waiter and the watcher, who can say nothing, but dies because he has learned too much.

He knew nothing about his brothers. These days they were only real to him in a play. Junius did not bother him. Junius took his natural place in *Julius Caesar*. He was no

20

real actor, he was too stolid, but he made an excellent Roman. When the play was over and the Civil Wars were done, he would fit into the New Rome and make an excellent businessman.

Nor did his own role bother him, for it had been assigned to him so early that he was used to it. By his father's whim, he was Hamlet to them all, and so might safely leave the world to Fortinbras. For him the world was unseasonable, and he was accustomed to that. It did not bother him. He was more worried about his daughter Edwina, who was in Philadelphia with his sister Asia.

He was himself in Boston, playing Sir Giles Overreach, an easy part that bored him, another item in the family repertoire, but the public loved it, and thinking about his brother Wilkes. There was something wrong with Wilkes. He was no actor. He was never the parts he played. His best and only performance was himself. Yet he had been good in *Julius Caesar*, obsessively good. Edwin had been disturbed at that. He had wanted to say: It is only a play, and the world is not a mirror, but an audience. Unlike a mirror, it never gives you back the echo vanity you search for, for an audience does not reflect the image you see in it. It may seem to, but there are a thousand faces behind the image the audience echoes back to you while you posture, and those are the faces which judge.

Such were Edwin's fears awake. His fears asleep were worse, for in his dreams he was never the actor. His dreams were not that simple. He was instead the watcher, like Hamlet, who cannot act, and yet events go on around him and act upon him.

Towards dawn, that Friday, he dreamed that he saw before him an immense billiard table, brilliant under its hooded light, in a darkened room. First he had heard the clack of his grandfather's toenails. Then he had seen the table. Then the cue.

Like the probing wand of a searchlight, it flashed out of darkness, smacked the moon, and vanished. The moon, hurtling across the poisonous green sky, hit the clustered balls and stopped. The balls separated out and went their

21

various directions. The one, the three, and the eight, which was of course black, went towards the various pockets, but just as they circled the holes, there was a shake, the table tilted upstage, and then, rushing towards him, ahead of all the other balls, and followed pellmell by them, was the eight. It struck the edge of the table and flew up towards his forehead.

He awoke in a sweat. "Wilkes," he shouted. "For God's sake, Wilkes."

But the room was still. The plush curtains were heavy at the windows. It had only been a dream. He got up, pulled aside the drapes, and found himself staring down at the prosaic and reassuring cobbles of Franklin Square.

While he watched, a gentleman in a black topcoat and plug hat came out of the house across the way, descended the stoop, and turned left down the street, as though to do such orderly and mundane things were not a privilege, but a right. Edwin let the curtains fall. It was the decorum of everyday life that he watched from the farthest distance, and with the tenderest of envy.

He was alone, as always, in a room.

II

In Washington City, Mrs. Surratt, a woman he had never met, also felt uneasy. But it was less distressing for her, this period just after the war, for she had her daily chores to do. They left her little time for worry. However, since it was Good Friday, and she was a devout Catholic, she was determined to attend morning Mass.

She was a woman who had not managed to become what she could have been. She knew that. Daily affairs unsettled her; yet instead of being the mistress of Surrattsville, instead of being the one thing which would have slaked her mild ambition, Mrs. Surratt of that ilk, she was the operator of a boarding house. She had to demand money. She detested that, but she had no choice in the matter, for in order to satisfy one's creditors, one must be creditor oneself.

She stopped in front of the mirror in the hall, while she waited for Honora. She was, who could deny it, a lady; but she was a lady much put upon. It was not right that a woman of her age, a little prim perhaps, no longer young, but still not old, should have her gentility interrupted by the realities of a world which contained only failure, a little music, and the clamourings of tradesmen. This afternoon she would have to drive all the way to the Maryland Shore in a rented gig, which was not cheap, to try for the last time to raise money long owed her. She hated to do such things, or to see Surrattsville for what it was, a depressing small bar and wayside tavern, in poor ground. She preferred to remember Surrattsville as a glory lost.

It was not her fault. Before she had married she had been as pretty as Honora or Annie was now. But she had made the wrong marriage; and how was Annie to be provided for? How could anybody make a good marriage out of a boarding house, whose only portion was a coaching stop hired out,

23

for the miserable rent it brought in, to an unreliable drunkard?

In the mirror she saw the face of a woman of forty-five, which was not fair, for she was not forty-five. The body may grow older, but alas, we do not. So we have to corset ourselves in. We have to be staid. We have to remember to control what was once charmingly instinctive, and the ageing body does something to our habitual gestures, it twists and confines them, so that we cannot make them with the same grace any more. What had once been the craning of a coquettish girl had turned somehow into the snappish head-turning of a turtle surprised by an enemy it cannot see around the protective bulk of its carapace. Mrs. Surratt's carapace was the dresses becoming to her age, black, trimmed with grosgrain ribbon, heavy and full; whereas another woman of her age, say the wife of the President, Mary Todd Lincoln, was rich and secure enough to damn the world and still persist in appearing in public in the white rosebud trimmed dresses of a girl of seventeen. It might not be seemly. No doubt it caused comment. But oh how it must satisfy the whims of the soul.

But then Mrs. Lincoln did not keep a boarding house and did not have to worry about whether or not, for example, the new coloured girl, Susan Mahoney, was a spy as well as the inefficient sloven she so clearly was.

Honora came out of the bedroom. Mrs. Surratt opened the front door, and the two women went down the stairway to the street. It was a relief to be out of the house. They walked to the church.

It is important, as she often told her daughter Annie, to walk with one's head up. She walked with her own head up. But the posture was no longer natural to her. Do what we will, time will make it droop. Then we can only keep it up by a firm act of the will.

Mrs. Surratt may have been an impractical woman, but she had a firm will.

At church she tried to concentrate, but she could not. That often happened these days. Easter was a solemn moment, but it happened every year, and she was worried about the menu for dinner. She could remember how she had looked in her confirmation dress. The incense was soothing, but the weather was bad and the church was cold. She was a convert, but no Catholic worships God. He worships Jesus, Mary, and the Saints. Concentrate on God and you see nothing. Concentrate on Jesus, Mary, or your favourite saint, and you see an intercessor and a friend, someone to take that hand you have not dared to extend since you were a small child, romping through the pasture behind the house, or waiting upstairs, in the dark, with one candle, for your mother to come upstairs to tuck you in.

Mrs. Surratt's lips tightened. Once you are older than ten, there is no one to tuck you in, not even your husband. Your husband wants something else, or else he snores, or else he dies.

Jesus, in plaster, on the cross in front of her, under His draping, had the same look the dead on the battlefields had, in Mr. Brady's photographs, crumpled, inarticulate, boneless, and yet somehow still uttering the last word they had had to say while living.

As for the Seven Last Words of Christ, they meant nothing to her, though in Mr. Haydn's version they were very fine. She had heard it once, in Baltimore.

Again her lips tightened. She could never quite see God, but she knew that He was there somewhere, just out of earshot, if only He would turn and she could catch His attention. He had a long white beard and kind wrinkles around the eyes and His wrath was terrible. Her marriage had been so unfortunate, that He was the only man she ever missed, except for her son John, who was never there even when he was there.

Why was it always she who had to help him?

She was worried about him. She knew he was up to something, though she did not know what. She had not heard from him for several weeks. He was so thoughtless. He never seemed to realize how much she was worried.

As for her boarders, she had no idea how she would get Annie married. Mr. Holahan was decent enough, but married already. Those strange people John had brought to the

25

house, the troll-like German Atzerodt and Mr. Wood, a giant bumpkin who said he was a Protestant minister, were gone and good riddance. Mr. Booth had been a little better. When he came, the parlour became courtly and gay. Despite herself, she liked him. But she did not trust him. He was an actor. One knew about actors, and Annie was an impressionable girl. Mr. Booth would not do.

Otherwise, the only men who came to the house were weedy clerks, in search of lodgings, like that wretched ex-priest Weichmann, who boarded with her and whose whey face and permanent snivel got on her nerves. She did not trust him either. Not only did he work for the War Department, but he was an eavesdropper, a coward, and a sneak. He had damp hands. All the same, he would have the afternoon off from work, because of the holiday, and in the absence of anyone else, she would have to ask him to drive her into Maryland about that debt.

To tell the truth, it would be agreeable to get out of the city and to see trees, open fields, and spring flowers again. Also, she had a little errand to run for Mr. Booth. That, at least, was a pleasure. She might not trust him in so far as Annie was concerned, but unlike her son, who was not, he was a southern gentleman. He had had no part in this dreadful war. He had sometimes given them theatre tickets. It would be a pleasure to do him a favour in return.

III

Booth made up his mind at noon, when he went down to the theatre to get his mail. Of course, he had made up his mind before, only to fail, but like that sort of swimmer who hesitates too often on the brink of what he wants to do, he had become impatient with himself, and this time would enter history with one enormous, ill-timed dive.

It was history he wanted to enter. He was not named John Wilkes for nothing. His namesake was famous for adherence to a cause. So would he be. He wanted his image carried down the ages, bigger than that of his brothers, like the ancestral portraits of a Roman funeral procession, bigger than the real image of the corpse.

About fame he had no doubts. He was an actor. More than that, he was *the* actor; he was always careful to be treated as such; he always was treated as such; but an actor is expected to act, and he was afraid to do that. Bad training had ruined his voice. He could not now, as his brother had recently done, play *Hamlet* for a hundred nights. He could, at most, appear once a month, in terror lest his voice grow hoarse and he would have to stop. It was not fair that Edwin, who was a haunted wisp of a man, or Junius, who looked like a side of beef, should have an accidental stamina that he, with a body that had never failed him, smooth muscles, and the best face in the family, at least so women always told him, had not.

That was his secret. When he was sure of his voice, he acted in a play. When it failed him, he played the actor. He was dapper, assured, elegant, and handsome. At the same time he raged that he should be so put down. Fame was the only thing he wanted. Now fame demanded another kind of act. Well, he was ready to comply with that demand. Besides, he was tired of acting. He belonged on a bigger stage than any boxed in a theatre. There are no great men in the theatre, only great actors. It is the same with every profession. One will never be famous merely by doing what one can do. One must do more than that.

Life and Washington had maddened him these last few months, even though the clear part of his brain was as mercilessly immediate as a stereopticon. That was natural enough. He had no feeling for words. He thought in images. It was not the acting, but the stage business that interested him, like that leap from the rock he made in *Macbeth*, when the witches began to jeer. Now that had taken skill. What did words matter? It was the stage business of life that had always meant more to him than its mere meaning.

The actress Cushman, that terrifying amazon, who was dying of cancer, when she took a benefit slapped her diseased breast, in order to produce the right sort of dramatic scream. That passed for great acting. At the world's benefit he would do the same.

Yet how was he to make himself a hero now, with no cause left to fight for? The war was over. Jefferson Davis had fled with his cabinet on the last train out of Richmond. The city stood empty for a little while. Then Lincoln had walked in its streets, surrounded by swarms of superstitious niggers, half of them down on their knees, until the President raised them up, telling them to pray to God, not to him. Jesus had said the same thing in his day, and if this man could ape the manners of the Son, then where was God? In Richmond Wilkes had commenced his career. Now the President had snuffed out his audience. The smoke had scarcely settled, yet the Union flag was back over Fort Sumter already. Or so they said.

And though the niggers may have followed that tall, shambling, plug-hatted nemesis, no one else had but his own troops. Still, in Washington, that walk through a sullen city passed for a victory. On Tuesday night there had been a high hissing in the air, and small orange flames, like fox, like St. Elmo's fire, with blue-green cores, had leapt to life on the Capitol, until that ostentatious building loomed over Wilkes like a columbarium to receive his personal ambitions, and

28

the whole city became a stage set against the night sky, against the cosmic opera house, like that crypt scene in which Romeo dies. He had done the play often, and always as Romeo.

It was Romeo's play. Once he had left them in the morning, he never gave a thought to Juliet. Juliet was a part, filled in by a supporting player, with no significance of its own, a player such as Ella Turner, who called herself Starr, the redhead whom he had left that morning, his mistress, part of his life's permanent stock company, who always knew her lines when he came back to play out his engagement for the night.

As for what she did the rest of the time, he didn't care. Perhaps she worked in her sister's brothel. It didn't matter. For five years he had had star billing. It was he the world came to see. And so he meant to keep it. He had no use for Lincoln.

On Palm Sunday, Lee had surrendered. That left only Johnston in the field. The cannon had celebrated all day. They were still booming. They had been booming on and off for two weeks.

And now it was Good Friday.

So far the day had not pleased him. His boots squeaked and that was annoying. It is impossible to get the squeak out of a pair of boots once it has gotten in, and these were new and expensive ones. He was conscious of himself all over in that way, down to the last handkerchief or disconcertingly renascent pimple. That was because he was an actor. He had no repose. He did not even exist, unless he kept moving, and the nature of his own existence was something he had never been able to face, even in sleep. So he had a discontinuous mind, like that of a woman, in which nothing had either cause or consequence, since the whole world was one unique event, himself, and everything a play.

People like that can be dangerous, for though they are bad at planning, who can tell what they are apt to do on the spur of the moment? They do not know themselves. They are dandies. For them life is immediate. They have no time for thought. And yet they think they think.

29

Washington City was a quagmire of brawling, drunken mud; pigs wandered across Pennsylvania Avenue, the Capitol still lacked parts of its facing, and those buildings which were not shanties lacked all elegance. There was no pink marble in those days, and no cherry trees. There were only veterans back from the wars, a good many of them cripples, ex-spies, copperheads, and above them, a heavy, leaden sky pendulous with undropped rain.

Booth turned into Ford's Theatre, stepping jauntily, like a fox back to its burrow after the night's successful hunt. In the world he was always bothered by the lack of some perpetual proscenium. But in the theatre he felt snug. The world was an alien place, but in the theatre he knew where things were. He knew what to do. He felt at home. Therefore, whatever he did, it would have to be done there. He began to feel better.

The sun had come out a little. He went into the manager's office, picked up his mail, letters from ladies to judge by the handwriting, and said hello to Henry Clay Ford. Ford was a boomer. He talked too loud. He told Wilkes that the President and General and Mrs. Grant were coming to the theatre tonight. They might even bring General Robert E. Lee.

That was raillery. Booth was annoyed, but paid no attention. Of course they would not bring Lee. But also he was taken by surprise.

He went outside, sat alone under an archway, and read his mail. As the handwriting had told him, it consisted of *billets doux*. He paid little attention to them. Instead he stared at the opposite house, number 453, which belonged to one Petersen, a tailor. It was a plain brick house, with nothing to catch his eye. Its front door was shut. And yet it did catch his eye. He had to look at something, for he had an awful feeling in his stomach, as though something had kicked him.

He had known for some time now what he had to do, but he also knew he was incapable of decision. Events would have to make the decision for him. And now they had.

He was very aware of himself just then. From an ache in the stomach, the awareness of what he had to do had turned

30

into gooseflesh all over him. He felt both bigger and smaller than he was.

What actor can act without a costume? He looked down at his shiny and immaculate boots, which caught so well the arc of his calves, but never caught the mud of this world, for he had that art of dandies never to spot his clothes or splash himself. He looked at his riding breeches, and at his hands holding their letters. He could see everything of himself except the one thing he wished to have remembered, which was his face. He blinked.

These were his daily and comedy clothes. For high tragedy one must dress differently, for half the secret of playing any part, and half the strength of the performance, lies in one's costume, though in our day the cothurnus of tragedy has somehow altered to a pair of spurs. A pair with efficient rowels. He had always liked spurs. He would sit twirling the rowels with his thumb, before putting them on.

He got up and went into the theatre.

It was as empty as the Cumaean Sybil's cave, and as over-decorated, except for the far end, where the stage, that is, the tripod, was. He stood at the rear for a while, to watch. There were no armchairs, only cane backs, as in a European church.

The play was *Our American Cousin*, which was what Laura Keene always played, and played very badly, too. She was billed as an international *comédienne*. Perhaps she was, but she could not act. His brother Edwin had had trouble with her. He had had trouble with her himself. She always liked someone to blame for her own miserable performance. This time she should have it.

Under the weak stage light, Laura Keene looked older, more drawn and haggard than ever. She was kept by a gambler, a man called Lutz, and passed her own daughters off as her nieces, but he had always thought her a scrawny horror. He shrugged his shoulders. Some men liked older women best. But at the same time he grinned. He knew his Laura. She would make capital of what was about to happen if she could, sincerely, of course, for as though to make up for her lack of ability, she was always sincere, but ravenously too. He had never been able to stand her. He rather hoped they flung her in jail.

The Presidential Box, a double one, yawned black and as yet undecorated to the right of the stage. He calculated the leap. It was not so extensive as that he was accustomed to take in *Macbeth*, and on stage or off, he always kept in whipcord trim, for the Booths had a tendency to dumpiness that would not look well in the sort of tight trousers his tailor built for him.

He settled down to time the play. It began at eight. By ten-fifteen the players should have reached that point in the action where the stage is empty, except for poor old Harry Hawk, who has a comic soliloquy to deliver.

There was much to be done before ten-fifteen. He left the theatre in order to round up his little company. Every actor has one, of course, a little circle of anonymous cronies who shore him up against the neaps of reputation, but his had been chosen for a different purpose. He would begin with Payne. Payne, at least, he could depend on. But first he would go back to the National Hotel to dress.

When he got to his room, Ella Turner was gone, as he had told her to be. He liked to keep his worlds separate. The women one slept with were not the women one cared to speak to in the daytime, if only because what they had to say was so boring. For daytime use he had his fiancée, Miss Bessie Hale, the daughter of the ex-Senator. Whether they would marry he neither knew nor cared, but the engagement enhanced his aura. It was his dashing clothes that Bessie liked, anyway. Thinking of her, he made that little gesture, his favourite, which was habitual with him, a quick tugging at the handkerchief in his breast pocket, with head modestly downcast, like that of a white cockatoo preening itself. It went so perfectly with the single syllable "m'dear", which only actors seem able to pronounce. That syllable came out so naturally after some young miss had played the piano or paid a compliment: "M'dear, you have lovely shoulders: you play so well." "M'dear, you flatter me." He had been photographed making that gesture. It was his favourite photograph.

32

When he thought of Bessie, he saw her always sitting white and cool on a wide veranda, above a croquet lawn, a game which flatters young ladies in wide skirts so beautifully, with the sound of practical laughter so cooing across an afternoon lawn; half green, half lavender. His trunks contained sachets of lavender. It was a smell he preferred.

Rummaging in his wardrobe, he searched out a costume for this event which was to make him so permanently famous. He had some of his father's stage clothes in that trunk; some of his own; the uniform he had worn when he went off with the Virginia Rifles to watch the hanging of John Brown, which had made him sick. He did not care for violence. He was upset if he so much as cut his finger on a piece of notepaper. He was careful always to remain inviolate. But he did like uniforms.

His favourite costume was a riding outfit, half Dangerous Dick, half country squire, and today, as was fitting, it should be black, for is not the avenger always black? Besides, with proper tailoring, and he always insisted on proper tailoring, a riding costume made him seem taller, and shortness was his only physical defect.

The spurs were important. He spent some time choosing the right pair. Then, looking at himself in the pier glass, he saw that here and there his boots were dull in their sheen. He went downstairs, found a bootblack, and had them perfected.

It was a gesture he liked, that stance with one foot up on the box, above the shoeshine boy. It had the right magisterial air. His boots polished, he went to Herndon House to tell Payne what to do. He was sure of finding him in. Payne never went out into the streets if he could help it. He was a preacher's boy from Florida: any town with more than one street not only confused him, but filled him with despair. Booth went upstairs and opened the door.

The room was almost dark, for the curtains were drawn. Payne was lying full length on the bed, which was too small for him, smoking a cigar and flicking the ashes into that ashtray he had made by shaving the top off the skull of a Federal soldier. Payne was like that. He seldom drank, but he did smoke, and he was very fond of that skull. It was not a trophy or a symbol exactly, but it was what an old bone was to a dog.

Payne swung to his feet, saw who it was, and then lay down again.

"I hoped you'd come, Cap," he said. That was what he called John Wilkes. His own father was a little man and not worth bothering about, and besides, a father wasn't what Payne wanted in this world. What he wanted was to be somebody's pet dog in a regiment. He had probably never heard of Patroclus and Achilles. But that was the limit of his emotional world, and he had taken Booth for his Achilles. He was a soft spoken, warm, obedient, and affectionate dog who could only serve one master. He was also, if told what to do and how to do it, a homicidal maniac, which did not bother Booth. He had never played in *The Tempest* himself, but his father had once read that play aloud, at home, and he knew perfectly well who was Prospero and what becomes of Caliban. And like Caliban, he did not care, for Caliban is scarcely human. He is only a dog who wants to lick your face and for that reason can be taught to retrieve what birds you shoot down.

Yet sometimes Payne made him uncomfortable. The boy had strength but no guile. He was proof of what love can do without a brain. And Booth, who could not love in that way, was one of those people whom only loyalty to themselves makes a little uneasy. None the less he could depend on Payne. He told him what to do. He had never even heard of Mary Shelley's *Frankenstein*, though he knew Shelley well enough. But when that heavy, blinking, overgrown child stood up, there was something shuffling and inexorable about his walk which always took Booth aback. The boy had a strangler's hands.

Even so, he was not really dangerous. It was just that his world contained only one person at a time, in this case Cap, and so it did not matter what he did to the rest of the world, for the rest of the world did not exist. It was as simple and as confused as that. He was so grateful to have an affectionate voice to tell him what to do, that he would do any-

34

thing, in order to have the same voice tell him what to do again. As another man would carry his address in his wallet, in case of accidents, Payne carried a *carte de visite* of Booth.

Booth told him what to do and thought no more about it. The ethics of what he was doing did not occur to him. Booth had no ethics, only manners. He never had had.

When he had gone, Payne sighed. He did not particularly want to kill anybody, but if he did, then he would see Cap tomorrow. Therefore he would.

On his way to Atzerodt, who was out, Booth stopped by to leave a card on Vice-President Johnson, who was also out. Johnson was out because he was feeling ashamed of himself. If he could not hide in his room, he could at least hide in a bar. A shrewd enough politician in his own state, he had found out that his own state was not the same as Washington City. He had made a fool of himself by getting drunk at the Inauguration and giving an ill-timed speech to the effect that he was a self-made man and not ashamed of it. That always went down well at home, but here he had misjudged his audience. Most of those in the government were self-made men themselves, but their autofacture had been directed towards concealment of the fact, not display. They had watched him with uneasy horror and then condemned him. As a result, the President would not even see him. He had made himself the laughing stock of Washington, and though he had many virtues, being hard-bitten enough to act disinterestedly when he chose, or when he thought he should do so, which takes more guts, a sense of humour was not among them. So he was out to the world these days.

His absence made Booth angry. He had met Johnson once, backstage in Baltimore, and had hoped, on the strength of that, to get a safe conduct to the Maryland Shore out of him. Now he would have to bluff his way across the Navy Yard bridge, instead. Then there was the matter of Atzerodt. Atzerodt should have been in his room above Johnson's, at the Kirkwood House. But the man was an undependable coward. He was probably out drinking some-

35

where, knowing very well what he would have to do, once Booth caught up with him.

But Booth did not catch up with him. The day was dwindling away, and he could find none of his instruments. Herold did not turn up, Arnold was in Baltimore, and O'Laughlin, though in Washington, had refused to help. Finally he managed to collar Atzerodt in the street, before that silly, distasteful, hunched over little man could slither away.

"I am in trouble," whined Atzerodt. "I will never be out of it." Which was quite true, but not what Booth had to tell him. He would have to do something to bring these weaklings into line. So at about four o'clock that afternoon he wrote out a letter to the newspapers, explaining what he was about to do and why, signed it with all their names, and gave it to an actor called Matthews to deliver, since he would have no opportunity to deliver it himself. Then he was ready. He had even remembered to stop by and give Mrs. Surratt a little package to deposit for him at Surrattsville. Field glasses, by the feel of them.

Mrs. Surratt had hired a carriage for ten dollars, and now jogged across the Potomac, into Maryland, with Louis Weichmann to drive her. Not even the presence of that man could quite spoil her day, though he had been infuriatingly curious about the package. But then he was curious about everything.

There was even a little sun, and the weather on the Maryland Shore proved warm. It was as though there had never been a war. She began to unbend. When she unbended, one could see that locked up somewhere in her, under all that defensive gruffness, was something vulnerable and charming, but Louis Weichmann did not see it. Charm was not a quality he sought in life, and vulnerability was something he confused with weakness. He lived like a rat in a wheel, always paddling away at the same treadmill; and his dignity, of which he had none, unless frightened, was that of a rat rearing up on its hind paws to defend itself against danger.

Whether he was in danger or not, he did not know, but he

36

did know that he had talked too much before his superiors about the Secesh tendencies of Mrs. Surratt and her boarders, and he did not want to be called a liar, any more than he wished to be unmasked as a spy. Yet he had no will to move. He was quite comfortable at Mrs. Surratt's. She kept a good house. But neither did he want, being weak willed, the responsibility of anyone's being arrested, guilty or innocent, on his word. Just the same he questioned her. He could not help it. Besides, though he liked her boarding house, he did not like her. He knew perfectly well what she thought of him. It was what he thought of himself.

For a moment Mrs. Surratt was alarmed, lest he was trying to ferret out something about her son John. Yet John was safe in Canada, she was quite the equal of Mr. Weichmann, thank you, and the country was so beautiful that in a while she forgot all about him, except for the badness of his driving.

You could tell from the way he held the reins that Mr. Weichmann had not been brought up among people accustomed to owning horses, whereas she had been, in Prince George County, and even at Surrattsville, a few years ago. She saw two mares, white, in a field, and automatically she said, "zit, zit".

It was a game they had all played when she was a child. Whenever you saw a white horse, when you were out in the carriage, you said "zit". Whoever said it first got a point. She could not remember what the point of the game was. Perhaps it had been its own point. But the memory of it made her smile.

So did the countryside. She did not care for the smell of Washington City, which was a mixture of whisky, dust and stale garbage in open drains. She loved the smell of green spring meadows flocked with flowers. Every winter she forgot it, and every April it was there again, like the memory of a happy childhood or of a happy day. She loved the world when it smelled young. She even loved the young themselves.

Along the low horizon, against the sky, the first redbud was in bloom.

It was as well she enjoyed the day, for her errand was fruitless. Her debtor was hiding somewhere and could not be found. But she did stop at Surrattsville and leave that irresponsible drunk of a tenant, Lloyd, Mr. Booth's package. She knew how scornful Weichmann was of Surrattsville. He was full of the scorn of those who own nothing towards those who prize the little that is theirs. True, it was little. It brought in only six hundred a year. But at least it was Surrattsville, it was named for her late husband, and any land one owns is Eden, if one has to visit it from town.

So she ignored Weichmann. As she drove back through the dusk, she could smell the drowsy odour of the redbud, and it soothed her as she had not been soothed in weeks. To relax so much, made her realize how tense she had been. But with John safe in Canada and the war over, and quite enough boarders at the boarding house, really, perhaps life would be better from now on.

Jounced, jostled, alone, but content, she sat in the dusk, listening to the horse, and smiled.

Mr. Lincoln's afternoon drive had not been so pleasant. He did not sleep easily these days. His nightmares were worse and more frequent, and they left him drained. He had made all the plans of a man who knows perfectly well that he is not going to live to fulfil them. He would take Mother, which is what he called his wife, to Europe with the children, once this second term had run its course. He would set up a law practice in Springfield again. He made plans the way a doctor reassures his patients. He talked of the future with everyone, for he knew he was not well. It was of his own death that he had nightmares.

The scene was always the same. He came back to the White House which was a disorderly, ill-run, and inhuman building, to find that a death had taken place. And the body in the coffin was always his own. It was when learning that that he always moaned in his sleep.

The guard in the corridor, Lamon, the one member of the Secret Service whom he trusted, because the man fussed over him so, sitting there in the half light, heard that moan

38

night after night. But not many other people heard it, and Mary Todd Lincoln, if she did, paid no attention. Lamon was in Richmond, but Mother was here.

As though state affairs were not burden enough for him, Mother was worse than ever these days. He had long ago ceased trying to understand her, and she could not be helped. Certainly, in this life, she did little enough to help him, or anyone else she knew well, either, for that matter, though she was kind enough to strangers. It was merely with her intimates that she had not the patience to remain human. No matter how tired he might be, no matter how heavy a schedule he might have, Mother had to have her whims, and his only defence was to give in to them. So tonight they must go to the theatre, which he had no wish to do, and this afternoon, for a drive.

Mother's hysterics were the best kept open secret in Washington, but he was grateful to those who helped him keep it. He knew perfectly well why the Grants had left the city rather than come to the theatre. He thought it tactful of them. But one could not explain that to Mother.

Yet by five o'clock, when he finally arrived, late as usual, but that was not his fault, to escort her to the carriage, her tantrum had passed away. Perhaps they would have a peaceful drive. His only emotion at that was a relieved sigh, which was the most he could summon these days, unless someone told him a funny story.

If the event had been Armageddon itself, Mother would have insisted upon dressing like a belle of seventeen. No doubt on the day of Resurrection, in which, privately, he did not happen to believe, which would at least spare him one spectacle, she would do the same.

And yet, in her own way, it was quite true, even though she was harrowing and never gave much thought to behaving any better, he knew she was fond of him, as fond, he supposed, as she could be of anyone not her father. He was wistfully a little tired of doing his best to be the world's father, when what he wanted, sometimes, was someone to bring him a shawl when he was cold.

But Lamon did that, not Mother.

They got into the carriage, which trundled briskly through the White House gates and out into G Street.

The Presidential carriage was a surprisingly elegant barouche, low slung and gleaming. Despite the mud and ruts of the road, it glided smoothly by. There were few to watch it pass. Mr. Lincoln was not a popular man, either with North or South, for he had defeated the latter and to the former was the advocate of what no man likes for others, which is clemency; and no one thanked him for the new hordes of blacks who wandered everywhere and who, these last few years, had gotten uppity above their station.

If people looked at all, what made them turn their heads was the sound of Mrs. Lincoln's laughter. It was whole hearted, but it was not easy. There was a ragged edge of hysteria in it which slashed the silence like a piece of glass, the laugh of a woman who can never be noticed enough, and who is most embarrassing when most spontaneous. She was happy now, but who knew what she would be half an hour from now? Even the cripples turned to watch, and there were a good many cripples in Washington these days. Mrs. Lincoln did not like to see them, outside of a hospital ward, where they belonged. Flat in a bed and grateful for flowers from the White House, they were less disturbing.

The carriage swerved past the Capitol, past marching troops who no longer had anywhere to march to, past strings of prisoners. Yet the city was gay. Like most capitals, Washington City was irresponsible. And the President was just as bad. He looked like a corpse, and yet he sat there laughing.

Mrs. Lincoln stirred uneasily. He was not well. And laughter from the ill is apt to be a symptom. Such laughter does not sound spontaneous.

He was only trying to amuse her.

"I never felt so happy in my life," he said. It was agreeable to be out in what was left of the sun, and to have the war over. That was all he meant. He did so want her to be pleased.

But she was thinking that laughter was unwise. The President had been in such a mood just before their son Willie died, at the beginning of the war. Her own father was dead. Who would she have left to turn to, if anything happened to Mr. Lincoln? He must not laugh this way. It was tempting fate. Her own face became serious. Whatever they did, they must not laugh.

Seeing the change in her expression, Lincoln gave up. There was nothing to be done with Mother in one of her moods. He blinked and looked at the crowds instead.

Those who looked at the barouche as it went by, saw only that Mrs. Lincoln was herself again. She might begin by smiling graciously, she was overweaningly timid, but it seldom took more than a city block for that worried look to come back again.

The wheels of the carriage went around and around.

At the Navy Yard Mr. Lincoln got out to stretch his legs, and was induced to walk up the catwalk to the monitor *Montauk*, which was anchored there. That little disk with steel turrets was already part of the past, victory had made it obsolete, but in early evening light the river was almost touching in its gentle swell and idle current. If they did not go to Europe, perhaps Mother would be satisfied with a farm on the Sangamon. He had always liked the Sangamon. But that was the river at home, and this was the Potomac.

He got back into the carriage and was returned to the White House. As they pulled into the *porte cochère*, they saw two men leaving, both friends from home, Oglesby, the new Governor of Illinois, and General Haymes. The President felt so happy to see a familiar face, that he stood up in the shaky carriage and yelled at them to stop. It was so seldom these days that he saw old friends, and they always cheered him up.

He knew what the world thought of him, though whether it was himself or the office the world hated most, he did not know. An office changes a man, so perhaps it did not greatly matter. But Oglesby and Haymes could remember the day when he was just a man, and seeing old friends was like being able to take one's shoes off, when they hurt.

He took them up to his office to swop jokes.

IV

Wilkes was in his hotel room at the National. It had been his intention to take a nap, but of course he had not really slept. He lay on the bed, with his spurred boots over the edge of it, so as not to damage the coverlet, which was nubby and had an unpleasant texture.

His pocket watch told him it was 7:45, but he had no real desire to get up. He had had too much to drink today. The brandy had been too sweet. He felt faintly nauseated and faintly furry. The room had a high ceiling and an unpleasant dado. His mind was made up. And yet some part of it was having second thoughts.

Perhaps if he stood up he would feel better. He stood up; and it was true, he did feel better. He walked around the room. His recitation to young ladies was a parlour piece called *The Driven Snow*. He was good at it. When their eyes widened, he could pretty well tell how the little affair would end.

Bessie Hale's eyes had not widened at all; they had narrowed. He wondered what she would think of him tomorrow, and if she was thinking of him now.

When he was by himself, he recited only Shakespeare. Tomorrow he would be a hero and a tyrannicide, but he could never be sure when Bessie was not laughing at him, even when she seemed to take him most seriously. She came from the North. Her blood was cold. But the women of the South never laughed at him, or at any man. They had read their Sir Walter Scott, and they knew a hero when they met one. Tomorrow morning, he would be well into the South.

Besides, he could not back out now. He had already given that letter, signed with all their names, to Matthews, and if it appeared in the *National Intelligencer* tomorrow and he had

42

not appeared at Ford's Theatre tonight, he would be an ignominious laughing stock to the world.

> *The aspiring youth that fired the Ephesian Dome*
> *Outlives in fame the pious fool that raised it,*

he recited to himself. That was Cibber, bettering Richard III. But what was the name of the aspiring youth that fired it?

He could not remember.

For some reason that annoyed him. He must hurry. He was already late. Out of the theatrical trunk he took a variety of things he would need, for he planned well. This life is largely a matter of appearances, and though he was impeccably dressed as the booted avenger, in order to reach the South he might have to play other roles along the way. It seemed to him altogether natural, therefore, to pack a false beard, a dark moustache, a wig, a plaid muffler, and a make-up pencil, for wrinkles and lines of anxiety, should those be called for. As a last precaution, he snatched up two revolvers, for though the deringer would do for the theatre, being small, dainty, and formal, for a chase one would need something heavier. To lean out of the saddle to fire a pocket deringer, apart from the difficulty of reloading it, would look silly.

There remained only the choice of some phrase appropriate to the action. This was a serious matter, and Shakespeare was the source there. Unfortunately he could not think of anything from *Julius Caesar*, *Richard II*, *Richard III*, or *King Lear*, the only Shakespeare he really knew. The immortal assassination line in *Caesar* unfortunately belongs to Caesar. Payne's *Apostate*, his other good role, though a good role, was certainly not immortal verse. Besides, if the words were to have any dignity, they must be in Latin. They must have a certain imprimatur, if that was the word.

Sic semper tyrannis, out of his little stock of Latin tags, seemed the best. It sounded well, and it was the motto of Virginia, his favourite state. Therefore it was easy to remember.

Sic semper tyrannis, he said to himself, before the pier

43

glass. He was a little hoarse this evening, but he looked well.

He went downstairs and left his key at the desk.

"Are you going to Ford's Theatre?" he asked the clerk. The clerk said he had not thought of doing so. The clerk, who did not like the theatre much, was accustomed to dealing with actors. He was in particular accustomed to dealing with Mr. Booth, who, though making him uneasy, also amused him.

"Ah, you should. You will see some fine rare acting," said Booth, and the randy little man strutted across the lobby and out of the door.

Did actors have no gestures of their own? wondered the clerk. That finger waggle of Mr. Booth's came out of the second act of *Apostate*. No matter who might play Pescara, the finger waggle was always there.

Booth was annoyed. The clerk had not been properly impressed. He went off to find his little company. The night was fantasticated by mist. Through the mist, the gas lights of the Capitol dome hummed as inimically as a dynamo. A parade was forming. This was Good Friday, an appropriate day, since Lincoln chose to pose as Jesus in Washington City as well as Richmond, but the crowds were still on their first bender after the war.

What a dreadful thing to celebrate, and yet the mob does not care what it celebrates. Booth, who had fetched his horse, sat above the crowd, like a public statue, and saw nothing.

The conspirators met on horseback. In the way they held their seat you could see their nature. The horses looked through the misty night larger than they had any right to be. Atzerodt, that miserable scraggly haired dwarf, like a statue of Loki in cheap plaster, almost hung on to his horse's mane. He was a dreadful Neanderthaler, a drunk given to tugging at the coat-tails of people who would have none of him. Murder, he said, was more than he had bargained for. He wanted out.

David Herold, with his young and affronted look, had scarcely the wit for conspiracy. Atzerodt might whine to cut

44

and run, but Herold was the type to sidle away instead. Whatever he might be saying to you, you knew he was thinking of his 'coon dog, the one with the twisted curl to the tail, and of duck hunting early of a morning, in the sedges of Maryland. But he would do to hold the horses.

Arnold, Michael O'Laughlin, and John Surratt were not there. Booth did not care. They were ribbon clerks got up as gentlemen, and so would not be missed.

Booth cleared his throat and told Atzerodt that he had no way out. He would be hanged in any case. He explained about the letter to the *National Intelligencer*, that explained the plot in all their names. So Atzerodt would have to shoot Vice-President Johnson. Atzerodt was desperate for friends, and that was the price of friendship.

Herold he despatched with Payne. Someone had to lead Payne out of the city. One of the horses whinnied and her flank rippled with the cold, with that same motion a pool has, when one casts a pebble into it, a little hurried, but customary. Then she was placid again. She was a good bay mare. Booth cleared his throat.

It was Payne's part to murder Secretary Seward while Herold waited with their horses.

Payne said nothing. He loomed immense there, without a hat, in black trousers and a dirty cast-off white duster, which Booth had once given him, which was why he wore it. His enormous clumsy black Conestoga boots were exposed, by the angle of his leg, to the calf.

"Yes, Cap," he said, in that low-pitched, heavy, emotional voice of his. He did not seem to be listening. But he would do it, Booth knew that.

For an instant he hesitated, he did not quite know why. Payne disturbed him. It was Payne's suggestion that he come with Cap. Booth could not have that. One had to go to fame alone. Yet as the conspirators broke up, and when Payne was gone, for a moment, as that bulky silhouette nudged its horse down the alley, he felt futile, and perhaps a little lost.

Then he, too, rode on.

The time was 9:15.

45

V

The first member of the Presidential party to arrive at Ford's Theatre was Parker, the Secret Service guard. He came to his post highly recommended, if only because that was the only way his employers could pass him along to the next poor devil to be saddled with him. He had that capon look of any policeman who has been in the force longer than a year, slow, servile to his betters, and insolent when he could be, much given to feeling the slights of this world, very lazy, and addicted to prostitutes and drink. He had been selected for duty tonight by chance, and he was bored. Nothing would happen anyway, and who cared whether the President was shot or not? He had no intention of losing his life for another man; he did not relish being reduced to the status of an usher of the great, when he loomed in his own world quite large himself; and he badly wanted a drink. When at last the Presidential party arrived, he ushered them into the theatre. As the President was on his way to his box, Laura Keene, from the stage, improvised a patriotic joke; the patrons in the dress circle stood up and began to applaud; the rest of the theatre did the same; and Professor Withers, in the orchestra pit, lurched into yet one more performance of *Hail to the Chief.*

Mrs. Lincoln, for once, did not seem to be wearing white, though there was something white about her, the lining of her bonnet, perhaps. Both she, and the President in his rocker, sat well back out of view.

Whenever the stage action paused, those in the front seats of the theatre could hear the creak of the rocker. But it was a very faint sound. If it disturbed anyone, it was only to make him smile. It had to be admitted, whatever his vices, and they were many, that at least the President was picturesque and quaint.

The performance continued. Though she was no actress, Laura Keene could play herself to perfection, and the part suited her. The audience settled down to watch.

Parker was bored silly. He left the theatre and went round to a pot house to cadge a drink.

Atzerodt was also drinking. That was because he was terrified.

He knew he could not do it, but it took as much courage not to do it, and courage, as time had taught him, came only out of bottles for such men as he. No matter what he might look like, Atzerodt had had the usual shanty backwoods education. He had read the *Bible* and *Pilgrim's Progress*, but they had given him no place in the human parable. He felt displaced and lonely.

Usually, at least in a bar, he could strike up some sort of acquaintance. He would stop at nothing to have at least the illusion of friendship. But he stopped at murder. Booth, he saw now, had not been his friend, but only Asmodeus, leading Christian astray.

All this talk of tyrannicide and the nobility of democracy, which is what his displaced liberal German relatives talked about in the old country, but never mentioned here, meant nothing. Murder was murder, no matter how praiseworthy the cause. It was a hanging offence.

By the time he left the Kirkwood House bar he was a little crazy. They had given him all these knives and guns. What did he know about knives and guns? He had not served in the war. He had killed no one. He was a coach painter by trade. He did not want to hang.

He staggered out into the nightmare streets, got caught up in the crowd, was carried along he knew not where, and threw his knife down furtively in the street. He did not want to be caught with these weapons.

The crowd carried him well beyond the place where he had discarded the knife. He wanted to cut and run. He wanted to cry. But he was already too drunk to run, though tears came easily enough. He watched the clock on the wall. The hands

47

stood at ten to ten. He had no friends in this country. He knew no one. Where could he hide?

He went on drinking.

Booth was also watching the hands of a clock. Somehow this evening, his habitual gestures did not satisfy him as they usually did. The bar was Taltavul's. Of the two bars which flanked the theatre, this was the one he preferred, for the other got mostly actors, who did not pay him as much deference as workmen did.

Brandy was not quite what he needed now. He ordered a set up of whisky and water instead. Taltavul thought that unusual and would remember it.

Booth had the eerie feeling that he was doing everything for the last time. He could not shake it. No doubt it was because an assassination, unlike a performance, is a unique act. It cannot be repeated.

There were too many drunks in the bar tonight. One of them lurched against him, lifted a glass, and said, "You'll never be the actor your father was."

That jolted him. It was ages since he had thought of his father, that benevolent madman with the sagging calves and flopping belly. Junius Brutus the Elder may have played country squire like Farmer George, but it was he the Booths had to thank for their illegitimacy, hushed up though that matter was. One could only be a gentleman by forgetting all about him.

The thought of that firmed Booth's purpose. "When I leave the stage, I will be the most famous man in America," he said.

"Hell, for all you act on it, I thought you left it months ago," said the drunk. "Croak something for us."

Taltavul knew how to handle a drunk. He handled this one fast. But it was funny, come to think of it, but it was true, Booth had not acted for months. And what was all that blarney about leaving the stage, anyhow?

To his relief, Booth said nothing more, drained his glass, and left the bar.

In the theatre it was hot. The house was almost full, and the audience had been sweating there for over two hours. Booth watched for a moment, and then slipped into the corridor leading to the boxes, closing and bracing the door after him with a length of wood he had stowed there earlier in the day.

In the State Box, Mr. Lincoln took his wife's hand. He was feeling romantic and contrite for having been irritated with her earlier in the day. She might now be merely a pretty pudding, but in the half light she looked as young as she liked to pretend she was; they had been together a long time; and she was his wife, after all.

Booth was watching through the eyehole he had drilled in the door that afternoon, but did not see the gesture. He had not been able to get the stage carpenter, Spangler, to hold his horse, but since Spangler was a drunk, that was perhaps just as well. A boy was holding it.

It had impressed him, walking down the stage box corridor, that the walk to the scaffold is much the same as the criminal's march to the crime. It has the same inevitable pace. Yet the corridor was empty and he was no criminal. He was the hero, girding himself for an heroic act. He could only deplore that the setting was so shoddy. Still, he could see the damnable villain's back.

Opening the door, he slipped inside, took out his deringer, cocked it, and shot the President. The time was 10:15.

VI

Payne dismounted in Madison Place and handed the reins to Herold. There was a fog, which increased the darkness of the night. Two gas lamps were no more than a misleading glow. He might have been anywhere or nowhere.

The pretence was that he was delivering a prescription from Dr. Verdi. Secretary of State Seward was a sick man. The idea had come from Herold, who had once been a chemist's clerk. The sick were always receiving medicines. No one would question such an errand. The bottle was filled up with flour.

Before Payne loomed the Old Clubhouse, Seward's home, where Key had once been killed. Now it would have another death. From the outside it was an ordinary enough house of the gentry. He clomped heavily up the stoop and rang the bell. Like the bell at Mass, the doorbell was pitched too high. It was still Good Friday, after all.

A nigger boy opened the door. Payne did not notice him. He was thinking chiefly of Cap. If their schedules were to synchronize, there was no point in wasting time. He pushed his way inside.

For a moment the hall confused him. This was the largest house he had ever been in, almost the largest building, except for a hotel. He had no idea where Seward's room would be. In the half darkness the banisters gleamed, and the hall seemed enormous. Above him somewhere were the bedrooms. Seward would be up there.

He explained his errand, but without bothering much to make it plausible, for he felt something well up in him which was the reason why he had fled the army. He did not really want to kill, but as in the sexual act, there was a moment when the impulse took over and could not be downed, even while you watched yourself giving way to it. He was no longer worried. Everything would be all right. He knew that in this mood he could not be stopped.

Still, the sensation always surprised him. It was a thrill he felt no part in. He could only watch with a sort of gentle dismay while his body did these quick, appalling, and efficient things.

He brushed by the idiotic boy and lumbered heavily up the stairs. They were carpeted, but made for pumps and congress gaiters, not the great clodhoppers he wore. The sound of his footsteps was like a muffled drum.

At the top of the stairs he ran into somebody standing there angrily in a dressing gown. He stopped and whispered his errand. Young Frederick Seward held out his hand. Panting a little, Payne shook his head. Dr. Verdi had told him to deliver his package in person.

Frederick Seward said his father was sleeping, and then went through a pantomime at his father's door, to prove the statement.

"Very well," Payne said. "I will go." He smiled, but now that he knew where the elder Seward was, he did not intend to go. He pulled out his pistol and fired it. It made no sound. It had misfired. Reversing it, he smashed the butt down on Frederick Seward's head, over and over again.

It was the first blow that was always difficult. After that, violence was exultantly easy. He got caught up into it and became a different person. Only afterwards did an act like that become meaningless, so that he would puzzle over it for days, whereas at the time it had seemed quite real.

The nigger boy fled down the stairs, screaming, "Murder".

It was not murder at all. Payne was more methodical than that. He was merely clearing a way to what he had to do.

He ran for the sick room, found his pistol was broken, and threw it away. A knife would do. From childhood he had known all about knives. Someone blocked the door from inside. He smashed it in and tumbled into darkness. He saw only dimly moving figures, but when he slashed them they yelled and fled. He went for the bed, jumped on it, and struck where he could, repeatedly. It was like finally getting into one's own nightmares to punish one's dreams.

51

Two men pulled him off. Nobody said anything. Payne hacked at their arms. There was a lady there, in a nightdress. He would not have wanted to hurt a lady. Another man approached, this one fully dressed. When the knife went into his chest, he went down at once.

"I'm mad," shouted Payne, as he ran out into the hall. "I'm mad," and only wished he had been. That would have made things so much easier. But he was not mad. He was only dreaming.

He clattered down the stairs and out of the door. Somewhere in the fog, the nigger boy was still yelling murder. One always wakes up, even from one's own dreams. The clammy air revived him. Herold, he saw, had fled.

Well, one did not expect much of people like Herold.

He unhitched his horse, walked it away, mounted, and spurred it on. The nigger boy was close behind him. Then the nigger boy turned back and he was alone. He rode on and on. He had no idea where he was. After some time he came to an open field. An open field was better than a building, that was for sure, so he dismounted, turned off the horse, and plunged through the grass.

He felt curiously sleepy, the world seemed far away; he knew he should get to Cap, but he didn't know how. He was sure, for he had done as he was told, hadn't he? Cap would find him and take care of him. So choosing a good tree, he clambered up into it, found a comfortable notch, and curled up in it to sleep, like the tousled bear he was, with his hands across his chest, as though surfeited with honey.

Violence always made him tired, but he was not frightened.

In Boston, Edwin Booth was winding up a performance of *A New Way to Pay Old Debts*. It was a part so familiar to him that he did not bother to think about it any more. Acting soothed him. On a stage he always knew what to do, and tonight, to judge by the applause, he must be doing it better than usual.

As Sir Giles Overreach (how often had he had to play that part, who did not believe a word of it), he raised his arm and declaimed: "Where is my honour now?"

That was one of the high spots of the play. The audience, as usual, loved it. He was delighted to see them so happy. If he had any worries, it was only the small ones, about Mother in New York, and his daughter Edwina and what she might be doing at this hour, with her Aunt Asia, in Philadelphia.

Everyone is ambivalent about his profession, if he has practised it long enough, but there were still moments when he loved the stage and all those unseen people out there, who might cheer you or boo you, but that was largely, though not entirely, up to you.

They made the world seem friendly somehow, though he knew it was not.

VII

Wilkes was quite right about one thing. Laura Keene had been in the green room. The commotion had brought her into the wings. Since she could not act, one part suited her as well as any other, and so she was the first person to offer Mr. Lincoln a glass of water, holding it up to the box, high above her head, to Miss Harris, who had asked for it.

She had been one of the first to collect her wits.

It was not so much that the shot had stunned the audience, as that they had been stunned already. Most of them had seen *Our American Cousin* before, and unless Miss Keene was on stage, there was not much to it. The theatre was hot and they were drugged with boredom.

The stage had been empty, except for Harry Hawk, doing his star monologue. The audience was fond of Harry Hawk, he was a dear, in or out of character, but he was not particularly funny. At the end of the monologue the audience would applaud. Meanwhile it looked at the scenery.

"Well, I guess I know enough to turn you inside out, you sockdologizing old mantrap!" said Trenchard, otherwise Hawk. There was always a pause here, before the next line.

That was when the gun went off. Yet even that explosion did not mean much. Guns were going off all over Washington City these days, because of the celebrations, and the theatre was not soundproof.

Then the audience saw a small, dim figure appear at the edge of the Presidential box. "*Sic semper tyrannis,*" it said mildly. Booth had delivered his line. Behind him billowed a small pungent cloud of smoke.

They strained forward. They had not heard what had been said. They had been sitting too long to be able to stand up easily. The figure leapt from the box, almost lost its

54

balance, the flag draped there tore in the air, the figure landed on its left leg, fell on its hands, and pressed itself up.

Harry Hawk still had his arm raised towards the wings. His speech faltered. He did not lower his arm.

The figure was so theatrically dressed, that it was as though a character from some other play had blundered into this one. The play for Saturday night was to be a benefit performance of *The Octoroon*. This figure looked like the slave dealer from that. But it also looked like a toad, hopping away from the light. There was something maimed and crazy about its motion that disturbed them.

Then it disappeared into the wings.

Harry Hawk had not shifted position, but he at last lowered his arm.

Mrs. Lincoln screamed. There was no mistaking that scream. It was what anyone who had ever seen her had always expected her to do. Yet this scream had a different note in it. That absence of an urgent self-indulgence dashed them awake like a pail of water.

Clara Harris, one of the guests in the box, stood up and demanded water. Her action was involuntary. When something unexpected happened, one always asked for water if one were a woman, brandy if one were a man.

Mrs. Lincoln screamed again.

In the Presidential box someone leaned over the balustrade and yelled: "He has shot the President!"

That got everybody up. On the stage, Harry Hawk began to weep. Laura Keene brushed by him with the glass of water. The crowd began to move. In Washington City everyone lived in a bubble of plots, and one death might attract another. It was not exactly panic they gave way to, but they could not just sit there. The beehive voices, for no one could bear silence, drowned out the sound of Mrs. Lincoln's weeping.

At the rear of the auditorium, upstairs, some men tried to push open the door to the box corridor. It would not give.

A Dr. Charles Taft clambered up on the stage and got the actors to hoist him up to the box. In the audience a man named Ferguson lost his head and tried to rescue a little girl from the mob, on the same principle which had led Miss Harris to demand water.

Someone opened the corridor door from the inside, and called for a doctor. Somehow Dr. Charles Leale was forced through the mob and squeezed out into the dingy corridor. He went straight to the Presidential box.

As usual, Mrs. Lincoln had lost her head, but nobody blamed her for doing so now. There was a little blood on the hem of her dress, for the assassin had slashed Miss Harris's companion, Major Rathbone, with a knife. Rathbone said he was bleeding to death. By the look of him he wasn't that far gone. Leale pushed him aside. To get rid of Mrs. Lincoln was harder. He finally got her deposited on the sofa at the other end of the double box, where she and Miss Harris sat waiting, a muffled, sobbing, double white blur. Miss Keene, who had come up the back stairs, joined them there.

Lincoln still sat in his rocker, but his head had slumped forward and his legs looked lifeless. There was no light in the box. It was necessary to strike matches in order to see him. Leale sent for a lamp, got the body on the floor, and while men stood in a circle around him striking innumerable matches, he searched, by that dim flicker, for the wound. The lucifers of that day burned down quickly. In a few minutes the floor was littered with charred sticks. The sound of scratching, as new ones were lit, was the sound of a nail drawn down a blackboard.

Leale had to feel with his fingers, which came away stained with blood. The wound was at the back of the neck. A clot had already formed. Leale removed it, and the body breathed shallowly. He lifted up one eyelid. The eye glistened in the match light, but it was out of focus and the evidence of brain injury was plain enough. The matches smelled abominably of sulphur.

Dr. Taft tumbled over the edge of the box. Everyone was breathing a little too fast. Together the two doctors raised the body, which felt heavy and old. It was alive, but Lincoln seemed not to be in it. They could then see the wound, and observe that it was mortal.

The two men let the body down again. Leale applied artificial respiration. A Dr. King arrived to offer his services. They did the best they could.

Some soldiers were trying to clear spectators out of the box. The flat surfaces of their natty forage caps reflected the light of the lamp that someone had at last brought. In that light they looked like the ghost of an army. The box emptied. It now contained only the three doctors, the body, and a circle of dead matches on the floor, which crunched under their boot heels as they moved about. The air was acrid.

Mrs. Lincoln sat on the sofa. She said nothing. Laura Keene sat beside her, she did not quite know why. Perhaps she had merely followed a humane impulse. She was human, after all, though life had drained most of the real life out of her. But she was no longer spontaneous. Perhaps she had realized, for word had gone round that Wilkes Booth had done this thing, though Spangler, the stage carpenter, denied it, that the safest place for an actor at this moment was close to the President.

Outside in the street, dimly, you could hear a crowd roaring the name of Booth and threatening to burn the theatre down. Leale asked if Lincoln could not be removed to some nearby place.

Dr. King answered that soldiers had been sent for the Presidential carriage, which had been turned round to face toward the White House.

Leale shook his head. "No. The wound is mortal. It is impossible for him to recover."

Except for the actors, who were still on stage, in deshabille, the theatre was almost empty. Sound carried all too well. The three women on the sofa heard what he had said, though Mrs. Lincoln seemed not to have heard it. She was in a state of shock.

Laura Keene, who, being an actress, believed all the funereal sentiments of the day, got up and asked if she might hold the President's head for a moment. Leale looked at her blankly. But there was something in her taut, snake-like face and the quiet way she stood which made him nod. She sat on the floor, her enormous pale yellow stage skirt crinkling around her, and held the head in her lap. Leale noticed, without really seeing it, that her fingers, long but knobbly at the knuckles, were those of a woman older even than, in this half light, she looked. Arthritis perhaps. What he was really worried about was the trip to the White House.

"If it is attempted," he said, "he will be dead before we reach there."

There were houses across the street. Dr. Taft asked an officer, for there were still soldiers waiting in the corridor, to run out and find a lodging nearby.

Four soldiers formed a human sling. Dr. King held the left shoulder. Dr. Leale held the head cupped in his hands, decided that to walk head first would be better, manœuvred the body around, and with the soldiers, left the box. "Clear a passage," he shouted.

Laura Keene sat on the floor, her skirt matted with blood, and watched Dr. Leale's face, as he backed out the door. Then she got up, and with Mrs. Lincoln between them, she and Miss Harris followed the body. They could hear the crowd roaring in the street.

At the head of the stairs the women paused, their wide dresses bent to the walls of the corridor. The body had reached the lobby and was heading towards the doors. The women started down.

"Clear out," yelled the troopers down below them. "Clear out."

Then the crowd saw the body, first the shaggy head in its broken posture, then the chest and feet. Someone began to cry. It was impossible to clear a passage. The doctors had to inch forward, and the street was fifty feet wide.

The crowd pressed in front and closed in behind. The captain of the troopers had to swing his sword in order to clear a passage. The night air was damp and sweaty, but the sky had cleared and there was a cold wind. In the moonlight, the shadow of Ford's Theatre covered the street and stretched half-way up the opposite buildings, as though it had been a pall.

Night would darken it.

The three ladies stepped out into the shadow. Nothing could be heard over the crowd, pressed tight and baying for someone to lynch. That person they had detested half an hour ago was already dying, but there was no one to tell them whom or what to lynch.

On the opposite side of the street the soldier, sent to find a house, could get no answer at 451. But at number 453 the door opened, and a man with a candle stood there motioning. Lincoln had found someone to take his body in. Leale headed there.

He got inside, though the crowd pressed in after him. The man with the candle moved ahead of the doctors. To the left was a parlour. To the right a stairway led upstairs, but in all the next eight hours, it did not occur to anyone to go upstairs. It was dark up there.

Behind the parlour was another sitting room, but under the stairs was a small bedroom. Someone pulled the bed out from the wall. It was a poverty stricken room. It contained a bureau, three straight backed chairs, a washstand and a stove. On one wall was Rosa Bonheur's *The Horse Fair*, with its Hellenistic horses like some equine Laocoön. The other engravings were by Herring.

Mr. Lincoln's body would not fit the bed. He was an even larger man than Payne. He had to be laid upon it diagonally, with his feet over the edge. An extra pillow was found to support his head.

Leale had the house cleared. Mrs. Lincoln, Laura Keene, and Clara Harris took up their vigil in the front parlour. Mrs. Lincoln was coming out of shock, which was unfortunate, since it meant just one more thing to be dealt with. Leale held a conference with the other doctors. The man with the candle went through the house, lighting the gaseliers. His name was Petersen. He was a tailor.

Mrs. Lincoln stood in the doorway of the sickroom. Leale got her out of there. He did not bother to look at her face. He was too busy. Lincoln might just as well have disappeared. He was certainly no longer in that body. But the body was going to die, and therefore Lincoln would not be back. The death watch had begun.

What on earth was the crowd out there shouting about? Such grief seemed obscene. An hour ago they had hated him.

Leale did what had to be done. He sent for Robert Lincoln, two more physicians, and Lincoln's pastor, Dr Phineas D. Gurley. Then he settled down to watch the body. The brain might be hopelessly damaged, but that face the brain had shaped was still intact. It was a sad face, everyone knew that, and an ugly face, but the approach of death made something evident in it that few had ever noticed, something youthful, ageless, and despite itself, commanding. It was something worse than a face born to rule, something far worse. It was a face doomed to responsibility, and therefore sad because of what it knew. As he lay dying, under the dry shimmering jet of the gaselier, the tact drained out of it, and one could see, what usually that tact concealed, the awful marks of knowledge. While Leale watched, the dark shadows under the eyes became darker. But the face itself became luminous.

The war was over, but the nightmare had become real. And perhaps, if that body was still aware of anything, it felt only the luxury of a final muscular relief. Slowly the muscles slackened along the length of that ramshackle, amiable, but worn out body. As they did, the face, slack on the chest, became dominant, until they were all uncomfortably aware of its expression. For the faces of the dying show us something, always, we would feel easier not to have to see. They show us something about ourselves and the human condition that we would rather not know.

VIII

As yet Wilkes was ignorant of what had happened.

Two more days, and there would be a chromolithograph for sale in the Washington shops. It was called the *Assassin's Vision*. Since the Potomac lay in the background, Booth had already crossed into Maryland. His horse was a prancer. Unwounded and elegant, he sat astride his horse, as unconcerned as a Lipizzan trainer. He was passing some trees. The branches and boles of the trees formed a standing figure of Lincoln, his arms folded, a pitying look on his face. The print was probably German work. Germans were good at that kind of thing. Better at it, anyhow, than Atzerodt had been as the hero of a liberal assassination plot. In the branches little heads of Lincoln hung like the homunculi of some sylvan witch. The picture was also available as a lantern slide.

But it was not two days later, and Booth had no such vision. His vision was of something else.

He was wounded. It was something he had not counted on and it maddened him. He had never been violated in any way. He had always, even as a child, had a horror of such things.

He no longer remembered the shooting. What he remembered was slashing at Major Rathbone. And he remembered standing at the front of the box.

"*Sic semper tyrannis*," he had said, but he had muffed the line. The sound should have come out rich, full, and memorable. It should have carried conviction. But at the time he had faltered. Why should he sound so uncertain, who possessed, for this one time in his life, such certainty?

It was because of the audience down there. He had never seen an audience from the side before. He had always faced it head on, from the stage, the way it wishes to see and be seen.

From the side you could see that the audience was not really interested in the play at all. Most of its members had not even turned their heads when they heard the shot. They sat there in the semi dark, waiting to be amused. They had no concern with real and glorious events. He could not hold them. Nothing could hold them for long. To those who did look toward him, he had been only a little man standing up in a box. That had been a shock.

It had shaken his nerve. That was why he had caught his spur in the flag, and fallen on his leg. He had been nauseated when he heard the bone in his leg snap. He had wobbled across that stage like a terrified spider shaken out of its lair, or like Richard Crouchback, after his dream, on the way to Bosworth Field. Yet it was not just his leg that had made him cower.

It was the obliviousness of the audience. He had expected applause or at least attention, since one does not applaud a tragedy until it is over. All he had received was silence. That was what had made him scuttle for his horse. That silence haunted him. Who can act to apathy?

He wanted Payne. He wanted to smile and smile and have that overgrown puppy dog call him Cap, and prove he was a villain still. He could not do everything himself.

Of the next hour he remembered nothing, except that his ankle began to swell, and try as he would, he could not prevent it from slapping against the plump flank of his mare.

The moon was up. There were mackerel in the sky. It was Tam O'Shanter's ride, for he could not hold the reins, the ankle hurt too much, so he had to hold the mane, with a whole coven of witches behind him, gaining on him through the air. He felt so small and thin and isolated. He had never run for his life before. He could not ride fast enough. It was as though one of those witches had grabbed his horse's tail and pulled back, with two hideous feet planted against the animal's rump.

Yet at the Navy Yard Bridge he had no trouble. He pounded over the water, which was wet with a few lights, and once on the Maryland Shore, breathed easier, for witches cannot cross water. In Maryland he would be safe.

Payne would be waiting for him here. He slowed down and went up the empty road at a secure jog. Maryland was still partially dead from the previous winter. The trees were skeletal. The bushes rattled. Once he met Payne, everything would be all right. He spurred up Good Hope Hill, heard hoof beats behind him, and not liking the sound, or the sudden fear in his stomach, took cover in a stand of trees. Perhaps this would be Payne.

It was not Payne. It was Herold. Nudging the mare out to the road, Booth yelled, "Halt".

There was no mistaking that whimpering face. But Herold, though not Payne, was better than no one at all. Booth began to feel better. The two men went on to Surrattsville to pick up the binoculars. They found Lloyd, the tenant, dead drunk on the sofa in the parlour. They got him up, and he shuffled off to fetch the glasses, came back, stopped behind the bar, and drew them a quart of whisky.

Booth was exhilarated. "We have killed the President," he said, "and Seward."

There was no expression in Lloyd's face. He might not have heard. He thought they were drunk. All he wanted was a dollar for the whisky. When he got it, he went back to the sofa again. That was the way his life went. He sold a quart and he drank a quart, and he did not care for the quality, and in particular, not for people like Booth, who had money to spend when he did not.

Who cared about the President or anything else, when Mrs. Surratt squeezed 600 dollars a year rent out of him, for a farm not worth the tending, and the obligation of running a tavern and franking the mail besides? Why the hell should he have to frank mail? When you lost a letter, everyone in the world was down on you.

The sofa was lumpy. Lloyd had another pull at his bottle and thought things over. There might be more ways than one of not paying Mrs. Surratt her rent, if what Booth had said was true. But on the other hand, he didn't want to do anything risky.

He heard the two men gallop off, and grinned.

They had a long ride before them. It was seventeen miles

to the nearest doctor. That would be Dr. Mudd, whom Booth neither liked nor trusted. Few people did. But the pain in his leg was terrible. He had to have help.

IX

M r. Lincoln was dying, and there was nothing to be said
about that. He was a great man, and greatness is an
enigma. It is also amoral, and we cannot have that. Nobody
likes to have his little game seen through. And yet it could
not be denied. A fire was going out. So few of them had ever
realized until now that it had warmed them.

Laura Keene sat on the horsehair sofa in the front parlour
on 10th Street, while the gaseliers hissed, with Mrs. Lincoln
and Clara Harris. The room was close, and Mr. Petersen,
who owned the house, could not be a successful tailor, for
the wallpaper was faded and the furniture was massively out
of date. It made her wonder, because the room was so old
fashioned, if all this had not happened a long time ago, instead of having to be sat through now.

It was a long time since Laura Keene had lived in the
present. On stage she played women younger than herself,
and her life had made her older. Somewhere along the way
she had got lost, but though frightened, she had always
wanted to be a real person again, for she supposed she must
have been one once. On stage she was a terror, after all, she
had a living to earn, two daughters to bring up, and a position to keep, but offstage she was not unkind. Clara Harris
seemed a sweet enough little thing. She should be sent home
to bed. But if real life was what Mrs. Lincoln was going
through, and if real life made you that futile, that terrified,
and that silly, then perhaps it was better to be on the stage.

There were crowds outside the house, but the crowds
were quieter now. The house was not. Lincoln would die.
What then was the use of Mrs. Lincoln's hysterics? They
accomplished nothing. The inevitable was something one
watched with quiet eyes, from a safe corner.

That was why Laura Keene was here. Lincoln had been

65

shot in a theatre, and on Good Friday, at that. The pious can raise a rabble faster than a sensible man, and there would be hard days for actors ahead. In that case the best thing to do was to take shelter as close to the eye of the storm as possible. Besides, she could not have fled if she had wanted to. Something held her here.

She was neither a clever nor a political woman. British by birth, she had always found America a little unreal. But this room was real to her. Lincoln was real to her. Say what the world would, yes, he was coarse and provincial, but he had had some kind of human warmth about him. He was lying, she supposed, motionless on a bed, and yet she thought of him as sitting in a chair, a little benign, a little gawky, but very like a father. One felt hostile to him for that very reason, even though one loved him. He was a father. He had gone ahead. He knew what came next.

One could not love Stanton, and Stanton was in the next room. That man had seized the government. He had marched in an hour ago, at a little past eleven. She had not seen him, but she had heard him, and she had smelled the passage of that violet pomaded beard and seen his bespectacled face, as he glanced in the door of the parlour.

Now he was holding interviews, and all through the slow passage of that night, the people he had sent for slipped heavy footed but on tiptoe down the corridor. He was less Secretary of War than Grand Inquisitor, and yet there was nothing grand about him. He had sent out, she heard, to arrest everyone at the theatre, including herself. And he was quite merciless. He suffered neither from pity nor from doubt. He believed in nothing but efficiency. But he was also afraid.

The person who knew that was Gideon Welles, from the Navy Department.

They had met in the shambles at Seward's house. Seward was not informative. He could only complain and haul himself upon his bed again. He was a man given to indignation, but he was also an astute politician. No matter how the wind blew, he contrived that it should carry him back into office. Now the unknown smiler with the knife had descended upon

66

him. And yet he would survive. He lay there and grumbled under his sedative.

Stanton was something worse than a politician. He was a fanatic. His trouble, thought Welles, was that he had no chin beneath his beard. Therefore he was that perfect security officer, the coward turned absolute. He had imprisoned tens of thousands to keep his own position, first behind the world's back, and then, as his own power had increased, to its face. Lincoln had been astute enough to be able to control him. Welles did not know who could control him now. He was one of the new men. There was nothing to be done with him. Welles suggested they should go to the house on 10th Street. He said he had commandeered a carriage.

For the first time, he saw Stanton hesitate. "I am going at once," he said. "I think it is your duty to go."

Stanton drew back. "This is not my carriage," he said. A Grand Inquisitor may not respect anything else, but he does respect property. So do the new men. Men, women, children, and the emotions count for nothing. It is their right to suffer, for they are guilty and deceitful. But property is real.

Welles was not of that temperament. He said it was no time to argue about the ownership of a carriage.

Stanton was forced to agree, but all the same, he leaned out of the carriage window and asked Chief Justice Carter, who had also been at Seward's, to come with them. That would give the commandeering of the carriage a respectability at law. For the rest, he saw this murder as part of an immense plot. He ordered the declaration of martial law. He set a guard around the other Cabinet members. He ordered everyone at Ford's Theatre arrested, from stableboy to manager, which is what had made life awkward for Laura Keene in the front parlour.

He had taken only the briefest of glimpses at Lincoln, and those unwillingly. Unlike the women, he had no affection for deathbed scenes. He did not like to be moved, and the sight of that inert, dying body moved him. He had intrigued against Lincoln for years. Lincoln had been too clement. And now it had come to this.

Stanton, it was his justification, acted always for the

public good, which was an abstraction, and had nothing to do with men or women. Yet that body in there had rattled him. As he had looked down at the President's face, the mouth had pulled sharply to the left, in a sort of jeer. The doctors said he was beyond conscious thought. But Stanton did not care for the look of that jeer. In fifteen minutes it stopped, and the face smoothed away. But Stanton remembered it. His master had been more astute than his daily kindness would have indicated. It bothered him, that jeer. It seemed a jeer at him, as though this murder were nothing but a reflection upon his own efficiency.

Now these witnesses said the crime was Booth's doing. That was impossible. No one man could defeat Stanton. His net was cast too wide. Therefore there must be some vast conspiracy.

He felt confused, not by the evidence, but by those who gave it. He seldom interviewed people himself. He found them too distracting to the cause of justice and pursuit. Besides, he was worried about his own part in all this. He had conspired against the President, lied to the President, evaded the President, and despised the weakness of the man. And in a funny, patronizing, grudging way he had loved him. For the first time in his life he wanted to cry. He did not do so. He had never had the habit. It was his duty to maintain order and to prosecute the criminal. Without him, the Union would have collapsed years ago. He had not the time for tears. As soon as he was through with the witnesses, he had them sent to the Old Capitol Prison. It *must* be a widespread plot. How else could he have been defeated?

When Andy Johnson arrived at last, to look in on the President, he did not even stop on his way out to ask how things were going. That made Stanton feel a little desperate. Johnson did not like him. He had to prove his efficiency, or be sacked, and what would happen to the country without its Secretary of War? He became more peremptory with his witnesses.

Johnson had been asked not to come, his well wishers had said the trip might be dangerous, but he had come anyway, walking all the way from Kirkwood House. His reasons were in part mere expediency. He wanted no one to say either that he had cringed indoors or that he had rejoiced at this tragedy. But in fact it was something else that had drawn him here. He could not stay away.

He stood at the foot of the bed, wondering what the difference between himself and Lincoln was. Robert Lincoln stood at the head of the bed, alternating between that post and the problems of his mother in the parlour. There was nothing much to Robert Lincoln. He had neither his mother's brilliance nor his father's brains. He was just a mediocre young man, capable of feeling, no doubt, but not of thought. Johnson recognized him at once as that simple but unpredictable thing, a born constituent.

The body in the bed was something more.

What was that difference, anyhow? He could not fathom it. Each was a self-made man. Each came a little from the west of this puzzling, treacherous, and so-called civilized world of Washington City. They had played the same political tricks. They had the same political wisdom, the same wariness. And yet the difference was more than one of mere cleverness. The difference was something they could always recognize in Kentucky, poor white trash that they were, even if folks didn't do so in Washington.

The difference was that Lincoln was a gentleman. Not one of the high flown, dangerous, New York, New England, mercantile kind, not even the ostentatious or the work-horse kind, like Lee, but still, the calibre was unmistakable. It always had been, and it was no less so here on the bed. He did not even die like an ordinary man. He was too big. The brain was gone completely, so the doctors said. And yet the cachet remained, rawboned, maybe, and defenceless now, but real.

What the hell was it that made the gentleman? It was not the habit to command and be obeyed, though some people thought so. Lincoln had commanded nothing. And yet he had been obeyed. Perhaps it was some kind of integrity that lay behind decisions, and had nothing to do with what one said or did. And yes, for oratory was sometimes accurate, as

69

well as moving, it was perhaps the ability to accept God as an equal. In that sense, to be a gentleman was nothing but the strength to walk alone.

He, Johnson, was a son of the people. That meant he always had to be justified. He had to ask for approval, and stoop to win it. But a gentleman, he saw, did not have to be justified, for a gentleman, in being beyond it, has no difficulty in accepting the world. His sigh may be a little sad, his smile a little withdrawn, but he does not really want anything. He is only there to do his duty.

Looking down at that body, Johnson knew that now he would do his. The mechanics of conversion are best casual. But really, no matter how beastly they may be, men only want something to admire, in order to become admirable, and in this poor living corpse Johnson had found it. Three weeks before, to win votes, he had said he would hang every rebel he could catch. He knew now that was one promise he did not mean to keep. He looked, saw nothing and everything, and turned away. A man in his late fifties does not cry. But sometimes we see things, once it is too late, which make us want to cry. He had seen, not Lincoln, but that selflessness which defeats the self. He had seen the burden, which is also the backbone, of the gentleman, for in this life, given self-respect, we must carry our own load.

That visit changed him. He went into the front room, which he would not have done in the same way ten minutes before, to hold Mary Lincoln's hand. Then he went back to Kirkwood House.

Others in that room did not take the matter so deeply. Sumner sat there all night. He was watching the death of an old enemy, and that was all he saw. Earlier he had bowed his head and begun to sob. But though he was moved, nothing inside him moved. He was a good hater.

But he was a bad everything else.

All the same he sat there, hour after hour. He was fascinated. Nothing would ever make him understand that a good man may have the manners of a labourer, or that a mediocre demagogue may yet be raised above himself. He came from Boston. In Boston life was not conducted so. In Boston they

70

had some feeling for the forms of life, for the forms, and for little else. Lincoln had been beyond those forms. Therefore, though Sumner was moved, he was not touched.

His only thought was that Johnson would be worse, and yet at the same time easier to handle than Lincoln had been; and that somehow the power of the land was ebbing from Boston, and that this death had something to do with that. The power was floating to what he hated, which was the far west, Kentucky and Kansas, and other lands of the unregenerate baboon. Sumner had also, had he but realized it, the face of a baboon, even in grief, but it was the face of a baboon trained to wear clothes. That is what he meant by the proper forms. And for that matter, what is grief? It does not touch us, and yet when we assume it it is real. It is the assumption, then, that is real. So much for forms.

In the front room Mrs. Lincoln screamed.

That was most unfortunate. Stanton had work to do. He was dictating the announcement of Lincoln's death. There remained only the time to be filled in. Mrs. Lincoln had heard him. He had to send her back to the parlour. Then she went to the deathbed. She was a nuisance there. "Take that woman out," he said loudly. "And do not let her in again." He had never liked her. She had no right to interfere, when there was so much to be done.

The night dripped by.

At three in the morning Stanton had to face the truth. He wired New York, and for the first time admitted Booth was the assassin. Then he went to work to catch him. Once caught, he could be made to confess anything. Jefferson Davis was in the matter somewhere, and if he was not, soon would be. Of that Stanton was sure. He worked on.

So did everyone. In the newspaper offices the staffs were up until dawn. The temper of the people had changed, and besides, there was the outside world to think of, and some sense of the fitness of things. Page after page of proof was ripped out and the set forms broken. The denunciations, the innuendoes, and the complaints about the President, the thought provoking, the witty, and the cruel editorials and

71

cartoons, all had to be scrapped, down to the last insulting poem by the least known poetess. Into their place went laudations and long descriptions of the nation's grief. In the offices of the *National Intelligencer*, the sleepy daily poet ran up some passably convincing verses. Lincoln had been felled by a lone maniac. How else could it have happened, in a nation where everyone had loved him so?

That was the tone to take, though a few followed Stanton's lead and wrote of a widespread conspiracy.

In Washington City it began to be sallow dawn. No matter what happens, the milk cart must start out at the appointed hour, and the taverns open. In the public buildings the janitors had worked all night in the usual way. They were ready to go home now. The gas went off. The windows went up. At the Navy Yard, the sentries changed, and in an open field, Lewis Payne woke up in his tree and did not know where he was.

Only in the front parlour on 10th Street did the light have trouble seeping round the closed drapes. But even there the light began to grow stronger. There was no sound but that eternal military tramping in the corridor, and then, at first quietly, but then heavily, it began to rain.

At six Lincoln's pulse began to fail. His respiration was twenty-eight. By six thirty the breathing became unmistakable. His face began to glisten. At seven came the symptoms of immediate dissolution. The President began to moan, those long, frightening moans Lamon and Cook, his guards, had heard so often in the White House corridor, when he had his nightmare. His breathing became swift, his lips were everted. But his hands did not move on the coverlet. They were now incapable of motion.

Leale held one of them. He had done so all night. Lincoln was beyond reason, but should he regain consciousness, Leale wanted him to know that at least there was someone there to hold his hand.

Barnes, the Surgeon General, went to fetch Mrs. Lincoln. She was brought in, looked at Stanton from a distance he did not understand, and then allowed herself to be led away.

Stanton remained. Sumner remained. Barnes looked at his watch. Dr. Gurley came in.

The chest of the body went up as usual, but did not inhale again. They watched it for a moment. The time was twenty-two minutes past seven. The world seemed motionless.

"Now he belongs to the ages," said Stanton. Dr. Gurley began a prayer.

He was gone.

They had no precedent for such a thing. Neither had they had a precedent for such a man. The sound of the rain was unmerciful. He was gone, but he was more there than ever. And now he had gone, they could not get over the idea that more than a man had died, that, living, he had protected them from something which was plain to be seen, but which none of them wished to see.

And so he had. He was the last of the old men.

X

The new world began at once. That left them at a loss. Not even Dr. Gurley seemed to know what to say.

At six a.m. the Presidential guard, Parker, had wandered into a precinct station. He was drunk, but he knew he had to account for those missing eight hours somehow. So he brought along Lizzie Williams, one of his tarts, to have her booked for immoral conduct. The sergeant on duty refused. Lizzie Williams was let go. But beyond that there was nothing to say to Parker. He was a policeman in good standing, secure in his position. It did not even enter his head to ask what had happened to the President. He went home with an easy conscience. His job was still safe, and that was all that mattered to him.

At 10th Street the body lay ominous on its bed. Dr. Gurley went on praying. Leale walked out of the house. He noticed neither the rain nor that he had forgotten his hat. All around him the church bells of the city were beginning to toll. One after the other, from every direction, they began to ring out, solemn, insistent, and unnecessary. From the Navy Yard came the first funereal crash of cannon.

Dr. Leale realized that he was weeping, and must have been weeping almost since he had left the house. The tears poured down, even though he was calm with fatigue, and he did nothing to stop them. Digging his hands into his pockets, he walked through unfamiliar streets, though he supposed he knew them well enough. The crowds he walked through were either silent or weeping too.

As Mrs. Lincoln was helped down the stairs of the Petersen house, she saw the cold brick façade of Ford's Theatre, moist with rain, across the street.

74

"Oh, that dreadful house," she said. "That dreadful house."

There was nothing to do but agree, and to take her back to that no less dreadful house on Pennsylvania Avenue.

At the station the actor Matthews was boarding a train. In his hotel room he had opened the letter Booth had left with him for the *National Intelligencer*. Matthews read it once and then burned it. He now hoped to be able to reach the Canadian border.

Stanton's net caught him anyway.

In New York, the *New York World* had its editorial in place. It contained much praise, since the paper would be quoted abroad, but the praise was grudging.

"The conspicuous weakness of Mr. Lincoln's mind on the side of imagination, taste, and refined sensibility," its editorial writer said, "has rather helped him in the estimation of the multitude. . . . Among the sources of Mr. Lincoln's influence we must not omit to mention the quaint and peculiar character of his written and spoken eloquence. Formed on no model, and aiming only at the most convincing statement of what he wished to say, it was terse, shrewd, clear, with a particular twist in the phraseology which more than made up in point what it sometimes lost by its uncouthness."

The editorial writer thought that rather handsome of him, for it was more than he would have said had the occasion been otherwise. New York was perhaps still a little out of touch with the new national grief.

In the White House, Tad Lincoln, who was only a young sprat, heard the carriage drive up and stood, wide awake, on the stairs to the second floor.

"Mr. Welles," he said. "Who killed my father?"

It was nine in the morning. Mr. Welles had brought the body back, in a rain splattered hearse. He had always trusted Mr. Welles.

Mary Lincoln appeared above him on the stairs and peered down hopelessly. It was Mr. Lincoln, always, who had known how to console Tad. She turned and went back to her

75

room, the one that connected with the other one, the empty one. The door between was shut.

There were so many things about Lincoln people could not see, that they saw now, and would forget soon enough, now that his body lay downstairs in state.

It was Stanton's turn to run the country. There was no one else to run it, for Johnson had yet to collect his wits. What Stanton wanted was revenge. Let Stanton have his way.

Part Two

XI

Dr. Mudd could not sleep. He had not slept for hours. His passion was to own land. He had no other. And now he was afraid.

He had qualified as a doctor only in order to qualify for the gentry, an important matter in Maryland. His practice was as small as he could keep it. In youth one believes in these things. Time, marriage, and his father had taught him better. Love and the professions demand responsibility. Business does not. So to business one carries off the pride, frustration, and terror of one's soul. It was revenge on the world and pleasure to one's self, to see the land one owned. He never looked at any other. And little by little, as his marriage decayed and he found himself puzzled by the silences at his own table, Dr. Mudd had extended his holdings. And now, because of this absurd humane profession of his, which prevented him, when appealed to, from turning any poor stray away from his door, he felt obscurely in danger. It took him most of the morning to puzzle out why. And when he had done so, characteristically, he mentioned the matter to no one, but dealt with it in his own way, by doing nothing.

The trouble had begun a little after four in the morning, when he had been roused by a knocking and halloing downstairs. As he lay in bed listening, he heard the hound dogs barking both in his own yard and across the fields.

He did not want to answer the door. On the other hand, neither did he want it beaten in, and there were Federals in the neighbourhood. He went downstairs in his nightshirt and found himself facing a country bumpkin with a moon face and a nervous, excited manner. That made him feel better at once. He knew how to handle bumpkins.

"My friend here hurt his leg," said Herold. "His horse threw him. He's afraid it's broke."

Mudd peered into the drizzly half light beyond the door. One horse, a cheap rocker by the look of her, stood grazing the lawn. On the other sat an erect, heavily wrapped figure whose features he could not see.

The nature of the call reassured him. He ventured on the lawn. He was wearing scuffs, but the wet grass tickled his feet all the same. He and the yokel carried the man inside and dumped him on the parlour sofa. Mudd went to get a candle.

The man on the sofa turned his face away.

A doctor, even one who practises as little as Mudd, pays more attention to bodies than faces, and remembers them better. But he had never examined Booth before, and so did not recognize him. He saw at once the man would have to be moved upstairs. He went to fetch his wife to light the way. Mrs. Mudd delighted in an interesting invalid, for her life was dull. Yet hold the candle how she would, the patient always twisted away. She could not see his features.

Upstairs in the bedroom, Mudd slit the boot and threw it under the bed, stripped off the stocking, which was sweaty and distasteful to him, and took a look at the leg. A look was all he needed. It was a simple case of Pott's fracture, nothing serious, but the man would not be able to walk for weeks. He could stay where he was overnight, rest, and fetch a carriage tomorrow.

Booth was so consternated he was driven to speech. Mudd turned to look at him. Perhaps the *crêpe* beard had slipped. Booth disguised his voice.

Mudd frowned and went out to get splints. He took his wife with him. She, too, was anxious now.

Mudd told her not to worry. Queer things happened these days. Perhaps the man was an escaped Reb. Perhaps he was a deserting Northerner, for though the war was over, one could still be punished for that. It was better not to ask questions. A doctor had certain legal privileges. It was his duty to treat the patient who came to his door, not to ask his name. But Mudd did not like it, all the same. When he went up with the splints, he refused either to look at his patient or to talk to him. He gave his wife the same advice. The less they knew about the man the better.

80

Then he went down to breakfast, taking the younger man with him. The younger man was if anything too talkative. He said his name was Henston, and that the injured man was a Mr. Tyser. They were ridiculous names. Clearly Mr. Henston was lying, but the doctor was grateful just then for a lie. Henston asked for a razor. Mudd did not want to know any more. Henston had no facial hair, and the man upstairs had a grey beard, even though his moustache was black. Why should a man in a feverish condition suddenly decide to shave? Mudd got out of there and went to supervise his field workers. He did not want that man in the house. He was a southerner. These days it was dangerous to harbour a southerner. Yet he could not very well turn the two strangers over to the authorities, either. Surely not even a war can make human loyalty and love of your birthplace a crime.

And yet Mudd knew that was exactly what the war had done. It had changed the world. Loyalty and love were now a crime. He did not know what to do. For though his life was directed by prudence, he was not yet so modern as to be beyond loyalty. He might detest that restraint, but all the same, it bound him in.

Upstairs Booth fell asleep. Like Richard, his best part, he could add colours to the chameleon. He was loyal only to himself. He gave no thought to the repercussions of what he had done. And besides, his bed was so soft. He had never before realized, since he had slept in them all his life, the utter luxury of a well-made bed. He had lived so high on the hog these last years, for that matter, that he had never before realized the sheer luxury of being alive at all. It was pain that made him aware of that. He had never felt pain before, either.

XII

As always in that family, Edwin was the first to suffer. He was only thirty-two, but his career had been an insane and jumbled confusion of extremes. He had played low comedy, and he had played *Hamlet* for a hundred nights. Yet the triumph meant nothing. In America, he had said once, not bitterly, but sadly, art degenerates even below the standard of a trade. Yet at the same time he knew that art is a trade. Like jewellers whom the public can no longer afford, artists still spend their little increment upon the adornment of the world, for that is all they know how to do, even though the world be too spiritually impoverished to afford any longer their luxuries. The artist cannot afford them either. So he who would become master of the revels winds up a victim of his own abilities. Despite himself, life had made Edwin a tragedian, yet alone of that family, he had had a sense of humour. No doubt that is what makes one a tragedian. As a child, when they had all play-acted for pennies in a Baltimore cellar, it was he who had wanted to be the clown. But comedy turns to irony, and irony to divine comedy, which, as in Dante, ends happily only in heaven. *Hamlet* is only the *Pagliacci* of the self. Circuses are no more than a parable. Last night he had played Sir Giles Overreach, who is all the world's jape, which no doubt is why the world loves to see the part performed. And who should he be today, as he woke up in Boston?

He found out soon enough. The news was everywhere. Wilkes had shot Lincoln.

That overwhelmed him. That was the madness of the family, showing at last. But it did not surprise him. Not, at any rate, now that it had happened. In an insane family, it is only the sane one who worries about his sanity. "You look like Hamlet," his father had said in California. "Why do you not do it for your benefit?" But Hamlet was a role to no one's benefit. It had too much melancholy in it. Now Wilkes had put them on a larger stage, and they would all die in Act Five. For no one gains from Hamlet, no one at all, except Fortinbras. That normal creature, that only member of the audience upon the stage, is moved, unmoved, and yet survives it all, to his own benefit. *That devil Wilkes*, in Wilkes' case, was no devil, but only a poor devil. If we are trained to do so, how easily we rant on; but that would not save the family.

Edwin stayed in his room. Yet he could not stay in his room. He would have to take some action. His mother, that simple hearted creature, alone in New York with his idiot sister Rosalie, would need his help. And so would Junius and his sister Asia, with her husband, Sleeper Clarke, who would be furious now. At least his own daughter was safe with Asia.

"If it be now, 'tis not to come; if it be not to come, it will be now; if it be not now, yet it will come: the readiness is all." Those lines summed up his life. They were his favourite lines. He had spoken them much more than a hundred times. He thought of them often. And yet he was not ready.

There was a note from the manager of the theatre, not so much to ask, as to point out to him, that it would be better if he did not appear that night. Edwin sat down and answered it. He wrote from the heart, for he had a heart, and he had always admired Lincoln. He would co-operate in every way. And he agreed. It would be better if he never acted again. How could he? He had tried to rise above his family, but his inheritance had once more pulled him down. Madness was all. An actor is limited. He has no right to make the world his stage, for then he reminds us of what we do not want to know, that we are merely players.

"I am oppressed," he wrote Jarrett, the manager who had decided to close the theatre, "by a private woe not to be expressed in words." And neither was it. He could only stare. Even Edwina's name would be besmirched by this thing Wilkes had done. It was all very well to say not so, but he knew how the world went.

In Cincinnati, Junius Brutus Booth had yet to find out.

In that family it was Junius Brutus who was the business-man. His nerves were as thick and as sensible as his legs. The eldest, he saw himself as the uncle of them all. He was also the sanest. But he did not know what had happened. He came downstairs after breakfast and told the desk clerk he was going for a walk. The clerk winced and told him there was a mob out in the streets, waiting to tear him to pieces.

Junius did not understand and looked bewildered. He knew about mobs, of course, and what they could do, for he had been a charter member of the Vigilantes in California. But that had been a small mob, acting only because there was no other justice to call upon. Here life was orderly and settled, as it was supposed to be. What had a mob to do with him?

The clerk told him.

Junius could hear the mob now. It was a sound he had never heard before, for in California he had been at the head of it. It was his first and only glimpse of what lies underneath the surface of life, and from what lies that surface is accreted. The clerk told him to take refuge in his room upstairs, and he went at once.

But he could hear them down there, and for the first time in his life he was afraid. He was afraid of what life was. Unlike Edwin, he was not a thinking man. He was merely clever. He had never before glimpsed the reality of the theatrical pretence.

It made him unwilling ever to enact tragedy again. The sound downstairs was inhuman. He could almost hear that mob knot a greasy rope. It did not even care that he was the wrong man. It merely wanted someone to play with.

Finally the hotel staff managed to smuggle him away.

For their mother, in New York, it was perhaps worst of all.

Mary Ann had felt lost for years. Without her husband, and uprooted from Maryland, she no more than existed in New York. A country girl snatched up from London flower selling, she had been whisked here, by a man who could not even marry her, and buried on a farm in Maryland. In forty years she had not yet caught her breath. She at least had the children. Their father's death had been almost a relief; illegitimate they might be, but now at least there would be grandchildren to play with.

It had not worked out that way. She did not understand the brood she had reared. They puzzled her as much as their father had done, and she loved them far less. They were so seldom home, and their children they kept away from her. Even Edwin, who meant to be kind, sent his daughter to Philadelphia and not to her. Asia was a witty, caustic stranger, ashamed of her own birth. Junius Brutus evaded her, Edwin, who had been so lively a child, had unaccountably darkened. He was kind to her, of course, but only because he wished to be. She was not taken in by that, even though she was grateful to him for being so. Rosalie was weak minded, though, since she stayed home, she was better than no company at all.

Somehow life had turned her into a useless old woman. Of them all, only Johnny had ever flattered her enough to remember she had ever been young. So why should she not have indulged Johnny? She had kept him home and let him play the gallant. She found that agreeable. And now he called himself Wilkes, and had done this dreadful thing.

She was a silly woman. She knew that. She had never aspired to anything else. Why should not a woman be loved and silly? She couldn't help that, could she? Silliness was all her safety and all her power. Silliness had kept her snug and warm for years, even though she had had to manage everything and yet find the energy to be silly, or at least to pretend to be.

Of course she had idolized her husband. In her day that had been the proper thing to do. It was certainly not a crime. At the same time she hadn't exactly been sorry when he had gone. He had been a difficult man to deal with. She had preferred to dote on Johnny. He broke her heart, of course. He refused to grow up, he was a devil with the women. But really, having one's heart broken was rather nice. It gave her

85

something to do during the day, which was more than any other member of the family had done.

Besides, he was so dashing. He had such a nice smile. How could he possibly have murdered *anyone?* In some fight over a woman, perhaps, or on the battlefield, though she had stopped that by forbidding him to enter the army, not wanting to have him hurt any more, she had seen, than he had wanted to go. But how could he expose them to this *public* thing?

She knew what her duty was. A mother's duty in time of trouble is to go to her children's family. The only family to go to was Asia's. She shrank from that. Asia was so inhuman. But all the same she made arrangements about the train. She had to do something. Her great hurt she would keep to herself.

Poor Edwin, she thought for a moment, up there alone in Boston, and then thought no more about him. Johnny often left letters with Asia. Perhaps there would be some explanation waiting there.

XIII

John T. Ford, the owner of Ford's Theatre, was in Richmond, supervising what could be saved from his properties there, when they brought him the news that Booth had shot the President, and where.

"Impossible," Ford said. "He's not in Washington." For like the rest of the world, when he thought of the name Booth, he thought of Edwin first. Then, with a shock, he remembered that John Wilkes had been in Washington City that night. The man was mad as a hatter, but that would make what he had done none the easier for the rest of them. Ford made plans to go to Washington.

Booth woke towards noon. He felt deliciously relaxed. Then the pain began again. What had wakened him was the familiar country noises outside the windows and in the fields beyond. It was raining. The familiar sounds gave him a childhood, soothed, and tucked in feeling. Then he remembered where he was.

He was frightened. He had to get away. He would not be a hero until he reached the South. As he swam up from sleep, his mind caught at various pieces of rhetorical flotsam. "Truly the hearts of men are full of fear: You cannot reason (almost) with a man that looks not heavily and full of dread." That was the citizens in Richard III, and not what he wanted. He grabbed at another speech.

> What! do I fear myself? There's none else by:
> Richard loves Richard; that is, I am I.
> Is there a murderer here? No. Yes, I am:
> Then fly. What! from myself? Great reason why.

No, that would not do either. He had almost drowned in that sea of words, but now he was awake. He was reduced once more to the status of a man. Therefore it behooved him to escape.

Before he could turn his head, Mudd was in the room, examining his wound. Mudd was still worried. He had seen something he had no wish to see, and refused to recognize, but it had made him more than ever eager to keep the patient upstairs out of sight, where the servants could not see him. Servants blab, and Negroes have a thousand ways of getting even with their former masters.

Therefore, when Booth demanded a carriage, Mudd temporized. He would do his best, but this was Saturday. Most of the local carriages were reserved for Easter Sunday. It would not be easy to find one.

Booth saw no signs of recognition in the doctor's face. Whether that blankness was real or assumed, he had no way of knowing. He paid the man twenty-five dollars. He hoped that would be enough.

Mudd said he was going into Bryantown. Booth sent Herold with him. Someone had to watch the doctor. Herold could not be trusted, and yet in some measure he was dependable enough. It was the best Booth could do. The two men left, and Booth was left alone. The afternoon wore on.

In Washington City, Stanton had decreed one last performance of *Our American Cousin*, to be held behind locked doors. The actors were led out of the Old Capitol Prison, where he had sent them, and into the theatre. They were innocent, all of them, but they had spent a night in prison. That had left them with a guilty look.

It did not improve matters that the play was a comedy. The stage was still set up for Hawk's monologue, but the theatre itself was empty, and so brilliantly lit, as to seem even more than hollow. The brilliant lights were for the photographers, whose shrouded boxes stood everywhere, with nothing to be seen except a white hand reaching out from under the cloth, to remove the lens caps.

Military guards also stood everywhere. Footsteps in the lobby could be heard on the stage. There was no one down in the seats but detectives and military officials. The whole play had to be run through. Stanton was determined to prove some collusion between the actors and what Booth had done. It was difficult to remember lines. As they approached that interrupted scene, they became more and more nervous. The auditorium, without an audience to warm it, was cold. Laura Keene shuddered. They all shuddered.

At last Hawk's scene arrived again. Mrs. Mountchessington left the stage. Harry Hawk stood there alone.

"Well, I guess I know enough to turn you inside out, you sockdologizing, you sockdologizing," said Harry Hawk, and his voice dried up.

"Go on," said the assistant from the War Department, speaking from a seat in the third row.

"You sockdologizing old mantrap," said Hawks. And because he could not help it, looked up at the Presidential Box. Nothing about it had been changed. But it was empty and dark. He heard a rustle behind him, Laura Keene, he supposed, in the wings. He paused, his arm extended.

From the box there was the creak of a rocker. Then somebody appeared at the box rail and jumped.

Laura Keene screamed.

The figure scuttled by Hawk, but it was only a young soldier, standing in for Booth. The performance was over.

Half an hour later they were led back to the Old Capitol Prison. Innocent they might be, and yet somehow their guilt had been proved.

Booth had shaved off his moustache. Without a moustache he looked callow and naked, which was how he felt. No one could hear him, but he could hear every noise in the house. He could not tell what was happening down there. Mrs. Mudd did not come up again. He paced the room. A coloured man brought him improvised crutches. He tried to hobble about. The room was beginning to get on his nerves. It was too much like a cell. The leaves of a tree barred the windows and sent a pattern of moving boughs across the floor, for the sun had come out weakly for a little while.

He heard a horse gallop up, and boots stumbling on the stairs. Herold burst into the room. There were Federal troops in the neighbourhood. They would have to get out of there, because Mudd knew who they were, and was going to turn them in.

He was lying.

Afraid to go into town with Mudd, he had reined off by the side of the road, at the entrance to Zekiah Swamp, waited for a while, and then made up his story. But Booth did not know that. He believed Herold. Putting on his false beard and his shawl, he took up his crutches and hobbled down the stairs.

A figure blocked his path. In the dim light of the stairwell it was hard to make out, but from the rustle of stuff he knew it must be Mrs. Mudd. She seemed bewildered.

He mumbled something to her, went out the front door, and hobbled across the lawn. Herold went ahead, riding one horse and leading the other. It was a long way across the lawn.

The servants watched them go. They had better memories for their own grievances than for facts, but they would remember Dr. Mudd was not a popular employer.

He knew that. He had heard all about the assassination by now, and what he did not know, he could guess. He began to sweat. Booth was tattooed with his initials on his left hand. So had been this man. That was what Mudd had tried not to see. Now, as he rode home, he could see nothing else. It was a coincidence, but he knew what a coincidence like that could lead to. There was only one way to defend himself. He would have to turn them in.

But when he got back to the farm, both men had fled. And so, since he knew he could expect no sympathy from the North, he decided to say nothing. That was what he usually said about things, anyhow.

It was his worst error. The game of hounds and hares demands a purse, and the reward posters were already coming from the printers. There was a hundred thousand dollars at stake. That was writ large. The death penalty for those

90

who aided or abetted their escape, in finer print, assured Stanton of a good trial. Some men might choose one reward, and some another.

But Mudd, who being cautious, preferred not to face any choice in this world, had not seen the reward posters yet. All he knew was that there were two thousand cavalrymen searching the county. He had not realized before, being a man of property, secure in the midst of his own extensive family, that the world we feel so secure in has such thin walls. He found the sound of the cavalry deafening, as it galloped by. Yet a doctor has defences of his own. He took a sleeping draught.

XIV

Herold pointed out a wagon track leading into the woods. The trees were slim and the cover far from dense. Booth turned down that way. The crutches bit into his armpits. The rocker mare rocked before him. Herold bent down from his horse.

Booth did not care for that. It was he who should be mounted, not this wretched underling. The ground was soft and muddy underfoot. His crutches sank into it, and when he pulled them free, he did not care for the sucking sound the effort cost him. Herold tempted him to ride, but he could not ride. It would be torture and he was in enough pain as it was.

They entered the Zekiah Swamp.

It was not impressive. Booth was used to better scenery. A swamp in a play has tall blue-grey trees, Spanish moss, will o' the wisps, willis, and dugout canoes, a mossy bank, and between the speeches and the Bengal lights, a nip of brandy in the Green Room, with someone to talk to. Here there was no one to talk to, except stupid Herold. The air was oppressive. He did not like this place. It had nothing in common with even that phosphorescent grandeur Gustave Doré produced to decorate Chateaubriand's Bernardin de St. Pierre America. Neither René nor Atala would have lasted a moment here, nor was there any kindly hermit to take them in. In one moment Booth had puffed all the kindness out of the world, as though he had been blowing an egg. He was left with the shell.

This swamp was low, muddy, uninviting, and treacherous. Booth looked at it and felt as though he were leaving the world forever. But Herold had cheered up. He felt sure footed. This was where he came when the world became too much for him, to hunt ducks.

Where was Payne? Herold was too weak even to support him while he hobbled. Payne was his courage. Payne made him feel himself again. He did not trust Herold. Herold was shifty and intractable. Near the open water the mud became viscous. Booth's crutches stuck fast and so did he. He shouted for Herold.

Herold was incapable of feeling pity and terror at the same time, and terror filled him up. They were not safe yet. "Either get mounted, or you'll stay here till the turkey buzzards get you," he said. Even the horses were mired. Booth was almost hysterical. Herold paid no attention. Hysterical himself, he knew hysteria was only another kind of drunkenness, and could be dealt with in the same way. He boosted Booth up on the rocker mare and then washed his hands in a patch of water, for Booth was covered with slime.

Irritated, Booth ripped off his *crêpe* beard and threw it away.

They had left the stream, neither man knew where. It was dusk already. All colours had faded, except those of the redbud. Frogs began to croak and peep. They rode on. Booth looked at his pocket compass, but could make no sense of it. The night was damp. Tree limbs and low bushes ripped at his exposed and wounded foot. Surely by now it must be Sunday morning?

Whether it was or not, a church loomed up before them, standing by itself at the intersection of several roads. It was a landmark of some kind, but Herold was lost. He could equate it with nothing. But if they were in the middle of nothing, at least they were safe there until it became something, and Booth could ride no more. He dismounted to wait on the church steps while Herold went off to find out where they were. He had decided to make for the house of a Southern sympathizer named Cox, which must be somewhere round here. Herold disappeared and he was alone.

All Maryland was being ransacked. He had to get to Virginia. The problem was how to get there. He no longer trusted Herold, for there was nothing to prevent the boy's running off. The cross roads before him were shadowy and the church behind him empty. He could feel the pressure of that emptiness. But he was weak and tired. He could not remain alert.

Herold came back, with a darky walking down the road behind him.

The darky seemed scared, but he was obedient. He had brought ham and bread. That was the way with darkies. They did as they were told until they could get away from you. It was ten miles to Cox's house. He would lead the way. When they arrived there, Booth told him to wait and faced the house.

Though the war had made him poor, Colonel Cox lived in a certain style, more style, anyhow, if on less money, than Dr. Mudd aspired to. The house was no plantation, but it was sizable, white with green shutters, and standing safely behind a barrage of picket fence. Herold pounded on the door knocker.

A light went on upstairs and Cox came down and opened the door. He had pulled on trousers over his nightshirt, and had a pistol at his belt. He knew it was wiser to go armed these days. He led them inside. Booth saw a sofa and lay down on it. Cox had a reputation for loyalty to the Southern cause. And so he told Cox who he was.

Cox said nothing. For the first time, as he looked about him, in the flickering candlelight of his own house, he saw that the room had too low a ceiling. He was not impressed by these gentlemen. The boy was a pewling afterbirth on legs, a druggist's clerk, by the look of him, or something like that. Booth was more complicated, but no better. He was that dangerous thing, a would-be gentleman. And besides, a gentleman shoots no one in the back, whatever the provocation. Even more than a Southerner, Cox was a Tory. He had the florid, square, businesslike face of some eighteenth-century provincial governor, but that did not mean that he was insensitive. Whatever else he might have been, Lincoln was at least a rational man. Cox looked at Booth with some contempt.

None the less, he could not turn him in. He was not an informer. Booth was a matinée idol, so they said. No doubt on the stage he did well enough. Now he was a wounded dog and had the same look in his eyes. It was a look Cox avoided. He was always kind to animals. He had learned enough of humanity, to be so. And besides, he had suffered enough in this war. The best way to suffer no more from this man, who had been born to bring suffering to others, you could see that in his face, was to help him to escape. But that would not be easy.

"Quarrel," he said.

Booth looked puzzled.

"Stage a quarrel, man. You're an actor, aren't you? There are too many ears in this house. I'll take care of you, but first I have to turn you out. So quarrel."

They quarrelled.

It did Cox good. He had no taste for politics. He thought them a dirty, self-advancing, Irish business. He merely loved his home, his way of life, his State, his adopted son, who lay wounded near Petersburg. What had politics to do with a man who sat on his own land and defended it, not out of principle or economic selfishness, but simply because he loved it?

Now this woods' colt, if rumour about the Booth bastardy was true, this silly play actor with the sensibility and the unreality of a Southern belle of seventeen, and none of the guts of the mistress of the house that belle had been educated to turn into, lay here and wanted help; without doubt he had brought new ruin on them all, not to mention upon his own family.

Cox talked on. He got rid of five years' worth of baffled sorrow. What he said meant nothing to the man, but at least it made him angry, and Cox was of the opinion that the impotent anger of weak men was exactly what they deserved.

"Curse as you go out, and curse loud," finished Cox. "I'll send you a man to guide you away from here."

He opened the front door. As he had expected, Booth had no trouble cursing. If his words lacked the right degree of coarseness, they had the right tone. Cox grinned as he slammed the door.

Herold and Booth went down the yard. At the gate a man was waiting to pick them up. He said his name was Robey

95

and that he came from Cox. Together the three of them stumbled through the wet countryside and came at last to a knoll covered with pine trees. There Robey left them to wait until Cox could send down someone with a boat to get them away, and perhaps with some food.

It was Sunday morning.

Back at the house, Cox stretched, yawned, spat in the fire, and found that he was still quivering with indignation. He cooled down and sent for his foster brother, Thomas Jones. Jones eked out these thin war years by poaching. Jones would be able to get them off, and would keep his mouth shut about doing so. The two men always owed each other a favour or two, so there was nothing to worry about there.

Because he believed what other men merely said they believed, Cox had managed to get through this world with an easy conscience. He went back upstairs to bed.

XV

Booth was furious. He did not care to be snubbed by the gentry. Cox was as bad, in his way, as Bessie Hale's father had been in his.

The copse of pines stood above the open fields, backed by a wood down to the unseen shore, and standing about a mile from the Cox place. Booth considered himself a gentleman. Whatever a gentleman did, he slept in a bed. He had never slept out of doors before, and the night was vile. The pine wood was no help for anything but cover. The trees were scraggly, with exaggerated needles so yellow and laden with moisture, that the slightest touch of wind discharged a volley of stale rain on to the faces of those below. Nor were pine needles comfortable to sleep on, either. He could not endure his situation for a moment.

Yet he was to endure it for five days.

When he woke the world was an oven of leaden grey as damp as the ground beneath his body. His hands and joints were stiff with moisture, and he had a fever. He shivered and huddled deeper in his blanket. No man should have to be exposed in this way.

Afraid he had been deserted, he shouted for Herold. At last the boy appeared, looking as though he were going to cry. Booth had no patience with that, and sent him to look after the horses. When Herold came back it was to say that Booth's rocker had tugged its rope loose and escaped. Booth said what he thought of that, saw by the boy's face he would have to go carefully, otherwise the bloated booby would run away, and sent him to fetch back the mare. That used up all his remaining strength. He had not the will to think. After a while he heard someone whistle.

He thought at first it was troops come to take him alive.

97

He did not mean to be taken alive. He sat up, against the bole of a tree, and took out his revolver. On his lip a little spirit gum glistened, where he had had the beard fastened on. He should never have thrown it away.

Peering anxiously, he recognized Herold and another, older man, approaching. The older man was leading Booth's escaped mare. The stranger had a long, gaunt face with a dreary moustache, but his eyes, like those of Cox, were bright.

"Mr. Jones has a boat," said Herold. "He can get us across the river."

Booth began to rail against Cox. Thomas Jones paid no attention. He had heard all that before, from other men, and he knew more about his foster brother than Booth did. He had only wanted to see the man before making up his mind. Saving them was a futile gesture. The war was lost. But now, from the look of Booth, he saw that the man would have to be got out of the way, if Cox and he were to save their own necks. A promise to Cox was a promise.

Besides, he felt sorry for the poor devil. Booth was still handsome, but he already had the marks of decay on him. Jones had seen him act once. He was a good, noisy, vigorous actor, more animal than anything else, but a speaking animal. He certainly had a good voice. But the vigour was beginning to go out of him. Being a fugitive didn't suit him; and somebody had to help him, since clearly he didn't know how to help himself.

Booth shrank away. The one thing he did not want was pity. He felt small lying there, before this faded denim man with the watchful face.

The niggers would be worst, Jones saw that. Every nigger in the country was weeping and wailing for Lincoln, as well he might. Booth would have to stay where he was, until it was safe to get him out, but he saw no point in telling the man that. He looked close enough to the end of his rope as it was. Jones gave them the food he had brought and said he would be back when he could, tomorrow maybe. Booth seemed to want only two things, brandy and the newspapers. Brandy was more than Jones could manage, this was corn likker country, but he said he'd see about the papers. He went away.

Booth fell asleep, and when he woke, saw Herold polishing up the guns, as though nothing had happened, and this were only a hunting expedition.

"Davy," he said. "Do you know the manners of good society?"

Davy just stared at him. No, he did not. He went on polishing the gun.

Before him Booth saw an enormous decanter of cut glass. He knew it was not there, but he had to have it.

"Davy, I want brandy," he said. His throat had gone back on him again. He realized he was whispering. How could he act, if he had bronchitis? Besides, there was no brandy.

"Davy, have you ever thought of dying?"

"No," said Herold, who at the moment thought of little else and was beginning to long to avoid the experience. He did not like the way Booth was looking at him. But then Wilkes' eyes glazed over, he swallowed hard, and began to carry on a monologue about the nature of good society.

That was what he wanted the papers for. He wanted to find out what good society had to say of him. Good society, when it is bored, which is most of the time, is only too delighted to have a hero worth the fêting, one who knows the difference between a knife and fork, and has a friend like Payne to help him, though Payne, poor loyal lad, was not instructible and would never appreciate that difference.

Everything would be all right once Payne came. Where was Payne?

XVI

He was in Washington City, cold, miserable, and lost. He could think of nothing to do, except to wait for Cap to come and rescue him. He knew Cap would.

He had spent his second night in that old tree, down by the Potomac. Now he walked across a dry vacant lot, his coat flapping in the breeze, turned round to watch the river and the Maryland shore, and went off to get something in his stomach. He did not care what the food was, just so he could fill up on it.

It was Easter Sunday, he supposed, to judge by the church bells, but he felt bedraggled and bored. A meal made him feel no better. He was in a poorer section of town. There were no fine ladies to watch, as they swept into church like great self-willed conservatory flowers. At most, a woman here and there had turned her bonnet or added a papier-mâché bunch of berries to it.

Having nothing else to do, he slipped into the back pew of the nearest church. It was that sort of church, with pitch pine pews and no stove, fundamentally cold, in which the preacher, knowing nothing of it, is chronically given to deploring the world. Payne grinned. His own father had been a hellfire preacher, which was one reason why he had left home. He was used to that kind of oratory.

"Would that Mr. Lincoln had fallen elsewhere than at the very Gates of Hell," groaned the preacher, who had a badly shaved Adam's apple. "We remember with sorrow the place of his death. It was a poor place to die in. The theatre is one of the last places to which a good man should go, the illumined and decorated gateway through which thousands are constantly passing into the embrace of gaiety and folly, intemperance and lewdness, infamy and ruin."

That was enough for Payne. He had learned those adjectives at his father's knee, and they were to him no more than what they were, a meaningless nursery jingle to soothe the fretful and the underprivileged. Still, they did not soothe him.

For its own reasons, the Government, or Stanton, anyway, agreed with the preacher. They had to arrest someone. That was why the whole cast of the theatre was in jail. But there was nothing to be got out of them. They had to be let go. Stanton turned his attention to the Booth family instead.

He was a little behindhand. The public had got to them first. The anonymous letters had already begun to come in, delivered by special post, so as to arrive on Sunday. Edwin was the chief recipient. "Bullets are marked for you," he read, before deciding to read no more. They all got them, from Mary Ann, to poor Junius's daughter by an earlier marriage, Blanche de Bar Booth.

Souvenir hunters streamed out of Baltimore to Bel Air, and tore Tudor Hall to pieces. Old clothes, dead leaves, and bits of the upholstery all went down that public maw. The newspapers were splenetic. Mary Ann, in New York, could only hope, as she boarded the train for Philadelphia on Saturday, that Wilkes would not live to be hanged. There was nothing else left for her to hope for. The papers were full of the whole sorry story of their lives. They were illegitimate. Their father had been a bigamist, and their mother, that is to say, herself, Mary Ann, not even so good as a common law wife. Junius's daughter had been born out of wedlock, while he was still married to his first wife. Edwin was a former drunkard, whose neglect of her had killed his wife.

He believed that himself, but he did not want to read about it in the newspapers. He held his head in his hands. Even their Jewish blood was dragged up against them, and not least in the Jewish press.

He sat down to write to Asia. Asia had treated him badly, but she was his sister, his child Edwina was with her, he hoped in safety, and someone had to advise Asia, who was fanatical about Wilkes and always had been. There was no telling what she might say or do.

"Think no more of John," he wrote. "As your brother, he is dead to us now as soon he must be to all the world, but

101

imagine the boy you loved to be in that better part of his spirit in another world." He had already had a broken-hearted letter from Bessie Hale, Wilkes' fiancée. That too had shaken him.

He had not himself loved Wilkes. He had not cared for his patriotic posturing and his incompetence. He had loved him only as the one member of the family who lived in a charmed circle, and so had been able to afford irresponsibility, and yet who was in some way weak.

Now they knew in what way, but it would not help Asia to tell her that. Poor Asia. She was a great hater. That would make it all the more difficult for her to bear the hatred of the world. At least she was in Philadelphia. But so was Sleeper Clarke. Sleeper Clarke had married her, Edwin had told her so at the time, only to get a leg up in the theatrical world by means of the Booth connection. Since Asia was ashamed of her connection with the stage, he had made little out of it, which had made him irritable to begin with, so goodness only knew what he would have to say to Asia now.

Sleeper had nothing to say. Others might go to church, but in the Clarke house in Philadelphia no one went there. They had not the stomach, the house had already been ransacked by the police, and Asia was under house arrest. That the Booths should consider it their house always infuriated Sleeper, who owned it, and he was no more sedate now. If that fool Wilkes had not been let in here, against his express orders, by Asia, they would not all be in this trouble.

Asia, who was five months pregnant, sat in a chair placed for some reason in the middle of the parlour, and, watching her husband, wondered how long she had detested him. She had married, it was true, in order to get away from home, but in those days Sleeper had been different. For one thing he had been called Sleepy; for another, he had not been so relentlessly businesslike. Edwin was right: he had tried to claw his way up by means of her. But she was a woman, not a ladder. Sometimes Sleeper forgot that.

Unfortunately he was a ridiculous man. He might not be very bright, though he schemed enough for two men, but he had that rare thing, a physical comic genius. Do what he would, pose as a man of affairs, and as a matter of fact, he was a good one, rant and rave, or upbraid her, that appearance of his always defeated his best domestic effects. He could relax an audience simply by looking at it and saying "whoops". But time had hardened him. It seemed impossible to believe that he had once gone out of his way to amuse her. On stage his best part was the title role in something called *Toodles*. It was years since he had played Toodles at home. She had to confess that she had shrunk from the vulgarity of it, when he had. But now she shrank from his rage.

For years he had hated all the Booths, and in particular, Edwin, who was everything Sleeper could not be. He loathed Mary Ann. Now Mary Ann was here, and they were going to open the packet Wilkes had left with Asia.

The packet contained two letters. One had been written to Mary Ann the previous November. Clarke read it by himself. It was a piece of fiddlefaddle, as one might expect, but at least it exonerated the family, if one could believe it. Clarke looked around at Asia and Mary Ann, and believed nothing.

The second letter was the more recent, the longer, and addressed, To Whom It May Concern. It was even worse than the first one. It had not even been sealed. It was nonsensical, dangerous taradiddle. He read it aloud, and went right on reading it, even after Mary Ann had fainted. The letter was a justification, if so one could call it, of the crime.

Asia did not faint. She was not the sort of woman who did. She revived Mary Ann and helped her upstairs. Then she came back and demanded to read the letter for herself. Clarke would not allow her to. He read it aloud. He wanted to make her squirm.

She did not squirm. But she remembered. Of course Wilkes had been some kind of Southern courier. Unknown to Clarke, many people had come to this house on his errands. She pretended not to see them. She also remembered something else. She had often heard Wilkes say that there was a fine chance for immortality, for anyone who might shoot the President, and she knew about Wilkes'

103

thirst for fame. She had always thought that nothing but guff. And yet, as she listened to Clarke's awful voice drone on she knew that, yes, Wilkes had actually done this thing.

She could not understand that. They had loved him so. Had he no thought for his family? Surely he had loved them in return. She knew he loved her. Looking at Clarke, she tried to hold on to that certainty.

XVII

No, he had not thought of his family. He seldom did. He had a mother and a brother who played *Hamlet*, that was true, and even a useful sister Asia, who coddled him, but he was determined to be the only Booth. He was himself alone. And so he did not even now think of them. He was more worried about his present situation. He was helpless in the hands of incompetents, he did not feel well, and he did not know what to do next.

He lay under that accursed hangman's tree of a pine, the biggest one, and wanted very much to shriek. He had had a bad night. It was Monday, if one knew what day it was in a wood, and still that man Jones did not return. He saw it must be dawn, which was not a sight he was often up to watch. Late rising was half his occupation, its hallmark, and its privilege. Not that there was much to see. There was a sluggish ground mist which streamed upward, changed colour, and drowned him in a shallow sea of sickly yellow fog. Herold was still asleep. The two horses were tied to trees. Off somewhere he heard a bugle sounding reveille. That meant soldiers in the neighbourhood. He roused Herold and sent him to quieten the horses.

No one came. Herold went into the underbrush with his carbine. Booth felt irremediably lost. It was hard to remember who one was, without an audience to play to. Never having been ill before, he had not realized what a tyrannical and terrible thing one's own body could be. He felt it would eat him up, if once he was so unwary as to lose consciousness. On the ground before him was the nibbled wreck of a small pine cone. He concentrated on that.

When he looked up, Jones was standing in front of him. Jones did not ask how he felt. He merely handed over a blanket, a bottle of whisky, a packet of food, and the news-

105

papers. There was no telling how long he had been standing there.

Hungry though he was for food, Booth was hungrier to know what the world thought of him. He opened up the *National Intelligencer.*

"There's a lot of soldiers around today," Jones said. Booth scarcely heard him. The paper was two days old, and full of nothing but Lincoln, page after black leaded page of it. From the *Intelligencer* he turned to the New York papers, but found them no better. They did not even mention his name.

What had Matthews done with that letter? It should have filled two full columns at least, for it had been a long letter which explained everything. It was one of the best letters he had ever written. Had that coward Matthews thrown it away, or had the damned Government deliberately suppressed it? Since it gave a true account of the matter, and the papers seemed to regard Lincoln as a martyr, which he certainly wasn't, perhaps the Government had.

He turned back to the *Intelligencer* again, and finally found his name in a short item. The account was uncertain, as though nobody knew who he was. In another despatch, Stanton was said to have said that John Wilkes Booth had played some part in the crime, but his name was not even in the bold type usually reserved for proper names. His trunk had been found at the National Hotel, and Stanton referred to O'Laughlin: General Augur offered ten thousand dollars for O'Laughlin's apprehension. Booth glanced at Jones. But Jones was helping Herold prepare the food.

Everything seemed to have gone wrong. A knife had been found on F. Street. It certainly was not his. A riderless horse had been captured. That must be Payne's. A small headline informed him that the route pursued by the criminals had been discovered, that one of them was Booth, and the other was supposed to be John Surratt. The authorities seemed to believe that it was Surratt, not he, who had engineered this thing. That was absurd. He stared at the papers with disbelief. He had staked everything on this one appeal to fame. And now his name was scarcely mentioned.

106

"Can't you get me some Southern papers?" he asked. He had always got a better press in the South. In the South they understood him.

Jones merely stared at him. Booth was weak enough to weep. Was there to be no eulogy?

"I want Southern papers," he said, and almost spilled his mug of coffee.

Jones felt sorry for the poor devil already. He did not want to see him cry. He couldn't figure Booth out at all. What did the man expect?

Behind them they heard a man's voice in the woods, and the sound of horses. A detachment of cavalry jogged by, so close that the flash of metal accoutrements could be seen through the trees. Then they were gone, but they would not be gone for long. Jones had jumped for the muzzle of his horse. Now he let go of it.

"You'll have to get rid of your horses," he said. "Otherwise they'll give you away."

Booth did not want to agree to that. Once the horses were gone he would be cut off from escape, and he didn't altogether trust Jones; but he was too weak to argue, and Herold was so scared he'd do anything Jones told him to do.

The two men led the horses away, and Booth went back to the papers. Now the sun was up, the ground steamed with damp.

Everything had gone wrong. Seward was still alive. The steel collar supporting his fractured jaw had saved him. There was no mention of Johnson at all, except the statement that it was suspected he had been marked out as one of the victims. Worst of all, there was no mention of him. So many people had wanted Lincoln dead. He alone had had the courage to kill him. Why then these eulogies of Lincoln, and none of him?

Far off, deep in the swamp, he heard the echo of two shots. The horses were gone. He was now dependent upon others for his escape. And from the way his own conspirators had behaved, right down to Lewis Payne, for Lewis had bungled the job and run away, he did not put much faith in others.

His letter had gone astray, and where were the other con-
107

spirators? Weak though he was, he would have to explain the whole matter again. He took out his notebook and opened to a blank page. The notebook was a diary for 1864, but he had no other paper. At the top of the blank page he saw he had once written *Te amo*. He could not for the life of him remember to whom that referred. He smoothed out the paper and wrote in the date. "April 12th, 13th, 14th, Friday the Ides." What Ides meant he was not sure, but he remembered the phrase from *Julius Caesar*. He also remembered that Brutus had died for his act. Because he was used to coming out after the death scene to take his bow, and he always did a good death scene, he had forgotten that, but now it struck him forcibly. Brutus is, however, the hero of the play. And so he should be, despite that cringing fool, Matthews.

The papers said he had been a cut-throat coward. That made him angry. "I struck boldly and not as the papers say," he wrote. "I walked with firm step through a thousand of his friends, was stopped, but pushed on." What if he had shot Lincoln in the back? What point would there have been in asking him to turn around? "Our country owed all her troubles to him, and God simply made me the instrument of His punishment," he went on. And then a little politics: "The country is not what it was. This forced Union is not what I have loved. I care not what becomes of me. I have no desire to outlive my country."

On the other hand, he had no real desire to die, either.

Jones and Herold loomed up in front of him and said that with so many troops on the move, Booth would have to stay where he was for another day or two.

Booth whimpered. It was too much. He did not see why he should have to suffer so. He sat there and went on writing as long as he could. It was necessary to explain about that letter to the *National Intelligencer*. Writing calmed him, but even so, he could not bear the thought of lying here like an animal another night, when others far worse than he lay in comfortable houses.

XVIII

They were not to lie in them long.

Monday, Edwin came back from Boston to New York. He had been questioned over and over again, but then released. Life might have no mercy, but he did have a few powerful friends. They saw to it that he was left at liberty, despite Stanton. It was not a liberty he much enjoyed, for overnight the whole world had become his prison. He could not bear to be seen. He would never act again. He dreaded even to descend from the train.

Tompkins, his host in Boston, had come with him. Edwin would almost rather have been alone. It had never occurred to him that anyone might find him lovable. Therefore, even when he needed it most, he shrank from help. Help was something he found it easier to give than to receive.

He was pale and tired. Life had bleached him out. For a mercy there did not seem to be any reporters about, but there was a plain clothes detective not far behind him, for though he was not to be arrested, he was to be watched. He looked around shyly. When he saw his old friend Tom Aldrich there, he smiled so hard he almost cried.

"Tom," he said. "You shouldn't have come." He was concerned. Tom Aldrich was a journalist who needed his job, and who could tell what might happen to anyone who spoke to a Booth these days?

They went straight to the 19th Street house. It was empty, except for Rosalie. Mary Ann was in Philadelphia with Asia. He had tried to make this house a home for Mary Ann, who certainly deserved one, but now the rooms seemed futile. He went right to his own bedroom. Poor Mary Ann, she was his mother, but perhaps for that very reason he never knew what to say to her. Now no one would know what to say to her. Johnny was the only one who was able to please her,

109

the only one she cared two pins about. For the first time, for he doted on his own daughter, he saw that willynilly, to be a parent is inevitably to expose oneself to loss.

He had forgotten. There was a portrait of John Wilkes on the wall beside his bed. He stared at it, while Tom Aldrich came in, glanced at it, and then tactfully looked away. In that instant Edwin knew he would never take it down. Whatever he had done, Wilkes was a member of the family. But neither could he bring himself to look at it any more.

The men settled down for the night. Through the shutters they could see the plain clothes man waiting down in the street. Booth did not dare to leave the house. As his father had once said bitterly, when someone he did not even know had greeted him on the street, "Everybody knows Tom Fool." The difference between fame and notoriety is seldom certain. Suddenly Tom Fool was exactly what Edwin had become. The wretched history of his family had finally tripped him up, as it was to do to how many others?

That was what Stanton wanted to know. How many others were there? Stanton had worked around the clock. Edwin might get away from him, but now he proposed to arrest everyone in sight. It was his usual method, for he had come to believe that all the world was guilty of something. It was merely necessary to discover of what, and that could be proven better in the Old Capitol Prison than in court. The writ of habeas corpus was still suspended. That gave him a free hand. He was in no hurry, but he was inexorable. He began with such of the conspirators as he could catch.

The first to be hauled in was Sam Arnold. He was easy enough to find. He was asleep in the back room of the store at Fort Monroe where he worked. Arnold was not surprised. He had read in the newspapers that the jealous and temporizing letter he had written Booth from Baltimore had been found when the police seized Wilkes' trunk at the National Hotel. What was the letter about? Nothing but that Booth had come to Baltimore and taken Mike O'Laughlin out to dinner instead of him. "How inconsiderate you have been," he had written.

How inconsiderate he had been. A kidnapping during a war was one thing. Murder after the war was over was another. Arnold had told Booth that. He had fallen in with the man only for the profit of knowing him, since Booth was involved in wartime smuggling. There was money in that. They ran quinine. Murder was another matter entirely.

Arnold did not have the look of a criminal. At twenty-eight he was a pleasant young man. And neither was he a criminal. When the arresting officers handed him a letter from his father, advising him to co-operate and to talk, he talked.

It was Booth the charmer, not Booth the assassin who had held his attention. He was not implicated in the assassination in any way. Why should he not talk?

With Mike O'Laughlin the matter was more serious. He had a deeper awareness of that vague Southern dream of the gentleman, and Booth had been kinder to him. He was small and delicate, but he had a firmer mind than Arnold. He knew what his own arrest was apt to lead to.

He had taken refuge at a boarding house, and so dodged arrest for two days. There seemed no point in trying to dodge it any longer. Those sent to arrest him seemed impressed by the fact that he apparently understood why he was being arrested and asked no questions. His only wish was to protect his family. He had been in Washington City that fatal night, and Arnold had not. He would undergo whatever he had to undergo alone.

Those were the only conspirators Stanton could gather in that day. Atzerodt, Payne, and Booth himself were still at liberty, as was Surratt, whom he wanted most of all. But if he could not have the son, the mother was available. Major Smith was despatched for Mrs. Surratt.

XIX

Out of some sad last minute whim, Mrs. Surratt had decided to play the piano, which she had not touched in weeks. She felt nervous, for she still had no news of John. She could not keep down some sense of dread. She raised the piano lid, stretched her fingers, and searched out a chord. The chord sounded sour, for the piano had got out of tune. Annie was dressed to go out to a party, and was waiting to be called for. Honora sat on the sofa. The other boarder, Olivia Jenkins, was equally quiet. But all four women had a lot to think about.

The house had been searched Saturday. The police were after John. Mrs. Surratt had told them nothing, but hoped John *had* had the sense to slip away over the Canadian border. Weichmann had left Saturday, and so had her other male roomer, Mr. Holahan. Mrs. Holahan had moved out Sunday, taking her child with her. So many departures were ominous.

The front parlour was not an agreeable room. One wall was decorated with a lugubrious lithograph called *Morning, Noon, and Night*. On another hung the arms of the State of Virginia, with two crossed Confederate Flags beneath it, and the motto written large. *Sic semper tyrannis* was the motto of Virginia, "Thus will it ever be with tyrants." Mr. Booth had admired it once.

And repeated it on Friday night.

What was to become of them all? Mrs. Surratt looked down at her fingers, and watched them search out the familiar melody, a piece by J. R. Thomas, "Bonnie Eloise, the Belle of the Mohawk Vale". It had been popular during the war. She had no real awareness of playing and no pleasure in doing so. She noticed only that her hands looked old.

The thing that had disturbed her most that day was some-

112

thing quite trivial. Happening to glance out the parlour windows, at about noon, she had seen a man across the street, his head under a black cloth, taking a photograph of the house with a large box camera on a tripod. As she watched, an arm reached out of the cloth, removed the metal cap, and she found the pupilless great eye of the camera staring at the house like the bore of a cannon.

She went right down the front steps and across the street. "What is the meaning of this?" she said.

The man said he did not know. He only knew that Mr. Brady, who photographed everyone and had photographed the war besides, had sent him to take a likeness of the house.

"But why?" she had insisted. "How dare you do such a thing without my permission?"

The photographer had given her a pitying look, snapped up his tripod, and walked away. It was a look she remembered now, even though her hands were playing this supposedly agreeable and sentimental music.

All four women heard the rattle of horses and then footsteps on the stoop, outside. Annie's escort, no doubt. He was a little late. The doorbell rang, Mrs. Surratt finished her phrase, and got up to answer it.

From the parlour the others could hear her gasp, as she opened the door. It was not Annie's escort. It was the military.

"We have come to arrest you and everyone in the house."

They heard that too. Annie glanced at the arms of Virginia on the opposite wall, but there was no time to remove it. Mama came back, sat down, and began to pray. The men followed. They did not like the job of arresting women. They were embarrassed. But they had no choice. Mrs. Surratt looked up and sighed. She would not be dragged through the streets like a common criminal. Nor would she have Annie treated so.

"May we have a carriage?" she asked. She was always a little timid with men, but it was a pitiable enough request. "It's cold and damp, and I don't want my daughter and these other ladies . . ." Her voice trailed off.

Major Smith was delighted to oblige. He would have done

113

anything to make his task less disagreeable. He sent one of his men out for a carriage and told the ladies to get their hats and coats. Mrs. Surratt rose to do so. Major Smith regretted that his orders were not to let her go through the house alone. A Mr. Samson would go with her.

She went upstairs, gathered up the coats and bonnets, and went back to the parlour. The women were tying their bonnets when the front doorbell rang again. Two of the soldiers answered it this time.

Outside they saw a tall man in a grey coat, black pantaloons, rather fine riding boots, and with the torn sleeve of an old shirt on his head. Over his shoulder he carried a pick axe. It was Payne. Seeing them, he turned around to leave. They would not let him leave. They asked him what he wanted. He said he wanted to see Mrs. Surratt. Perhaps he had mistaken the house. They asked him in and shut the door behind him.

Major Smith called Mrs. Surratt out of the parlour. The man said he had been hired to dig a gutter. Mrs. Surratt swore that he had not. She was short sighted and the hall was dim. But she recognized him, she thought. He was the man Booth had introduced to her as a preacher named Wood, who had stayed in the house a few days, about two months before. She saw no point in identifying him. Booth had caused her enough trouble already.

Payne said he had never seen her before either.

He only did that to save her. When he had stayed here as Wood, she had been kind to him. He had only come here because he had hoped Cap might be somewhere about.

They made him sit on a bench in the hall. He hauled out his oath of loyalty to the Union and showed them that. That was how they knew he was Payne. Even Mrs. Surratt had not known that. He had no will to resist. He knew the jig was up. But neither did he want to get Mrs. Surratt in trouble. When the soldiers told him to stand up, he shambled out between two of them, the way he guessed they wanted him to. If Cap wasn't here, it didn't much matter where he went.

Mrs. Surratt had gone back to the parlour. The ladies were in there, on their knees, while she led them in prayer.

It struck Major Smith that they had not asked, even obliquely, why they were being arrested. That made him thoughtful, but he was gallant enough to give Mrs. Surratt his arm, as they went out to the carriage.

In the carriage she sat as erect as she knew how and told the girls to do the same. She did not want the neighbours to know they were being hauled off ignominiously to jail. Looking up, she saw her own front door being shut. In the front parlour the lights were still on. That startled her, but she fully expected to be back. It did not occur to her that anything worse was going on than that she was to be grilled again about John's whereabouts. It was a mercy she did not know them. Otherwise these men might have been able to get them out of her, somehow. As the carriage left the familiar street, and headed she knew not where, she could not help but panic. She did so at that moment when she could not see her own house any more.

In the house Eliza Hawkins, the old coloured woman, went upstairs to turn off the gaseliers. When she got back to the kitchen Susan Mahoney was having hysterics. Mrs. Hawkins didn't like Susan, who was an ex-slave belligerent about standing up for her rights. She'd been working here two weeks, and didn't care two pins about anybody, white or coloured. All she wanted was her wages. That was what she was having hysterics about. She was afraid of being cheated out of what she called her rights. Mrs. Hawkins told her she'd be paid. Mrs. Surratt always paid her bills, if it took her the last cent she had. But that wouldn't do. Susan wanted the money now.

Eliza wanted to be shut of the wretched girl. She told her to be off to bed.

XX

A night's sleep made Susan feel no better. This house gave her the creeps, and she wasn't going to be cheated by no whites, not now the Negroes were free. She wanted to get even. Tuesday morning she got her chance.

The detectives had come back to search the house. They kept Susan and Eliza in the dining-room, while they did so. She knew now what Mrs. Surratt had been arrested for; and what was going to happen to any darky, now Mr. Lincoln was dead? She wasn't taken in by Mrs. Surratt either. Eliza might say she was good, but Susan knew she was just picky and stingy, so she could help Mr. Lincoln get shot.

From time to time a detective came into the room to ask questions. Two pictures of Booth had been found behind the *Morning, Noon and Night* lithograph. Whose were those?

"Dose belong Miss Annie," said Susan. "Miss Annie, she dote on Mr. Booth. She thinks she love that man."

Eliza slapped her face.

The detective got interested. "Tell me some more," he said.

"Sho, but not here," said Susan, and gave Eliza a wounded, down-trodden, cringing look.

The detectives took her away and she told them more. They offered her 250 dollars for everything she could remember. That was better than waiting round for a lot of lousy little ole wages. Besides, she liked the attention she was getting.

It wasn't any trouble at all to say that three men had come to the boarding-house after the assassination just to whisper so she could overhear it, that John Surratt had been at the theatre that night.

After she'd said that twice, she believed it. There were an awful lot of pretty dresses you could buy for 250 dollars.

Why couldn't she have the money now?

In his town house, Senator Hale was getting ready to corner his daughter. He had never approved of her crush on that man Booth, but he had been wise enough to wait for the thing to collapse by itself. Now he was angry. The assassination was vivid to him. He had had an interview with the President that same Friday. He had never had much use for Lincoln, but the man had appointed him Minister to Spain, which was decent of him, and this wasn't exactly the time to say what you thought. Now he had discovered, to his horror, that the foolish girl had actually written to Edwin Booth.

Didn't she know that any connection with the Booth family could ruin him, that Edwin was being watched, and that even though he had been defeated in the last campaign, once his tour of duty in Madrid was over with, he planned to run for re-election in New Hampshire?

He was red with rage.

But as it turned out he didn't have to say anything to Bessie. She had written Edwin on impulse, nothing more; she had had two days to think things over; and she would never be so foolish as to act on impulse again.

She had had her romance, which is to say, her scare, and perhaps she was as glad now to have it terminated as he was. The softer sides of her tightened up at once. She looked older. He had expected a fight, and instead she had become worldly in five minutes, if perhaps a little lost.

Looking at her, he saw that he had worried needlessly. No matter how bad a crush she might have had on Johnny, she came of good sound stock. She would have found some way to break off the engagement, even if this thing had not happened. It made him proud of her. It made him sigh with relief. It was balm in Gilead to discover that the thing you love is after all well worth the loving, and he did love his daughter. She was so like himself.

She agreed with him that the sooner they both left for Madrid, the better. He told her to pack at once.

He was so pleased. Now everything would be all right. She would do what she had been educated to do; she would

117

always be charming, and with luck, even a good hostess; and she would make a good marriage. From being a silly girl, she had turned overnight into the sort of woman he admired, a woman like her mother, someone who could be trusted to put up apple butter and cranberry jelly at the country place and handle her own stocks and bonds, who understood the mystique of never spending money foolishly, dressed simply but well, and if she had children, no matter how much she might dote on them, could be counted on to put whatever money he might have to leave her into a self-renewing trust; a woman who would teach those same children not only their catechism, but that other catechism whose first sentence is a stern directive that whatever we may do in this life, we must never touch our capital.

Good may come out of evil, after all. He had always believed so. And by the time they returned from Madrid, all this scandal would be hushed over and forgotten. By then nobody would remember Lincoln, let alone a man called Booth.

XXI

Lincoln's funeral was held on Wednesday. Having no precedent for grief, the authorities had had to put it off until then, while they invented a ceremonial. The body had been in the White House all that time. So had Mrs. Lincoln, Robert, and Tad.

That house now had a terrible reputation. Overnight, from being the fairground of an office seekers' carnival, it had become a mausoleum. Johnson stayed away, partly out of consideration towards Mrs. Lincoln, partly because he did not wish to enter that building until he had to. He took the oath to the Constitution in his hotel bedroom, and did nothing all day long but sign papers sent to him by Stanton. There would be time enough to remove Stanton later, when his usefulness was done.

Every night Mrs. Lincoln roamed the now deserted upstairs corridors. Sometimes she caught a glimpse of herself in a console mirror, but apart from that image, the mirrors reflected nothing. She did not think they would ever reflect anything again. From now on she would have to live surrounded only by nothing, and her own image there no longer meant anything to her. She had had her glance at the future. She refused to go downstairs, because the body was down there.

On Wednesday morning, she could hear the company arriving. They had come to take away something that belonged to her. Mr. Lincoln lay in the Green Room. Its mirrors were draped. There was a guard of honour. But it was considered a singular evidence of the poverty of his origin, that no blood relatives could be found outside his own immediate family, and of those Tad was too young, and Mrs. Lincoln too violent, to attend. It was her relatives, however, who were down there. They had not much cared

119

for him living, Mary had married beneath her, but now he was dead nothing could keep them away. Dr. Lyman Beecher Todd, General John B. S. Todd, C. M. Smith, a cousin, and Mr. Ninian Edwards, a man of much better family, would not have wanted to miss this, their last contact with the White House. The Todds were well pleased. Yesterday Mary had somewhat inconveniently been the Chief Magistrate's Lady, and today, as the papers said, she was a widow bearing only an immortal name. That was much more convenient.

At a little after eleven the clergy came in from the reception room and the obsequies began. The clergy were followed by those people who counted, the Governors of New York, Massachusetts, New Jersey, Iowa, Illinois, Connecticut, Ohio, Maryland, and Wisconsin, all solid men, of whom the Todds approved. They even approved of the funeral. It was very fine. All those people they would never have known in Springfield and Kentucky were there. The Diplomatic Corps was there. And at noon President Johnson arrived.

That made everybody feel better. It brought life into perspective again, for Johnson was a man they could all understand, a wily hardbitten rogue with cold eyes and something evasive in his manner. He was, he had said so often, a common man. They had nothing against that. Politicians were always common men, who did the work that statesmen could not stoop to do. It was the uncommon attributes of Lincoln which had disturbed them. About Lincoln there was always the reserve of a kindly judge who, kind or not, still sits up there, fingering the dossiers of both sides of the case, whether he admits to doing so or not.

Johnson stepped forward to the bier and looked down, at that head from which Willie Wright, in whose bed the President had died, had saved some of the brains on a handkerchief, with the thought of giving them to Robert Lincoln, at the appropriate time. When a corrupt man becomes incorrupt, that merely means he uses the forces of corruption for incorrupt ends. Unlike a man born good, he is hard to dislodge. But as yet nobody had had the chance to find that out.

120

Johnson stepped back.

The sermon, by Bishop Simpson of the Methodist Church, was short. The oration by the Rev. Gurley, who relished death as much as most of his auditors did, was much too long. Whether they wanted to or not, the Todd family had time to think. And yes, they could see it now. He had been a great man. They would have seen it at that time, if only his family and manners had been better.

They also thought of Mary. She would be more of a problem than ever now. She would be back on their hands again. In all likelihood Lincoln had not left any estate worth mentioning, and surely her pension would not be large.

The room smelled of death. They would be glad to be out of there. For though the age was one in love with the idea of easeful death, and everybody read the threnodies of that brisk, productive, cheerful little body, Lydia Huntley Sigourney, whose river of ink flowed out of Lethe, and who, said Mark Twain, had added a new terror to death, they did not particularly care for the smell. It was sweet in the wrong way, like saccharine.

After the oration the coffin was placed on an enormous hearse topped by a gilt eagle. Fifteen feet above them it tottered and swooped, as the catafalque headed up Pennsylvania Avenue towards the Capitol. The muffled beat of the funeral drums, as though someone was in slow motion emptying faggots into a wood bin, kept the pace of the company. The sky was clear, the avenue, as usual, an accordion of dried mud.

A Negro regiment, marching to the procession, met it, reversed order, and so, against all the plans of the War Department, which had prepared so swiftly and with such protocol, led it instead of trailing behind.

One could not really complain, one had no right to do so, but the Todds did not take it kindly that of all these crowds lining the street, most were a rabble, and the rest coloured, peering out over the white spectators like hired hands in the shrubbery of a newly cleared world.

The funeral march, composed by Brevet-Major General J. G. Barnard, in great haste, whoever he was, did well enough. Behind the hearse came the saddled horse of the deceased, in accordance with a ritual older than the Old Testament. There were those who could almost see the President mounted easily upon it, the homely shambles of a man, bending down to say something kind.

Yesterday the papers would have interpreted that friendly voice as the bellowing of an incompetent fiend. But it cannot be denied: death makes a difference.

Behind the Diplomatic Corps marched the Justices of the Supreme Court, slightly fusty, like so many talmudic Jews, blinking in the daylight of some new diaspora.

Had Lincoln been the savage some men had taken him for, though a wily savage, the horse would have been shot to follow him, rather than trailing empty after the catafalque. Now it preceded the Judges, with its white, liquid eyes.

There were picnickers on the lawn of the Capitol. Hastily they bolted their cold beef sandwiches, rolled up their napkins, and got to their feet. Lincoln's coffin was carried past them into the Rotunda of the Capitol, where Dr. Gurley delivered a few more words. It is appointed, he said, unto men once to die.

And so it was. But that was no reason to explain why P. T. Barnum had offered him 1,500 dollars for Abraham Lincoln's hat.

Gurley finished and the mourners departed. They had contrived an impressive ceremony, after all, out of bits and pieces of a hundred rituals as old as the Europe from which they derived. At last, at nightfall, the body of the President was left alone there, under the burning gas lights at the spring of the dome, with a few guards the blades of whose drawn weapons glinted in a muscularly retracted shimmer, under the hissing lights above. The crowds would be admitted tomorrow, to that greater than Rome's Capitol, as the journalist, Mr. Shea, called it, and who was to know if he was wrong?

XXII

Booth still lay in the woods. The one thing he wanted now was escape and some release from this endless pain. Yet it was not safe to move. More troops had arrived at Port Tobacco on the night of the 18th, and were fanning out over the peninsula, between the creeks. There were fourteen hundred cavalry alone, not to count Pinkerton men and hired detectives. It was the detectives Booth feared most. Jones had been offered a bribe by one of them, at Port Tobacco, which was where they were holed up. He had refused it. He promised to get them away tonight, in a small boat. But money was money, and the reward was up to 100,000 dollars now, dead or alive. Who was to tell what Jones might do? Booth loved money enough, not to rate it too low against the claims of honour. Jones was only a dirt farmer, anyway.

While he waited the long day out, he looked at the papers, for he did not dare to look any longer at his leg, which was distended, pustulous, and of an unwholesome colour. He had the Southern papers now, but the world in which they were printed seemed farther off than ever. The South had repudiated him. No doubt they did so only out of a fear of reprisals. That must be the explanation. When they got there, they would understand. It would be a matter of Cox again, cursing him only to help him. It must be that.

For the Northern papers were no better. Mrs. Surratt had been arrested, Payne had been arrested, O'Laughlin and Arnold had been arrested. That left only Atzerodt to account for.

On one of the back pages, in a short item, he read that Ella Turner had attempted suicide at her sister's brothel on Ohio Street. She had been found with a chloroformed rag over her face and his picture under her pillow. Nellie's house was behind the White House. The police had hauled all the girls in.

It meant nothing to him. He had almost forgotten Ella. He could scarcely remember her now. It was such ages since he had slept in a bed, let alone felt any human warmth there. Yet she had been pert enough. He was touched. It was just that he had more important matters to think about. Where was Atzerodt? Why hadn't he killed Johnson? He sighed. It all seemed somehow abstract now.

It was not abstract to Atzerodt.

That miserable troll knew perfectly well what the world had in store for him. The night of the assassination he had not even been able to find a friend to put him up. That showed him what the world was. He had stayed at a glorified flophouse instead, and then, sure he would be caught in any case, had fled to enjoy his last few days of freedom. America had always frightened him. It was too large. It had no corners to hide in. He pawned his revolvers, and with the ten dollars he got for them, went on a spree. For five days he lived life as he had always wanted to live it. He went to Germantown, in Maryland. He ate in taverns and talked to the other guests, like a normal man. He was accepted by them. He called himself Attwood. That was the name he always took on his drinking expeditions, when he impersonated a normal man. It was wonderful. He stayed in the house of a Mr. Richter. He ate meals in the dining-room, and slept upstairs in a room with two other men, instead of the six that slept in the same room at his flophouse. Not since Mrs. Surratt's, where he had boarded until she had flung him out, had he been treated so well. He got drunk every night. He was terrified.

When they came to arrest him, which was done before dawn on the morning of the 20th, he was ready to tell them anything and everything, pellmell, just so they would let him go. Who *they* were he did not know, but clearly they were persons in authority. He told them everything.

But they did not let him go.

In Philadelphia the arrest of Sleeper Clarke and Junius Brutus Booth was conducted with more decorum. They were men of property.

Asia was under house arrest. Her brother Junius had arrived the night before. Edwina was still upstairs, with Junius's own daughter, Marion. Junius was no help. He was too stolid. And he and Clarke got on each other's nerves.

Clarke was bad enough to begin with. He was furious about the house arrest, when Edwin went scot free. He could not denounce Edwin. He denounced his wife instead. It was she who had brought all this upon him. Only she.

She did not bother to answer. Did he expect her to repudiate her whole family, just because he had made the mistake of marrying her? After all, she had made the mistake of marrying him. She did try to keep out of his way. She blushed for shame enough, without having the detective hear what Clarke had to say. Why should she not be loyal to her family, for certainly Sleeper Clarke was not loyal to her.

It was almost a relief when at last the Federal Marshal took Clarke and Junius into custody. She was not pleased with June. He knew how she felt about Wilkes, and yet all he could say was that he wished John had been killed before the assassination, for their family's sake.

Clarke was arrested on the grounds that he could have read Wilkes' letter, since it had been unsealed, and so could have prevented the plot had he chosen. That business was the sort of farce he was so good at. But it was not a good farce. The charge against Junius was even less substantial. He had written John Wilkes about their oil investments in Pennsylvania, and the government suspected that the plot numbers were really a cypher. June knew nothing about such things. A life of concentrated self-interest had left him with a curious innocence about the ways of the rest of the world. He went along to jail almost cheerfully.

Asia was at last left alone with that grief she did not even dare to mention, yet she had no will to weep. Thoughts were her grief, not tears. She saw herself as a Roman matron. Roman matrons do not weep.

The detective took pity on her. He begged her to let his

125

wife take over his duty. Asia was so patently both ill-treated and ill. Would she not prefer a woman in the house? Asia said to thank his wife kindly, she appreciated the offer, but she would rather be watched by ten men who could keep quiet, than by one chattering female. That was true enough. Asia had not only the soul of a man, but a man's hatred of gossip. Do what the world would, she would not be seen humiliated by her own sex. She went upstairs to write to Edwin.

It was true she had been unpleasant to Edwin about his first wife. The woman was an actress, and Asia received no actresses in her home. But of them all, he, apart from herself, was at least loyal to the family, when even Junius was not. On her way to her room she stopped in to look at Edwina, who seemed to be taking her afternoon nap. Edwina, too, had doted on her Nunkee Wilkes. She gazed down at Edwina, and then slipped back into the corridor. It was as Edwin had said. That jolly man Clarke had never loved her at all. And she had tried for so long to believe that he did. Why had Wilkes done this to them all?

He could not have said himself.

In Concord, the previous Sunday, Ralph Waldo Emerson had delivered his own eulogy upon the passing of a great man. Try though he would to hobnob with the great and deal with the problems of poor, self-educated Thoreau, at bottom Emerson was an American. Therefore, it did not matter what he had said to Carlyle, he was also a snob. If one cared for things of the mind, in the America of his day, one could not be anything else. So he had had some trouble with his eulogium. But he had finally found the right words. Lincoln, he had said, was remarkable in this, that he was a great *worker*. And great workers were so rare, for everybody had some disabling quality.

Though he had yet to admit to his own, he was quite right. Everybody had. In Washington City the public had filed by all that dreary rainy day, from six in the morning until nine at night, just to see what a great worker looked like. They wanted to see if that face had survived death.

126

The funeral train was already made up. It was to leave Washington City at eight the next morning, a procession of nine cars, preceded by a black-draped locomotive, that was to visit Baltimore, Harrisburg, Philadelphia, Cleveland, Indianapolis, Chicago, and finally, to arrive at Springfield on the 3rd of May. It was almost the same route Lincoln had taken to his first Inaugural, and now they were taking him back.

His stepmother, when told of what had happened, was not surprised. She had reached old age, she knew something of the world, and she had not expected him back alive anyway.

Tacked on to the train was an ordinary Mail Car, which had been fitted up as a pullman for Mary Lincoln. She refused to use it. For five weeks she would not leave the White House, who had expected to remain there for three more years. But whether she was alive or dead, she scarcely knew.

Neither did Wilkes. But he had had one good piece of news. Jones had learned at Allen's Fresh that the soldiers had turned south. That was his chance, and he was eager to take it. It was now safe to put Booth and Herold out on the river.

Booth was more than willing to go. He had exhausted the papers. It was at least something not to have to face another night in this hopeless and deserted swamp. Why did the world hate him so today, when they had loved him so yesterday and hated Lincoln in his stead? Could the world love only a dead man?

He let Jones and Herold boost him back on a horse, but he was too weak to sit erect with ease. He had been very ill. The two men guided his mare, wet branches swept across his face, and at last they came out on to an empty road, eerie in the cold night. They passed below Jones's house.

"Can't you take me up there and let me have a cup of hot coffee?" Booth begged, and did not know he was sobbing.

Jones said not. The darkies at the house would see them. They had to go on.

Booth had expected that answer, but he did not like to hear it. It seemed strange to him that he should be reduced

127

to begging for a cup of coffee. He allowed the horse to jog him on.

A little later he heard the wind rising. The horse was picking its way downhill, towards the shore of the river. Herold and Jones told him to wait, and went off to drag a small skiff from the weeds to the water. Then they placed him in its bow. The skiff shipped no water, but he could sense the wetness of the water slapping at the hull. It was to be in a cradle, or that barge in which the dead body of King Arthur drifted down the pages of Malory. It was many years since he had thought of Malory.

Herold and Jones got in, Jones pulled at the oars, and they drew away from the shore. Booth felt drowsy. Once across this water, and he would be safe. He hauled himself up and tried to make out the dim blur of the Virginia shore, but could not. The night was too misty.

That was what saved them.

Jones could see what Herold could not. He shipped the oars and let the boat float with the current. There was a gunboat above them on the river.

Booth turned to look, and it was there, all right, a long shape on the surface of the water. As he watched, the turret gleamed and there was a red glow of fire. They were being shelled.

Jones slipped off into the mist. A shell fell into the water to the left of the skiff. The splash poured down on them and the skiff began to rock, and then shot aground in the bulrushes. Jones and Herold grabbed Booth and dumped him into some bushes. Then they ran to hide the boat.

The gunboat was so close that men could be heard talking on its deck.

Jones came back and said it was not safe to try again that night. They must wait a day. He rowed them back to a bluff below his farm and left them there.

Herold said nothing. Neither did Booth. But if the boy's thoughts were half so terrible as his own, then there was no hope. There was no hope at all.

XXIII

On Friday the 21st, Dr. Mudd got up early. He was feeling better. He had got over his scare.

But he had not quite recovered from Booth's visit. Oh, he remembered the man well enough now that the whole world wanted him. And he knew him well enough. Booth was not a man to be trusted. He had met him the previous November, at Church, through Dr. McQueen. Booth had chattered on about the Confederacy and the war, oil stocks and the family property of Tudor Hall. He had wanted to buy horses one moment and land the next, but he had never shown the colour of his money. That had not surprised Dr. Mudd. Whatever else actors might be, they were flibberti-gibbets. Dr. Mudd had spent his life among settled people. He knew a poor financial risk when he saw one. He had not wanted anything to do with Mr. Booth, he had tried to make that plain, but the man had plagued him anyway. He per-sisted in posturing as a country squire in search of property. Mudd found that annoying, for a genuine offer for his land would have greatly pleased him. He wanted to sell, and he did not like his time tantalized in that way.

No gentleman comes to your house in disguise. That ridiculous false beard had shown what a man like Booth thought of other men's acumen. He was like a child, a dangerous child, and yet it is not the duty of a doctor to turn a wounded man away. Actors were half-cocked crea-tures. Then, on Saturday, at Bryantown, he had found out what had happened. So when two officers had appeared at his house the following Tuesday, he had had his story ready. They had accepted it, gone away, and then come back. So he had told them his story again. He could not deny that he knew Booth, for that could be proven. He could deny that Booth had come to his house Saturday morning, for that could not be proven. He had given the officers a statement in writing, and hoped the matter ended there.

All the same, he had remained uneasy until today. Friday was the day he usually had noonday dinner with his father, who lived close by. For once he was glad to get out of his own house. He put a little pomade on his moustache, combed his beard, and went out into the hall.

His wife was waiting for him there. She had been cleaning, and had a duster round her head. She looked frightened. In her left hand she held a slit riding boot, still elegant and shiny.

"I found it under the bed, when I was dusting the front bedroom," she said.

"Throw the damn thing away."

"The niggers will get it. It's good leather."

Dr. Mudd could think of no answer to that. His wife was very pale.

"The man who was here, it was Booth, wasn't it?"

He hesitated, and then nodded.

She did not ask him why he had not told the officers that. "I'll hide it," she said.

He went down the stairs, got on his horse, and rode over to his father's house. They talked of small things there. The matter was not something Dr. Mudd wished to confide to his father. When the two men were most intimate, they talked politics and land. Those were the subjects they had in common. They shared no others. That had not occurred to Dr. Mudd before. He had always admired his father as a shrewd man, and that, heretofore, was all he had demanded of men. But now, as he sat there concealing his own fright, he saw that it might be possible to expect more.

The other guest at table was Mr. Hardy, a fellow land-owner in the neighbourhood, and a friend, he supposed, for they had known each other for years. When a message came that Dr. Mudd was wanted at home, Hardy rode back with him. They found Lieutenant Lovett in the yard. He was wearing civilian clothes.

Dr. Mudd did not ask him what he was there for. He thought only of the boot. He told Lovett about it and sent

130

his wife to fetch it. When the boot came, Lovett turned it over in his hands and said it was a fine boot. Then he arrested Dr. Mudd.

Like the others, Dr. Mudd did not bother to ask what he was being arrested for. That impressed Lovett, and so he told him. Besides, the legality even of martial law demanded that he do so.

The charge was quite clear. It stated that the said Samuel A. Mudd "did, at Washington City, and within the military department and military lines aforesaid, on, or before, the 6th day of March, A.D. 1865, and on divers other days and times between that day and the 20th day of April, A.D. 1865, advise, encourage, receive, entertain, harbour and conceal, aid and assist the said John Wilkes Booth, David E. Herold, Lewis Payne, John H. Surratt, Michael O'Laughlin, George A. Atzerodt, Mary E. Surratt, and Samuel Arnold, and their confederates, with knowledge of the murderous and traitorous conspiracy aforesaid, and with the intent to aid, abet, and assist them in the execution there, and in escaping from justice after the murder of the said Abraham Lincoln, in pursuance of said conspiracy in the manner aforesaid."

With the exception of Booth and John H. Surratt, who must be the son of that woman whose boarding-house he had once entered, in order to meet Booth, Dr. Mudd had never heard of any of them. The charge was conspiracy and treason. The punishment was death.

Dr. Mudd asked to be allowed to change, and then came back. As he rode out the gate, he noticed that Frank Washington, the coloured man, had forgotten to repair the shakes of the fence, and that Hardy had gone into the house as soon as the arrest had taken place and had not come out since. Neither was a matter he wished to mention to Lovett.

The other person arrested that day was the stage carpenter, Spangler. He had been in and out of the precinct station all week, there seemed as little in him as they had got out of him, but Stanton was determined to have him all the same. True, it was clear from the evidence that Spangler had known nothing of the plot until at least two hours before its

131

execution, if he knew even that much, but he had been inside the theatre, and when one of the stage carpenters had shouted, "That was Booth. I swear it was Booth," while Booth was galloping down the alley, Spangler, whom the uproar had brought outside, had turned and smashed his face in. "Be quiet," he had said. "What do you know about it? Don't say where he went." He had been drunk at the time, but it proved conspiracy, that statement. For that he would hang. Somebody had to hang. For that they would all hang.

The trouble was to find him. He had been homeless since the death of his wife. He slept at Ford's Theatre and took his meals at a boarding-house. Sometimes he forgot to eat, but he never forgot to drink. When finally cornered, he was having dinner at Mrs. Scott's boarding-house. The other guests sat as far away from him as they could, for they all knew the police had been after him, so clearly he must be guilty, and guilt can be contagious. They wanted no part of him. He knew that, but since he had felt very hungry, he had sat with them anyway.

When the officers arrived, he stood up and blinked at them. Of course he hadn't wanted Booth to be caught. Why should he? The man had always treated him square, lent him money when he needed it, set him up a drink, and acted as though he were a man and not a middle-aged laughing stock. He'd just returned the favour, that's all, without stopping to think about it. Surely that wasn't something they'd hang you for.

He begged them not to arrest him. He made a scene about it, for, as everybody knew, he had no self-respect. He didn't want to die.

They arrested him anyway.

XXIV

Booth still lay on the riverbank, with Virginia unattainable across the water, though he could glimpse it through the trees. He was feverish again, to judge by the sound of him.

Here in the woods Herold didn't feel so bad. In the woods he always knew what to do, even if he didn't know exactly where he was. But Booth felt lost out here, he guessed. He was pretty worried about Booth. Herold wasn't too bright. The furthest he could think into the future was five minutes ago. From the way he was raving, Booth wanted to go back to Washington, and Herold was afraid to do that. He felt safer where he was.

From Great Hero Booth had passed to Great Sinner. He had to justify himself some way, and even when delirious he thought about that. If he could not be the great hero he wanted to be—and the papers told him he had misjudged his audience there—then he would impress the world with the enormity of his sins.

He saw the scene so vividly that in amongst the scraps of feverish Shakespeare, as he raved, Herold could see it too; for Booth had reached the stage of self-pity, and that is always a vivid emotion. Herold had had such visions himself, though on a simpler level: A great hunter, and a rich man, too, like John Jacob Astor, he came back from the West to impress his sisters. But he did not understand the Shakespeare.

Booth was in the midst of the tent scene from *Richard III*. They had all come to haunt his dreams, Prince Edward, Clarence, Seward, Lord Hastings, Ella Turner, Anne, his wife, Buckingham, and Lincoln. The dawn came. The ghosts vanished. The scrim went black. The house was silent. He

133

started from his dream and grabbed the readiest words. It was time to arm.

King Richard: *Give me another horse* (he should never have allowed the horses to be shot). *I did but dream.* (What was happening to him could not be true.) *O coward conscience, how dost thou afflict me!* (Not true either, but what is a Great Sinner without a conscience, cowardly or not?) *What! do I fear myself? There's none else by.* (Yes, he was beginning to fear himself. He feared the fever. Yet, *I am I.*) *Is there a murderer here? No. Yes, I am: Then fly. What! from myself? Great reason why—lest I revenge. What! myself upon myself?* (Why had he shot Lincoln, anyhow? It had brought him nothing but trouble. He could no longer remember.) *I am a villain. Yet I lie. I am not.*

Of course he was not. Somehow, despite Matthews and the lost letter to the *National Intelligencer*, he must explain. He would go to Washington, as a simple ordinary man. He would explain, and he would move the authorities to clemency. His speech would take place in an enormous cool pillared hall. Perhaps the Rotunda of the Capitol, but if so, why were the senators wearing togas and sandals, and what was Stanton doing there? There was no such scene in *Julius Caesar*.

He would explain. He would move them to tears. The misunderstood Great Sinner would be seen for what he was, the Hero. Dressed simply in black he stood there, holding them by his oratory. He was so afraid his voice might give out.

All I want, he would say, is *a grave.*

A little little grave, an obscure grave.

He had always been adept at pathos. But he remembered now. Those lines were from the wrong play. They are spoken by Richard II, before he is betrayed by the pretended clemency of Bolingbroke into giving himself up, not by Richard III.

He opened his eyes. He was rational again.

Relieved, Herold went off for a walk in the woods. Booth had given him a bad scare.

No, thought Booth, he could not go to Washington. He saw that. But neither could he allow the world to say what it would of him. He must right that misconception. Opening the diary, he began to scribble. The endless work of self-justification went on. *"Friday, the 21st,"* he wrote. He must explain that he had been punished too much. "After being hunted like a dog through swamps and woods, and last night being chased by gunboats until I was forced to return, wet, cold, and starving, with every man's hand against me, I am here in despair. And for why? For doing what Brutus was honoured for—what made William Tell a Hero. My act was purer than either of theirs. I am abandoned with the Curse of Cain upon me."

Despite his bitterness and the awful pain, he felt a little like Byron, sitting under that tree. He had always wanted to perform *Cain*. Herold was no Dorsey, of course, but he was better than nothing. Dorsey, to Byron, had been no Patroclus either. But *Cain* was an excellent part. "And for this brave boy Herold, here with me, who often prays (yes, before and since) with a true and sincere heart, was it a crime for him?" he wrote. "I do not wish to shed a drop of blood, but I must fight the course. 'Tis all that's left to me."

He did not like that last phrase. It sounded too true. Herold he saw was back and watching him. He shut the diary.

It was perhaps a relief to both of them when Jones appeared with a candle, led them down to the shore, and showed them where to row. He recommended Machadoc Creek. A Mrs. Quesenberry lived there, and would help them. He then explained to them the movements of the tides and how to compensate for the current. He even drew a map for them. Whether they understood what he was saying or not, he could not tell and did not dare to ask.

Herold did not understand, but he was eager to get going, lest Booth demand to go back to Washington again. He got into the boat.

Booth was himself again. He appreciated the dramatics of the scene and was grateful to Jones. He gave the man 18 dollars for the boat.

Jones did not want to take the money. He had not protected them for pay. But he was a poor man, and a boat was

135

a boat. Gruffly he told them to watch out for the monitor which was still on the river. Then he left them.

There was a flash of lightning down the sky, which only made the dark seem the darker. The river was very wide. Herold rowed silently and then stopped.

They both heard voices. They both saw the shape on the water downstream. They had almost hit the gunboat.

Herold let the skiff drift. The returning tide caught it and swept it up to safety again, but away from where they were supposed to be going.

They were lost, and the sky was beginning to lighten. They would have to make for shore. Once the skiff was pulled up in the weeds, Booth took out Jones's map and his own compass. The needle pointed the wrong way. All the estuaries of the Virginia shore ran west to east. The needle showed them north. They were still in Maryland. They would never get away.

XXV

He sent Herold off to reconnoitre, while he lay in the boat and stared at the clouded sky. There were still a few hours of darkness ahead. Like hope, the dawn had been false.

Herold came back to say that they were in Maryland all right, at the mouth of Nanjemoy Creek, wherever that was, Herold recognized the place because he had gone poaching there. A Colonel Hughes lived up the creek. Colonel Hughes was all right.

Booth was starving. That didn't bother Herold any. He said he'd go ask Hughes for food. Booth told him not to say any more than he had to, but with Davy that was usually too much. The boy suffered from a helpless compulsion to gabble while he ate. It was his way of making friends. Not having shot anybody himself, Herold still didn't quite see where their danger lay.

He was back in an hour, happy, healthy, and well fed. Booth might be driven half mad by this existence, but Herold liked it. To him this desperate flight, except for its cause, was a vacation. He throve on it. Booth's cheeks had fallen in, his skin was grey, and his eyes stared out of deep shadow. Herold had never looked better. He had had a good breakfast and had brought back food for Booth, a bottle of whisky, and the newspapers. Colonel Hughes had told him that if they caught the tide after midnight, it would carry them right to Machadoc Creek. He'd had a nice long talk with Colonel Hughes. He'd told him everything.

Booth opened the package of food. It contained a blue-pink ham, glistening with age. For five days he had eaten nothing but ham. He was sick to death of it. But he ate. He had to eat. And while he ate, he read the papers. Atzerodt had been arrested. "It was with difficulty that the soldiers could be prevented from lynching him," he read. He knew what that meant. It meant that Atzerodt would talk, and talk, and talk, until he had talked their lives away. The same page of the paper carried a reward notice. His own price was still 50,000, but Herold was worth 25,000 now and had his name in bigger type. When he pointed that out to Davy, the boy's face quavered. He looked like a porcupine. When he was scared, the rattle of his quills was almost audible.

There was also a quotation from the Southern press. It spoke in sorrow, an emotion the South had recently learned to maintain at all times. But it repudiated him. "At the moment he struck down Mr. Lincoln he also struck himself from existence. There can be no more a J. Wilkes Booth in any country. If caught he will be hanged. If he escapes he must dwell in solitude. He has the brand of Cain upon his brow." That had not the air of an editorial. Rather it seemed the description of something that had already happened, factual because all the world believed it. He believed it himself. "God try and forgive me, and bless my mother," wrote Booth in his diary, who had not thought of her for days. Then he asked Herold to hand him the whisky.

Space it out as they would, they could not make it last until midnight. Sometime after dark, Herold asked him if he did not smell something. Booth said he did not, and indeed he did not. He smelled only the slimy marsh smells that had surrounded them now for days. Herold let the matter drop.

It was the gangrene. Not only had it bubbled up in his leg, but was spreading into his bloodstream. But how were they to know that? Neither of them had ever seen a wounded man before. They went on drinking.

What was in this wretched Lincoln anyhow, that had made people love him overnight, now he was gone? Booth did not know. He could conceive of a scapegoat, a saint, and a Machiavel, but had not the wit to see them in one body. To him Machiavel was a villain, and not a man who knew that good is only a chestnut we pull from a fire of other men's lighting. His mind wandered. His costumes were in the South. He had shipped them ahead weeks ago. Why was not he? He longed so much to lie in a bed of warm linen once again.

At a little after midnight of the 22nd-23rd, Herold shoved off the skiff and they floated down the river, unmolested, towards Machadoc Creek and Mrs. Quesenberry. From that name Booth derived much comfort. It was a motherly, maiden aunt, no nonsense and gruff kindness sort of name. From it he could legitimately expect lemon butter and lavender scented sheets, a foot warmer, and a small snug room with flower sprigged wallpaper. He held himself in against that promise and refused to look at his leg. When they arrived at the shore, he sent Herold off to find the woman.

While Herold was gone, a straw-footed white wading bird flapped down to peer at him, as he lay at the bottom of the skiff. That startled him, but he had not the strength other than to stare back at it until it went away. When he looked at his once white hands, he saw them mottled with liver spots, like those of an old man. He got out of the skiff, hauled himself ashore, stretched out beneath a tree, and watched the estuary. The tide was moving up over it, sea birds waded in the shallows, and Herold seemed gone a very long time. It was Sunday again, he realized, the 23rd. Who could have thought a week could have been so long? But at least he was in Virginia at last.

His leg was worse, but he did not notice that, for he lay in the midst of flowering shrubs, whose heavy odour muffled all others. He felt drowsy. He did so long for Mrs. Quesenberry's cordials, maternal atmosphere, and bed.

When Herold at last came back, it was to say that Mrs. Quesenberry would have none of them. But her daughter had said that perhaps a farmer called Bryant would help them.

XXVI

So he would for a price. He would have done anything for a price.

Mr. Bryant was a cracker. He had been one all his life, and had a white beard to show for it. His jeans were old, soft, and faded, and fitted him like a second skin. His eyes were on the small side. He had a tight face and a cantankerous manner. Poverty and pellagra had made him an animal. He had an animal's ambitions, an animal's cunning, and far less than an animal's self-respect. For self-respect the baffled farmer's poor white trash substitute did him just as well: he was touchy.

The truth would never sway a man like that. What he would want was a bargain. Booth passed himself off as a wounded Confederate soldier trying to avoid the Federal patrol.

Bryant accepted the explanation. "It'll cost ya," he said. "Your brother here said you could pay. Otherwise I wouldn't have bothered none."

Booth had trouble holding in his temper.

As usual with his sort of man, the hope of some advantage made Bryant tight-fingered and sullen.

Booth took out some greenbacks. "I can't walk. I need a conveyance. A carriage of some kind, and a horse."

Bryant spat. They didn't look like Confederate soldiers to him. They were in worse trouble than that. If that were so, he could get more for even less than he would normally have offered. He asked them where they wanted to go and how much they'd pay to get there. The beat-up one said he wanted a doctor to dress his foot. The nearest doctor was Doc Stewart. Stewart probably wouldn't lift a finger to help, but that wasn't any of Bryant's business. His only job was to get Booth there.

Booth said Stewart would do and told Bryant to hitch up his horses.

Bryant had been waiting for that. He didn't have any carriage, he said. Just horses. Booth almost sobbed when he heard him. Bryant decided he could hope to get ten dollars in gold, waited until Booth paid it over, and then said the two men would have to walk up to his place by themselves. He didn't have the time to bring any horses down to meet them. He walked away ahead of them, chinking his gold. Ten dollars wouldn't go far. Maybe he could get more out of them.

The more desperate of the two men seemed to have trouble hobbling up the dirt lane. Bryant grinned and led the way to his shack, a tumbledown shanty whose housekeeper was a slovenly Negress. Booth sat down on a ricketty chair and closed his eyes. Herold asked for something to eat. Bryant said that would cost them, and sold them some soggy biscuits and three cold slices of bacon for a dollar. Herold ate them. Herold wasn't choosy about what he ate. But Booth was in a hurry to move on.

Bryant was enjoying himself. Out of sheer cussedness, he said they couldn't have the horses until the day's chores were done, which wouldn't be until evening. Having gotten his money in advance, he wasn't in any hurry to go out of his way to earn it. But he did allow as how Booth could lay down on the bed for free, if he wanted. Then he went out.

The bed was filthy, but the rest did Booth good. He wasn't too worried about Bryant's turning him in. He knew the type. It was too cunning to plan for anything but immediate advantage. Ten or twenty dollars was the limit of Bryant's experience; 25,000 or 50,000 wouldn't mean anything to him at all.

Nor was he wrong. By late afternoon Bryant was back with his spavined horse, Herold boosted Booth up to the saddle, and by the time darkness fell they had reached Dr. Stewart's house.

It was a good while since Booth had seen a real house, and Dr. Stewart lived well. The building was two stories high, with a wide porch along the front of it, and faced ten acres

141

of lawns and pasture, backed by trees. The glow of lamps at the windows was heartbreakingly cheerful. He would present himself as a Confederate soldier and, if Dr. Stewart seemed sympathetic, would tell him the truth later. A little forlorn on his horse, he sent Bryant inside to fetch the doctor.

Stewart came out and asked him what he wanted and who he was. His voice was curt. Booth said he wanted help. Looking down, he saw he would not get it. There was something hostile about Dr. Stewart.

"I'm a physician, not a surgeon. I doubt whether I can be of much assistance," said Stewart, though his voice betrayed no doubt of any kind. "But come into the house, if you wish. I suppose you want something to eat. Every soldier who comes by here seems hungry. I can't feed them all."

Too much call upon his good will had drained off Stewart's southern sympathies. He had been arrested several times during the war, and now the war was over, he did not propose to be arrested again. People think that because a man is a doctor, they may ask anything of him.

Booth would have turned away. But before he could do so, Herold had him out of the saddle and on to his crutches. Herold was hungry. They went into the house.

The sight of that large and comfortable parlour made Booth blink. A woman, obviously the doctor's wife, sat with his elaborately dressed daughters. The girls were weedy, but the mother had plump, complacent arms decked out with gold bracelets. He would have said something courtly, in his customary, half-forgotten style, had not one of the daughters raised her hand to her mouth and gasped.

That reminded him. He looked a tramp, so that was what they thought him. Young girls like their soldiers to be officers, and smart with boot polish at that. He was stubbly and filthy, probably wide eyed with fever, and the bandage on his foot must look like a piece of marbleized paper soaking in a gutter. In the expression of their faces he could see that he was something they did not want to remember, the exact image of what civilians hate most in a war, though they cheer loudly enough when the troops go off.

He did not try to speak. He allowed Stewart to lead him to the study. It was a heavy, red rep room. Stewart glanced at the bandage, poked his fingers in it, and realized that the sooner he washed his hands the better. And yet he couldn't turn them away, nor would he accept money from a Confederate soldier for so slight a service. At the same time, he most decidedly would not put them up. He did not like the look of them. But he did say he would see that the servants got them something to eat. He led them to the kitchens and left them there.

Herold saw nothing demeaning in that. The closest he had ever gotten to the gentry was their kitchen offices. The room was warm and the food plentiful. He had no objection to sitting down at the plain plank table, said the doctor was very kind, and began to stuff himself. Opposite him some copper pans and dessert moulds hung on the wall. They gleamed. Dr. Stewart must be well fixed. Why didn't Booth eat? The food was good.

Booth didn't bother to answer. He raged. He felt the humiliation of sitting here all the more deeply, for being so feeble. The one thing he had always insisted upon was entering life by the front door. It was his due. It was a demand he had always bought with his appearance, and not even Bessie Hale's father would have dared to send him to the kitchens. Now Lincoln had reduced him to this filthy discarded scarecrow whom nobody would have dreamed of asking to sit anywhere else. He felt for the first time some of the terror, but none of the resignation, of the middle-aged character actor, who earns his living by pretending to be less than he is, and so becomes what he is forced to impersonate. He would not be degraded so. He got up and hobbled off in search of Dr. Stewart. The man could at least tell him of some place where he might stay. He had never before realized how much of a man's position in this world comes from a razor and a good suit of clothes, how little from his character.

Stewart met him in the front hall, barring entrance to the living room. Booth missed none of that. The nearest place to sleep was a Negro shanty down the road, owned by a freed

143

man called William Lucas. Stewart said he would not ordinarily send a white man to a nigger, he apologized for that, but there was no other nearby house. Booth fetched Herold, got back on Bryant's horse, and rode off into the woods. He had put all the sarcasm he could manage into thanking Stewart for his hospitality, but he had not been able to say enough.

In the first clearing they came to he drew rein, got out the diary, and scribbled away by the light of a candle stump. He did not realize that all he achieved was a written whine.

"It is not the substance, but the manner in which kindness is extended, that makes one happy in the acceptance thereof. 'The sauce to meat is ceremony; meeting were bare without it.' Be kind enough to accept the enclosed five dollars (though hard to spare) for what we have received," he wrote. The trouble was he could not afford even five dollars. He rewrote the letter and cut the price to two and a half. That humiliated him still further, for the one way a gentleman has of showing his contempt for scoundrels, is to pay them more than their services are worth. But he could no longer afford to be a gentleman. Two fifty would have to do.

He signed the note, "A Stranger", and sent the note back by Bryant. He hoped it would give Stewart a bad moment or two. Instead, it was to save the man's life. Then he took a swig of whisky and rode on.

The Lucas shanty was nothing but a clapboard ruin badly chinked. At first, Lucas would not come out when summoned. When he did come out, he was a shivering darky of the kind that makes you want to kick them as soon as they open their mouths. He wouldn't let them in. He said his wife was ill, and besides, he only had one room. Booth would have to go away.

What right did a nigger, freed man or not, have to tell a white man what he could or couldn't do? Booth hit him with one of his crutches. It was the first time he had struck a nigger, but he had had enough. He barged inside and told Lucas to get his wife out of there. Lucas decided he could do

144

that. Herold sniggered. Booth had the bed stripped, because you never knew what bugs a nigger might have, lay down and went to sleep.

He had had enough. He had had enough.

XXVII

Edwin had not yet left the house on 19th Street. It was night, and he found the nights worse than the days. During the day he hid from the world. But at night the world was sleeping, he could not, and so it was himself then he had to hide from.

He thought he should have done something to prevent this. He had known Wilkes was crazy on the subject of Lincoln. He had even heard Wilkes say that awful sentence, that there was a great way for a man to immortalize himself, by shooting the President. But he had thought that only Wilkes's posturing, and had believed that Wilkes was too concerned to posture ever to take part in real events.

Now he had. That one shot had shattered the whole family. How could any of them face the world again?

His only consolation was that he himself had once saved Robert Lincoln's life. It had happened on a train. Robert Lincoln had missed his footing and started to fall under the wheels. Edwin had hauled him safely up. He told everybody about that, the way an old pensioner shows his certificate of service to strangers who do not even remember the campaign he served in, let alone the man himself. The Booth family madness had come out at last. Against that, nothing weighed on the balanced side.

Junius had been arrested. Nothing could be done with that optimist. He wrote confident, bubbly letters from prison, telling Edwin that it would be over soon enough and that the world would soon forget. Edwin knew better. It would never be over and the world would never forget. Sleeper Clarke was in the next cell, raging against them all. June did not say that, but Edwin knew it. Sleepy would never forgive Asia for getting him into this, and Asia was under house arrest. It could not be easy for her, though she

146

made it no easier for anyone else, in refusing to condemn Johnny. She spoke out too much. Edwina was still with her, and if Asia's correspondence was being opened, Edwin shuddered for the safety of his daughter.

Few of his friends wrote to console him. That did not surprise him. He was only surprised that a few did, which touched him deeply, and he answered as best he could. It was the other mail that disturbed him, the anonymous letters, the signed threats, and the charitable communications from acquaintances who wrote to say they had known how terrible the Booth family was, right from the beginning. John Wilkes was not dead yet, so far as was known, and yet he had received three letters from hysterical women claiming to be his widow, who wrote to ask about the estate. If it had not been for Aldrich, he would have gone mad.

Sometimes late at night the two men slipped out of the shuttered house, to take a constitutional in the streets. As far as Edwin was concerned, those streets could never now be empty enough. He shrank from everyone. As Asia had written, "Those who have passed through such an ordeal, if there are any such, may be quick to forgive, slow to resent; they never relearn to trust in human nature, they never resume their old place in the world, and they forget only in death."

Yet he could not shrink from meeting everyone. As his father had once told him, everybody knows Tom Fool. In this life we knot our own noose. He had always known that. But at least one might be allowed to kick away the box one's self.

" 'Tis a mere matter of time. I feel sure Time will bring all things right," wrote June. How could June be such a fool?

XXVIII

On Monday, the 24th of April, Lincoln's body arrived in New York, escorted across the water from Newark on the train ferry. To New York it was a procession, and New York loves processions. The window sashes were removed from the windows, so that people might have a better look. But a look was all they wanted.

Edwin had determined to stay indoors. And yet, though he told nobody, he knew he had to look. He found a place in the crowds which lined the streets.

As the catafalque entered the street, it seemed to sway down upon him like the cart of juggernaut. Its wobbling motion, behind its horses, was something he would never be able to forget. The crowds seemed unmoved. He did not understand. Perhaps fright had sobered them into their best behaviour, but our best behaviour is often our worst. This did not seem to mean anything to them at all. And yet he had only to open a newspaper to see how they cried for vengeance. Was grief, then, only the pretext for vengeance? Somehow he did not himself find it so. Grief should make one gentle, not venomous.

The catafalque was hauled out of sight, and he went back to his house. Did these crowds not realize that they were watching something much more terrible than even the worst raree-show? Or was a raree-show all they made out of the real meaning of life?

Perhaps.

The body was removed to City Hall, outside of which a chorus of eight hundred chanted the Pilgrims' Chorus from *Tannhäuser*. It was the latest music. New York believes in keeping up to date. A little puzzled by the vast world out there, beyond the Hudson, it only feels secure in novelty. That is its only pre-eminence.

Yet the obsequies, and in particular the decorations, left nothing to be desired. Other cities might place an eagle over the catafalque. New York had a silver eagle whose wings were folded and whose head appropriately drooped. It was a triumph of artistic expression, and yet the mourners, as the papers pointed out, seemed chiefly to be impressionable shop girls. Observers noted that though the respect was beautifully paid, there was less feeling and less sorrow in New York than elsewhere.

To tell the truth, the mourners found the body exposed and dusty. He was only a man, and a dead man at that, and the parade was more impressive than its occasion, they thought. It had, indeed, a magnificent allegorical float. When the body had been seen off on the train, the city took down the black bunting and went about its usual affairs, which were, after all, of some importance.

However, it had been a good procession, the citizens of the Fifth Ward of Brooklyn had been particularly impressive, and of course the Negro population had been deeply moved. Everyone had applauded the devotion of the Negroes. As a cheap labour pool, they would be invaluable.

The Honourable George Bancroft delivered an oration in Union Square. The Rev. Osgood recited an ode, and William Cullen Bryant, who was still alive, though his recovery from tuberculosis had been the death of his muse, had distributed among a few friends a little hymn.

But at Mount Vernon, near Yonkers, the Sisters of Charity, with veiled heads, stood on the lawn before their convent, surrounded by their two hundred pupils, and watched the slow funeral train go by, until it had vanished around a bend, leaving in the air behind it only a low, dissolving tube of black smoke. The countryside was more devout. Bonfires lit the hills, and sometimes the stations. In Ohio, at Richmond, the bells of the city rang out across the dark, to summon the citizens to the station. People came in from the country, through the hot, sticky night, in their farm wagons, and sat on their buckboards, as the train slowly passed by. Guns fired. And at Urbana, the young

149

ladies of the community, stiff in new frocks, entered the funeral car and dropped flowers on the bier.

It was incredible: the farther the train got from the urban centres which had processed the most, the deeper into the real country those politicians in Washington City thought they knew so well and knew they ruled, the more, as the train passed on, the real tribute came down to the trackside and flared on the hills, although the train did not stop.

As the train moved through Ohio into Illinois, the people brought not silver eagles, black velvet, and a gaggle of Bishops; not hymns, odes, and the latest music from Europe, but flowers.

From everywhere, that late spring, they brought flowers, from the fields, wilting already in the hands of those who held them, from the gardens and nurseries, arranged in set pieces and in vases, white roses, immortelles, amaranth, orange blossoms, and the emblematical justicia, for in those days people knew, what we have forgotten, the ancient language of flowers. They brought evergreen boughs and the flowers of the season, which meant more to them than laurel.

The eagle, which in New York had so artfully drooped, in the back country was larger and more triumphant. And at Chicago they did him proud. It surprised everyone. No one had realized that there were so many to care in Chicago. Again, before the coffin departed on its final journey, there were more flowers, that most ancient, prechristian, pagan, and perpetual of Man's offerings, which he offers in his fist, when it is too late, to he knows not what. Most of these people were of British stock. They might not understand each other or themselves. But they understood the meaning of flowers.

At 9:30 the cortège left Chicago for Springfield. Along the way it passed through the hamlet of Lincoln, a place named after him, in whose origins he had taken an interest. There, there was an arch over the railroad bed, and a choir in white, but the train did not stop.

From now on, the name of Lincoln would never stop.

150

XXIX

Booth was approaching Port Conway.

It was as though that dusty grey curtain behind which he had been skulking for days, had suddenly furled up to the proscenium, to reveal a gorgeous golden world. The sun was out. The play was on again.

He had been lying at the bottom of William Lucas's commandeered spring wagon. It was the sort of broken down vehicle a Negro would have, creaking, and without springs. Herold was on the seat with the driver, Lucas's son. Mile after agonizing mile, Booth had lain on his back, staring at the pendulous sky which sagged over him like the dingy sateen lining of a cheap coffin lid. Now, marvellously, a pale sun was out. It was a resurrection. After this death, he would come into his own again. Booth sat up.

Port Conway was a small enough town. Beyond it lay the Rappahannock, sparkling sedately in the April light, with Port Royal on the farther bank. Though small, Port Royal had once been a tobacco port. Scattered across that stretch of rural equanimity were a few stately houses. He was enormously cheered. Once on the farther side, and he would be himself again. The ferry was moored on the opposite bank.

Herold told him to lie down. He lay down. He felt lighthearted and happy. The sunlight was so good, so dry, so warm. Like a man in surgery, who is injected against despair, he gave way drowsily to that anaesthetic, and put his arm over his eyes. Whatever misery he was in, the sun would heal. He had had Herold shave him and put his clothes to rights. Since he had no mirror, he could not know how little that had helped. For the first time in days he felt the return of self-esteem.

The wagon stopped. They must be at the riverside, from

the odour of fish, tidal flats, and slime. Herold jumped to the ground and went to parley with the boatman. Though this closeness to freedom made Booth calm, Herold had turned shrill. That guileless child's voice was babbling too freely to the boatman. Booth lay there, listening to the soothing noises of a quiet countryside. So had he lain upstairs, as a child, at Tudor Hall, the Booth home, sure that if anything was wrong, or if he had been caught out and was due for punishment, for some prank, his mother would take care of him. He had that feeling now.

Behind him he heard the approaching clatter of hoofs and harness. It was a sound too dilatory to be pursuit, but it did not have the sound of farmers, either. He hauled himself up and peered over the edge of the wagon. What he saw was a posse of Confederate cavalry, three officers, no more than boys, slim, fresh faced, and natty in clean and polished uniforms. They looked at rights with the world. One of them swung down from his saddle with that physical, self-contented and accomplished grace which Booth, who had so much enjoyed innocently to swagger so, envied now, whereas ten days ago he would have had it himself.

Herold, who had gotten nowhere wrangling across the water at the boatman, ran shrieking to them. His rattled treble voice was too froward. Booth winced and lay down again, but he could hear the jabber well enough. How young the lads sounded. Younger than he had sounded, even when young.

Herold had chosen a new pseudonym this time. He was announcing that their name was Boyd. He came back to Booth and asked him to get out of the wagon.

"They're from Mosby's command," he whispered, as though that made everything all right. "They must be headed south somewhere. Maybe they can get us across the river."

Booth climbed out of the wagon and got his crutches under his arms. The sunshine made him blink, but he felt affable. He was with Southern gentlemen again. He could see that. And then, they were so very young, scarcely more than boys dressed up in soldier suits. They stood about so easily in their well-cut uniforms, elegant, with their weight on one hip, and maybe even a little shy. They would not refuse the simple demands of a fellow veteran since, by the looks of them, they had not seen much service. Embarrassed by someone who had so clearly been through more than they had, they would be kind. He introduced himself as John William Boyd, of A. P. Hill's corps. It was the first combination of the initials on his tattooed hand that he could think of.

They said they were on their way to pay a private visit. But they would arrange about the crossing. The ferry rested so tantalizingly on the opposite bank. Booth looked at the ripple of water against that bank, and the beaten track leading down to the slight wash on this one. Once over the river, and there would be nothing between him and Richmond. He would be in the heart of the South.

Herold was desperate. He was afraid of pursuit, and if he could not beg for help, then he could force it. Besides, had not Booth told him how gratified the South would be? What could be more Southern than three fine young gentlemen fresh from Mosby's Rangers?

"We are the assassinators of Lincoln," Booth heard him tell the sandy haired young man, whose name seemed to be Bainbridge. It was a loud and unmistakeable word on that bucolic air. The jig was up. He hobbled over to Herold, who gave him a fatuous, shame-faced grin and introduced him to Lieutenant Ruggles.

Ruggles stared hard at both of them. "If you are what the man says you are, you must be John Wilkes Booth," he said.

Booth admitted the name.

None of the three cavalrymen said anything. Instead they looked at him and they looked swiftly away. There was a price on his head. If they helped him, there would be a price on theirs. He thought it his duty to point that out. Why should they help him? No one else had.

Ruggles was the first to speak. "I guess we can't exactly turn you in for blood money," he said. "So we'll help you, I reckon."

Jett, the youngest one, hesitated and then agreed. But

Bainbridge, who was their leader, had had the time to find out that this world is full of traps for the unwary.

"We were told that the person who killed the President had already been apprehended," he said, and waited, staring at Booth.

Booth understood. He too had learned to be wary of traps these last few days. He held out his wrist with its tattooed initials. He handed over a bill he still had in his pocket, a draft against a Canadian bank.

The three men did not like it. A man should have some preparation, before having to thread his way through so many conflicting loyalties, particularly at a time like this, when they could all see where loyalty had got them. But they couldn't leave him alone, they'd met him, it was too late to remain unimplicated, they couldn't turn him in, the best thing to do would be to pass him along. He didn't look as though he could last long, by the looks of him. Poor devil, he'd had a hard time.

There was only one way they could go through with it, and that was to treat it as a lark. They looked at each other, and then Jett went down to the water's edge and cursed the barge nigger into bringing the ferry over. Action is what the young are good at. Ideas merely confuse them. Once Jett had started things in motion, Bainbridge and Ruggles fell in soon enough.

It was a poled ferry. It took the devil's time to get across. Booth gave Lucas's son ten bucks to keep his mouth shut, to be rid of him, and opened up to the lieutenants. He appealed to their spirit of adventure, he said. They were willing enough to have that appealed to. They had been defeated, and no man likes defeat. They said they were on their way to join Johnston, who had not yet surrendered his army.

The ferry touched the bank. Bainbridge and Jett rode on to it. Booth was boosted on to Ruggles' horse and followed. The nigger began to pole. The ferry approached Port Royal. Now everything would be all right. Booth managed a smile.

But at Port Royal, Jett could not find anyone to put up a wounded Confederate soldier. One woman agreed, but changed her mind. Now the war was over, she saw no

154

patriotism in running the risk. Jett remembered Garrett. Garrett owned a farm off the road to Bowling Green, which was where Jett and his friends were going. It was as simple as that. Jett and Ruggles led the way up to the house. They would drop Booth off there, while Herold went into Bowling Green with them. Herold needed some new shoes. Booth gave him the money. He was in a good mood. He rode up to the farm. There he met the Garretts. They were a populous, well meaning clan, and besides, he could see at a glance, they had the instinct to be kind.

He told them he was John William Boyd and that he had been wounded near Petersburg. He was planning to work his way south, he said, in order to join Johnston.

They said Johnston had surrendered. That set him back for a minute, but he was too tired to think about it. They gave him dinner and a cot upstairs, with the two Garrett boys. Bill had been discharged from the Confederate Armies only three days before, and was still in uniform. He had no wish to hear about the battle of Petersburg. Unfortunately, Bob, the younger brother, did.

When the stranger wouldn't talk, they thought maybe he was a little peculiar, but they didn't think any more than that. If Jett had brought him, he must be all right. The Garretts had known Jett all their lives. They trusted him not to saddle them with anyone who wasn't all right.

XXX

The next morning, which was Tuesday, the 25th, the Garretts had to admit that Mr. Boyd looked better.

He also felt better. The world pleased him. He had spent so much time in the theatre and on trains, that he had never had much occasion to look at it before. He found it delightful.

The men were already out working the farm, but Mrs. Garrett was in the kitchen. She nodded, smiled, wished him good morning, and went on telling the coloured help what to cook for supper. She was not the sort of woman he found it easiest to charm. She had neither the faded vanity of a Mrs. Surratt, nor the bewildered indulgence of his mother. She was brisk, cheery, and did not mince her words. He was best pleasing the unhappy, but Mrs. Garrett was so clearly satisfied with what she was, that there was no crack in her anywhere.

He went out on the porch and tried his charm on the smaller children, instead. They were on the lawn. He went down there and told them stories until about noon. They were well brought up children, scrubbed, rambunctious, and mannerly. He sat on the prickly grass and told them about his own childhood at Tudor Hall. He had not been happy as a child, but as he talked, he could see that the Garrett children thought he must have had a wonderful time. Perhaps he had. While he talked, he looked around him.

The farmhouse was smaller than its outbuildings. Instead of Corinthian pillars, it had plain square posts to hold up its porch. But it was painted white and had a gracious look to it, all the same. The barns were prosperous. The Garretts seemed exactly to fit where they were. The yard was planted with slim trees. He did not know what kind of trees. He would very much have liked to know. Behind the barns the woods rose up to rolling hills. The yard had an agreeable,

156

pungent smell. He leaned back to savour it and closed his eyes. If only he could stay here he would be well again.

The children asked if his wound hurt him.

He opened his eyes and said no. He had forgotten his wound.

At about noon the gate in the fence opened and Miss Holloway came in. She was Mrs. Garrett's younger sister, a schoolteacher who boarded at the farm. She had returned for lunch. She was the first gentlewoman he had met since last he had seen Bessie Hale. She thought him wistful, and felt sorry for him. She asked about his leg and then told him Lincoln had been shot. It was the latest news.

Booth was surprised. "Why, he's been dead for ten days," he said.

"We lead a secluded life here," she told him, and sat down on the bench beside him.

So that explained why the Garretts had been so charming: they lived outside events. He wished she would not tell them the news. He did not want this dream to end.

"What did you hear about it?" he asked cautiously.

"Not much. He was shot by some maniac. I suppose the man must have been a maniac, to kill him at a time like this. Besides, you probably know more about it than I do. Why don't you tell me how it happened?"

A maniac. He stared after the children, who having lost him to a grown-up, were straggling up to the house.

"I heard that the man who shot him was a Southern patriot. He did it for reasons that were purely patriotic."

"He must have curious notions of patriotism. What was his name?"

"He was an actor called John Wilkes Booth."

"Oh, an actor," she said, and examined her parasol.

That nettled him. "What do you suppose an actor would be like?"

"Always acting, I guess. You know. Always strutting around speech making."

His last speech had been three words, and those not even in his own language. *Sic semper tyrannis.* "Why should he not be a patriot?" he asked. She made him curious. Young

157

girls sometimes know more than we do. It is because they do less.

"Patriotism isn't the same as loyalty," said Miss Holloway, looking up at the house. "I mean, actors don't have any home or anything, do they? So they just act." She bid him good day and wandered up to the house, took off her bonnet, and joined Mrs. Garrett in the kitchen. Mrs. Garrett had been looking out the window.

"What's he moaning about down there?" she asked.

"I don't know. I think he's just lonely and wants someone to talk to. At least he looks lonely."

Mrs. Garrett gave her a sharp look. "You don't know anything about him," she said.

Miss Holloway blushed. "Don't you like him?"

Mrs. Garrett looked out the window again. "No, I don't. He's too smooth and there's something wrong about him."

"He's just wounded." Miss Holloway had found him puzzling, but charming.

"That's not what I mean," said her sister. "You'd better call him in to dinner."

They sat at the round table in the kitchen, eating and talking while the coloured help served them. Booth found his hosts somehow changed. The news of the assassination, perhaps. But he didn't like the look on Mrs. Garrett's face.

Bill Garrett said he reckoned Old Abe had it coming to him. Old Abe had done a lot of wicked things in his time. As for the reward, that was a lot of money. If the man came this way, he'd like to try for it.

That was too much for Booth. "Would you really turn him in? He probably did it for the South, you know."

Mr. Garrett shut them both up. As far as he was concerned, the war had been bad for trade, and that defined the war.

It seemed to Booth that Mr. Garrett was watching him too closely. He was glad when dinner was over. He went outside again. But he didn't feel as at his ease as he had that morning with the children.

158

During the afternoon Ruggles, Bainbridge, and Herold came back. He went down to the gate to meet them.

Herold looked happy. He had a new pair of shoes. That was all Herold cared about. The boy was no Patroclus. His raw voice jarred on Booth's nerves.

Bainbridge was curious. "Why did you do it?" he asked. "A few months ago it might have helped us, but now?"

The question made Booth angry. The only way he could justify himself was to point out how much he had suffered. That needed no pointing out. Bainbridge and Ruggles saw before them the ruin of an indoor man. Even after ten days in the woods, they wouldn't have looked like that.

"And now?" asked Bainbridge.

Booth shrugged. "I've thrown my life away for nothing at all. My only hope is to get to Mexico. But my foot . . ."

Ruggles, who had had some experience of wounds, offered to look at it.

Booth refused to have the splints removed. He pulled up his trouser leg, and Ruggles looked. The flesh was swollen and greenish purple. Ruggles had seen gangrene before. He told Booth that unless he could get medical attention, the leg would have to be amputated. But he knew the matter had gone farther than that. The man would die.

Old Mr. Garrett was in the parlour, waiting for Ruggles. When Ruggles came in, he wasted no time on preliminaries.

"How long have you and Jett known that man?" he asked.

"We met him at the ferry last night." Ruggles was cautious. "He's pretty badly chewed up. So we offered to help."

"In other words, Jett doesn't know him at all?"

Ruggles shook his head.

"Sure his name is Boyd?"

Ruggles said yes, his name was Boyd. Why get the old man into trouble by telling the truth, and besides, what difference did it make? Ruggles knew gangrene when he saw it. Booth didn't have long to run, in any case.

"Funny he isn't in uniform," said Garrett. "Maybe you

boys should get out of here. You don't have any parole papers, do you?"

Ruggles said they hadn't.

"Remember me to Jett," said Old Man Garrett. "And tell him not to bring anybody here he doesn't know." He turned and left the room.

He didn't leave the house. He stood in the kitchen, watching Booth and Herold on the bench down under the elm tree. Then he went to the outbuildings to help Bill with the chores. While he worked, he kept an eye on them; and he began to feel uneasy.

"You really think they're soldiers?" he asked Bill.

"He doesn't talk much, but that doesn't mean anything."

"I've been watching them," Old Man Garrett said. "If that boy's Mr. Boyd's brother, it doesn't seem to me they'd talk together quite the way they do. I don't think he's his brother at all."

The two men looked at each other. "What do you think?" asked Bill.

"I don't know what I think. But I'd like to get rid of them."

While Old Garrett watched, Bainbridge and Ruggles galloped up to the gate again. Booth pulled out a revolver. There was a parley, and then Ruggles and Bainbridge went off. Herold headed for the house, with Booth hobbling behind him. Old Garrett and Bill met them there.

Booth wanted to buy their horse for a hundred and fifty bucks.

The horse wasn't worth half that. The price made the Garretts suspicious. They temporized. Bill said he'd drive them into Guinea Station in the morning.

"I'll pay anything within reason, but hurry," said Booth.

It might be the best way to get rid of them, at that. Old Garrett nodded, and Bill headed for the shed where the horse and cow were kept. That was when the bugle sounded somewhere down by the main road. There wasn't any mistaking that military sound.

Herold whirled round. "Good Jesus," he said. He grabbed Booth and headed for the back of the farm, where the woods were. Garrett didn't move, but his eyes narrowed.

160

There was a downpour of hoofbeats. All four men watched the opening to the lane. Booth whipped out his pistol. Garrett was worried. He'd lost just about everything movable in this damn war. He didn't intend to lose his last horse and his last cow.

The horses pounded past the lane, without stopping. Nobody said anything. Then Herold began to giggle. The boy was unbalanced and the man was dangerous. That gave Garrett a lot to think about. Booth headed for the woods, went into them for several hundred feet, and sat down. What he wanted was a drink. Fortunately Herold had some whisky with him. You could depend upon him to have whisky, if nothing else. They stayed in the woods all afternoon. The cavalry did not come back. They were both hungry. And then there was the matter of the horse. They had to have the horse. They wandered back to the house. Its kitchen windows were lit. It was dinner time. The kitchen door was fastened. Old Man Garrett opened it for them. He looked stern. Herold didn't notice.

"We're hungry," he said. "Besides, we wanted to talk to you about that horse."

Garrett hesitated. "All right, you can eat," he said, and let them in. The others made place for them at table. But nobody spoke. Even Miss Holloway looked aside. Garrett waited for them to finish their food. Then he came out with what he had to say.

"I want to know why you were so scared of those Federals," he said. "What have you done?"

"We haven't any parole papers," said Booth.

"That's not a shooting matter."

Booth tried to smile, but his smile didn't feel right, even to him.

"I assure you we're not criminals."

Maybe they weren't, but they were something bad. And they sure wanted that horse. Garrett said he wouldn't sell it. And he wouldn't let Bill drive them at night, either. Not with all those Federals about. Maybe in the morning. But they couldn't sleep in the house. They'd have to sleep in the barn.

161

It was Stewart and Cox all over again. But Booth had not much dignity left to stand on. He agreed to sleep in the barn. And about the horse, could they leave before dawn?

Garrett cut him off. He said there was hay in the barn, and Mrs. Garrett would give them some blankets, if they wanted them.

They did want them. Herold carried the blankets and the lantern. They went to the barn.

It was a tobacco barn, about sixty feet long and fifty feet wide. Its sliding doors were walled up, the walls were mere slats, to admit air for the curing. At the far end was a pile of hay. When Herold went to investigate the hay, he found there was furniture underneath it, but they were both too tired to haul it out. Herold made two pallets of hay, and they lay down on those.

Booth was full of plans. Now he knew about his leg, and sensed he was dying, he was eager for life again. They would escape to Mexico. Maximilian was still Emperor there. Mexico City had an international court and a theatre. There would be a place for Herold, too. Once they were in Mexico they would be safe. Booth might even go on to Europe, on a triumphal tour. He talked on and on, and he didn't believe a word of it. Herold could tell that from his voice. Herold wanted to go to sleep.

Outside they heard a rustling in the shrubbery. While they listened, it stopped.

"Go out and look, Davy," said Booth.

Herold didn't want to go, but he went over to the door and tried to push it open. It wouldn't give. He shoved again.

"We're locked in," he said.

Booth was startled. Then he thought of an explanation. "It's just Garrett," he said bitterly. "He thinks we're thieves."

Up at the main house, Old Man Garrett chuckled, turned over, and began to snore. He hadn't been able to lock up the horse, but he had been able to lock up the men who wanted it. He'd out-foxed them. He had nothing to worry about until morning.

162

XXXI

Jett was awakened by an immense knocking downstairs. He was at the Bowling Green hotel, a large, deserted-looking building which only made these knocks on the door the louder and more ominous. He listened alertly, and heard voices. He could not hear what they said, but he recognized the feminine voice of his hostess. The other voices sounded Northern.

He looked towards the other bed, as he heard boots on the stairs. Mrs. Goldman's son was in the other bed. He was badly wounded, but he was awake. He had been one of the last casualties of this endless war.

There was a knock at the door. "Willie, will you come to the door?" Mrs. Goldman sounded timid.

There was no escape. The door banged open and a Federal officer came in, nattier and better fed than any Confederate was these days. The yellow stripes down his blue pants leg glowed in the candlelight and wriggled like a snake. His boots gleamed. He had a gun in each hand. Willie looked at the candle and at the guns. The candle was dripping on the floor. The officer stared at him. He had two men behind him.

"Take your prisoner," he said, went over to the bed, and looked down at the boy in it. With a flick of his hand he turned down the sheets. The boy's chest was a mess of bandages. Gently the Colonel put the sheets in place again and turned to Mrs. Goldman.

"I'm sorry, Madam," he said. "I had to make sure. Take us to another room. We don't want to disturb your son." He led the way to a bedroom at the other end of the hall, and there turned to face Willie Jett.

"I'm Colonel Conger," he said. "I want to read you something." What he read was Stanton's proclamation of

163

the reward. He dwelt lovingly upon the death penalty offered for those who aided or abetted Booth.

Jett asked if he might speak to Conger alone. He could not bring himself to grovel before his own people.

Conger put his revolvers on the table in front of him, stretched his legs out, and said yes. "You've got yourself into a lot of silly trouble," he went on. "Where is he?"

Jett told him. A lark is a lark, but no one wants to die for it. Besides, Booth was not one of his personal friends. He asked if he would be hanged.

"Not if you co-operate," said Conger. He knew nothing was to be accomplished by hanging foolish young boys. He was tired of Stanton's dirty business.

Jett co-operated. Herold, he said, was also there. Conger told him to get dressed and summoned the bugler to sound assembly.

Fifteen minutes later they were on their way. The road was empty. There was a narrow moon in the sky. And Jett felt utterly miserable. He did not want to see what would happen next. At the entrance to the Garrett lane he asked if he might wait there. Conger gave him a thoughtful look, and said he might.

Then, with the rest of the 16th New York Cavalry, he trotted up to the Garrett farm.

XXXII

The dogs had begun to bark from hill to hill. Since the night was crisp, the sound carried well. It gave Herold the shivers. Then the Garrett dog joined in. A moment later they heard the trot of cavalry coming up the lane.

Conger led his men into the farm yard. Six he sent to guard the escape to the woods, behind the barn. When they had gone, he rode slowly through the inner gate and stationed his men in a circle around the house. The yard was empty and seemed watchful. Perhaps that was a trick of the night sky and of the deep blue shadows. His men held their rifles in their hands, in order to prevent their rattling against their saddle slings. Cavalry can be quiet when it chooses, though not so quiet that Booth could not guess that something was going on. He could smell the horses.

Lieutenant Baker dismounted, went up to the kitchen door, and banged on the wooden panels. A second floor window flung up and Old Man Garrett asked what they wanted. He sounded sleepy.

"Never mind who we are or what we want," Baker called. "Light a candle and open the door."

The window slammed down. One of the horses snorted and pawed the ground. Conger drew his pistol, Old Man Garrett opened the door, and as he did so, two men pushed by him and went inside to search the house.

"Where are the two men who are stopping here?" demanded Conger. He had had experience of stubborn farmers.

Old Man Garrett raised his candle, saw the blue uniform, and said they had gone into the woods that afternoon, which was true enough. A light went on in the kitchen. The soldiers sent to search the house must have found a lamp. Somewhere on the second floor a child began to cry.

"It may interest you to know those two men are the murderers of President Lincoln," said Conger. "Anyone who shields them or abets them incurs a capital charge. Now, where are they?"

Garrett's face did not change expression. When frightened, he froze. He always did. There was nothing to be got out of him. Conger turned to one of the soldiers behind him. "Bring a lariat and we'll string him up."

Baker came round the house with a young man dressed in Confederate grey. "He's been hiding in the corn crib."

"That's my son," said Garrett. He didn't want anything to happen to Bill.

"In that case, he's just in time to see his father strung up," said Conger. He had the soldier throw the lariat up over a limb.

Bill didn't need long to think that over. "They're in the barn. We locked them in there, and my brother and I slept in the corn crib to watch them. We were afraid they were horse thieves."

Conger glanced at the house. The women were at the windows, scarcely visible, but watching. He bit his lip. "Keep them under guard," he told his men, "but take them inside." He motioned to Bill. "You come with me."

He led the way towards the barn.

Booth stood in the middle of darkness. There had to be some way of preventing capture, but he could think of none. Even in the woods, he had not felt so afraid.

He could see nothing but dim chinks of light between the slats of the walls, and yet he was aware of men moving out there. They no longer bothered to keep silent. They must be sure of themselves. Someone had lit a torch. Its flickering light spread long streaks across the floor. He heard the padlock unhasped, but the door did not open. Herold neither moved nor spoke. There was nothing to be done with him. His jaw was wobbling. Booth reached for his carbine.

The barn shook as someone kicked against it. "Wake up in there. We have come to arrest you," shouted a man's voice. "We have the place surrounded. Open the door."

There was no answer.

Baker put his candle on the ground and confronted Bill Garrett. "I'm going to send you inside. Tell them to surrender."

Bill didn't want to go in there. He was afraid of getting shot.

"You go in there, or we'll shoot you right now." Baker swung the door open, shoved him in, and slammed it behind him.

It was dark inside, but the bars of light cast by the torches flickered over Bill Garrett's legs as he stumbled forward.

"Damn you. Get out of here. You have betrayed us," shouted Booth.

Bill Garrett stood stock still and began to plead. His voice was a whisper. As far as anybody outside could tell, nothing happened. In a minute he was at the door, begging to get out. Conger said to let him out.

He came out trembling. "They don't want to surrender."

"Did you tell them who we are?"

"They didn't ask."

"No, they wouldn't ask," said Conger. He was a professional soldier. That gave him both a decency and an understanding that Baker, a ferret in uniform and nothing more, lacked. Baker was one of Stanton's men. Baker doused the lights, put his mouth to one of the slits of the siding, and told the men inside they had just five minutes to surrender their arms and come out, otherwise the barn would be fired.

Booth had been grateful for that abrupt dark. It was like a last blanket, pulled over his face by a man who wants to go on sleeping, even though he is at last awake. But he was afraid of fire. Herold was crying.

Booth spoke up, making his voice as rich and as assured as he could. "Who are you?" he asked. "Whom do you want? We are guilty of no crime." He could not help but plead for time.

Neither could he get it.

"It doesn't matter who we are," said Baker. "We know who you are, and we have fifty men around this place. You can't possibly get away. Come out peacefully and you won't be harmed."

"Give us a few minutes to think it over." If this drivelling, snivelling fool had been Payne, rather than Herold, he would not be in such a fix. But there was nothing to be done with Herold. "I am a cripple," he shouted. "I have only one good leg. Give me a chance for my life. Withdraw your men a hundred yards from the door, and I'll come out and fight you."

It was a proposal so ridiculous it made Conger spit. "Tell him to go to hell," he said.

"We can't do anything like that." Baker tried to sound patient. "We came here to take you prisoner, not to lose men fighting with you."

There was a pause.

"Fifty yards," the voice begged.

Conger cursed. The soldiers standing behind him grinned. The man was mad.

"Surrender and come out, or we fire the barn and shoot," said Baker.

There was another pause.

"Very well, then, my brave boys, prepare a stretcher for me," shouted Booth.

"What the hell does he mean by that?" Conger asked. "We've had enough of play acting."

Booth would never have enough of it.

Conger told the Garrett boy to get some brush and pile it against the building, so they could fire the barn. The man in there had shot the President. He saw no reason why he should be allowed to shoot innocent soldiers as well.

Bill remembered that his father had a neighbour's furniture stashed in that barn for safe keeping. He hesitated. Conger told him to do as he was told.

"We'll give that idiot in there just two more minutes. Then I fire the barn."

They could hear two men arguing inside. One of them sounded on the verge of tears. That was Herold. Herold was whining not so much for his life, as for just five minutes more of it.

Booth felt rather Roman. If it must be this way, then it must, but he would grant Herold his life. The manumission of a slave is the last act of a Seneca.

"Let me out quick. I don't know anything about this man. He's a desperate character, and is going to shoot me," yelled Herold. Fear had stimulated him to a certain worthless cunning.

Booth did not even hear him.

He was himself again. The curtain was about to go up. A noble Roman was about to open his veins, rather than be executed by the Emperor Nero (it was Nero, wasn't it, who asked Seneca to despatch himself?). But stoicism is a private affair. We do not demand that our servants be slain with us. We are not so primitive as that. Besides, he could not stop Herold.

"All right, Colonel," he called. "There's a man here who wants to surrender."

"Let him come out, then, but he must bring his arms with him."

"He has no arms. He swears to you he is guilty of no crime."

That was exactly the way Herold felt about it. He was guilty of no crime.

"For Chrissake, let the poor bastard out," Conger told Baker. "I'd hate to be in there with that lunatic. He seems to think he's still on a stage."

Baker opened the door. In the dark opening he saw a pair of extended hands. Then Herold came capering out.

"I always liked Mr. Lincoln's jokes," he simpered. "I thought he was a fine man. I always liked his jokes."

Baker yanked him aside by the wrists and turned him over to the soldiers. Herold began to cry.

A faint glow appeared at the side of the barn. With a snap, it blossomed out of its pod and spread up the building. The wood was old. The slats began to blaze at once. Through the slats Baker caught sight of Booth. The man was standing motionless in the middle of the barn. In that lurid half light he resembled his brother Edwin, and the flickering shadows

169

made him seem taller. There was no expression in his eyes.

He was looking at the fire. It had caught at the straw which hid the furniture, and flamed up from the varnish on it. The smoke was getting heavy. At first he was blinded by so much light. He stared at it almost idly, and remembered the name of the man that poem was about, the man who fired the Ephesian dome. The man was Herostratus, a white skinned young fanatic. He looked at his own hands. They were spotted and dingy.

The smoke made his eyes smart. He looked at the gun in his hand. The flames cast deep shadows and lurid lights on the roof beams. The barn, which was big enough to begin with, now seemed immense. The carbine was too clumsy. He dropped it and took out his revolver. No doubt he was being watched from outside. He had an audience. He took three or four steps forward. But what was forward, here? Whatever happened, he would not be led through the streets of Washington like some king of Armenia. He saw the scene, the crowds, the top hats, the togas, the crinolines, and the chains. And then reality struck him.

He was going to die. This was not a performance. It was real. It was something for which there would be no applause and no demand for a benefit. This was what reality was: to die.

He could not believe it. He wanted to cry out. Did they not realize it had all been a game? If this was reality, why should he not be allowed to live? The other had not been real, the assassination. It was only a pretence they would burn or hang him for. He had died on the stage quite often. That did not hurt. But this would. These villains meant to kill him here.

He tried to face the audience he could not even see, but the effort was too much for him. It was reality that was the pretence. The pretence was horrible.

"I am in this body," he thought. "Oh, my God. They are going to take it away from me. I won't be able to act through it any more. I won't even be any more."

Couldn't they take something else? Why couldn't they?

Couldn't they let him go on acting? For any body would do for him to act in. He didn't care what it looked like or what was wrong with it, just so they let him have one. Couldn't they torture him instead?

But when one says Oh, my God, it isn't because one believes in Him. There isn't any God to intervene except on the winning side. It's because there isn't one that one calls out for Him. One realizes that at last, and the realization is horrible. God is as indifferent to our affairs, as Manitou or Brahman.

He remembered himself. He saw a hundred cartes-de-visite, of Booth gallant, triumphant, white skinned, leaping on his horse, muscular, popular, sleeping in a warm bed, the idol of everyone.

It was the performance that was real, not the reality. For where else but on a stage could a man be himself? What else was the world, and society?

Raising his pistol, for he could not bear the sight of it, to a position out of his line of sight, he cocked it. A bullet whizzed by his ear. No. Only the performance was real. He shot himself behind the same ear. It was where he had shot Lincoln. It was where one administered the *coup de grâce* to a dying animal. But he did not think of that.

Sic semper tyrannis.

But at least he had been one. Ambition had made him one. Every idol becomes one. It is so with everything we applaud, and he could hear that applause. It had a curious rush, like leaves in a gust along a corridor. And then he fell.

Baker went into the barn at once, and had Herold dragged in after him, to identify the body. Conger followed.

"He shot himself," said Baker.

Conger said, "No." He could not admit that the man had shot himself. If he did, he would then have failed to carry out his orders.

Herold, his face hot with flames, who did not want to burn and felt his eyebrows singeing already, said yes, it was Booth; and knew he had condemned himself with the admission.

171

The officers could not be bothered with Herold just then. Some soldiers were detailed to tie him to a tree in front of the house. Conger and Baker dragged Booth out of the flames.

Sergeant Corbett stepped forward to say that he had shot the man. Conger looked up and saw who it was. He knew all about Corbett. The man was a hysteric renegade, with the naked, shaved look of an insane man. He had mad eyes and a cracker's cunning. He was also castrated. That was what an earlier fit of religious fervour had led to.

"I shot him," he repeated.

Baker told Conger he was crazy enough to have done anything. Conger took the hint, but he had to dress Corbett down.

"Providence directed me to do it, Sir. I heard the voice of God," said Corbett.

Perhaps he had at that, thought Conger, but there were one or two legalities to be thought of. "He was trying to shoot one of us, I suppose."

It was Corbett's turn to take the hint.

The barn was now blazing up to the rooftree. The light was both misleading and dazzling. Herold was praying, the tears trickling down his face. And Booth was still alive.

Some soldiers carried the body to the porch. Baker asked for brandy, Miss Holloway brought it, and soaking some on a handkerchief, ran it over Booth's lips. Baker held a candle over his head and moved it to and fro. Yes, the man's eyes were open.

"Is there anything I can do for you?" he asked Booth.

Booth had died so many times on the stage. He knew how to do it. He had killed himself, and yet he had not died.

"Turn me over. The pain," he said, and when they did, the pain was worse, so he asked to be turned back again.

"Did Jett betray me?"

Nobody answered him. He realized his body was paralyzed. Herold, tied to the tree, could see everything and heartily wished that he could not. He wondered if he would be killed there.

An officer bent over Booth. Booth could see him plainly.

172

He could also see Mary Ann. "Tell Mother I died for my country," he whispered.

"Is that what you say?" asked Conger. He was aware of himself, was Conger, kneeling there. He felt sorry for the poor fool.

"Yes," said Booth. It was only play acting, after all. Then he panicked. He felt himself slipping away. He could not bear that inevitable and giddy motion.

"Kill me. Oh, kill me," he begged. He would rather be killed than go through the terror of dying. He had had enough of reality.

Conger could not do that. He straightened up and looked across the yard. His soldiers stood about, young, ample, and easy in their spick and span and graceful uniforms. As the flames flickered, now one, and now another of them emerged from the darkness. They were oddly silent. There was something terrible about that dying body, something they did not want to hear about.

All men are actors, perhaps, but Conger, who was an older man, did not care for the silence of these. Corbett bothered him. That fanatic had the face of a barbered Medusa.

Booth fainted, but he was not dead yet. There was nothing to do but wait. The man took two and a half hours about dying.

Roped to the tree, even Herold was silent now. He had cried himself out.

Somewhere under consciousness Booth's body made a last effort. It was scarcely audible, because of the creak of leather-clad legs around him.

Conger bent over him to listen. It was only a little murmur, but Conger was not soon to forget it.

"Useless," said Booth. "Useless." And then he died.

So it had been, no doubt. Conger straightened up, his legs cramped with kneeling. What was not? Perhaps that was what the men had not wanted to hear. Looking down from the porch, he saw Corbett's greedy eyes.

Miss Holloway stepped forward and asked if she might not have a lock of the dead man's hair.

XXXIII

They sewed the body in a sack, slung it over the saddle of one of the horses, and jogged back to Washington. The men were dead tired and didn't have much to say. Neither did Herold. He could see the sewed-up sack in front of him, slapping against the flanks of the pack horse.

At Washington Herold was sent to the Old Capitol Prison, and Booth's body to the ironclad *Montauk*, the boat on which Lincoln had taken his last constitutional, two weeks before. There doctors came aboard to identify the corpse.

They had trouble in doing so. Dr. May, who had once treated Booth, found it hard to recognize the body. He remembered Booth as being white skinned and muscular. This man was emaciated and had freckles on his hands. But it was Booth, all right. The freckles were premature liver spots, signs of senility. Such things could appear as a result of extreme stress. There were cases on record. Shock can sometimes produce the symptoms of senility.

There was also trouble about getting the corpse out of the way, for crowds lined the river in an effort to catch a glimpse of it. Booth had fame of a sort, and at the War Department it was feared that someone might try to dig him up again. Therefore a dummy burial was performed, from a ship sent down the Potomac, and the body itself was hustled into an anonymous grave in the yard of the Old Capitol Prison. No one was supposed to know that had been done, but of course the prisoners knew. Prisoners always know such things. Stanton had arrested everyone. He would let no one out of his net. And with Herold his menagerie was complete. It was time, now, for the show.

Mrs. Booth received the news of Booth's death the day of

his burial. Asia was ill and had sent for her. Aunt Thomas was driving her to the ferry for Jersey City, where the rail terminus was. Hearing the newsboys shouting the news in the streets, he slammed down the carriage windows and drew the curtains, talking as loudly as he could to drown out the shouting. He was a family friend. But of course he could not drown out that cry. It could be heard on every corner.

When the carriage arrived at the ferry slip, he settled Mary Ann into a quiet corner on deck, and made the trip with her across that seagull madding water. No one recognized her, for she wore a widow's veil. At the train he bought a paper and gave it to her, folded. Better she learn the news from a paper at least given to her by a friend, than from a paper bought from a stranger.

"You will need all your courage. The paper in your hand will tell you what, unhappily, we must all wish to hear," he told her. "John Wilkes is dead."

She did not lift her veil. She did not move. "Thank God," she said. Death was the only mercy he or they could possibly have expected. But it was not until the train was well into the countryside that she opened the paper.

"Tell Mother I died for my country," she read. But whose country was that? Not hers. She was not sure. A grief like this had no natural outlet. She sat motionless. It could only be lived with.

Asia, in Philadelphia, had much the same reaction, but being younger, had not Mary Ann's self-control. She was bed-ridden. Life had levelled her. It was old Mr. Hemphill, one of Clarke's employees, who had the decency to bring her the news, though he could not come out with it. But she guessed why he was there.

"Is it over?" she asked.

"Yes."

"Is he dead?"

"Yes, madam."

She was so relieved she was almost happy. She turned her face to the wall and wept. She was so very glad for Johnny. Of the others, she did not think at all.

It was Edwin, as usual, who had to deal with the others. So, though he did not much like the job, he sat down and dealt with them. That was his way. Yet, if anyone had praised him for doing so, he would have been surprised. It was Junius, in that family, who had the reputation for being practical, not he. He was merely the one who earned money, and until this terrible thing, had hoped to become an artist. As he had said, "In America art degenerates below the standard even of a trade." So it was up to him to do odd jobs for the family. To them that was all he was good for. He was their odd job man.

"There is no solidity in Love, no truth in Friendship, no steadiness in Marital Faith," Asia wrote him. He would not have gone quite that far, but Asia had provocation. Her nurse patriotically refused to tend her through her pregnancy. Her doctor was nervous about being seen making house visits. Clarke had denounced her, publicly and privately. Only a minor actress she scarcely knew, a woman named Effie Germon, good in comedy parts, had asked if she might be of help. As Asia said, it was enough almost to revive belief in human goodness. Almost, but of course not quite.

Clarke and Junius Brutus had been let out of prison. Junius was tranquil enough. If the world had frozen over, Junius would have been tranquil. But Clarke was furious. The Booths were all Iagos, he told Asia, male and female. He demanded a divorce. Divorce from her was his only salvation, now. He almost hoped the child she was carrying miscarried. It was half a Booth. For that reason, if it did not miscarry now, it would be sure to do so later.

Then he went out and left her. She could only write to Edwin. Though she had once treated him badly enough, by refusing to receive his first wife, and by denouncing her as a cheap actress, Edwin, she knew, would not hold that against her.

Nor did he. But he remembered it. His poor dead Mary was still the only woman he cared about. Edwina, her daughter, was with Asia, and he did not even dare to go

176

fetch her home until the public outcry against them all died down. Not even friends quite made up for the malice of the world. Yet at least John Wilkes could not bring any more ignominy upon them now. Like the others, he was glad Johnny was dead.

So was Stanton.

Stanton was setting up the trial of the conspirators; and it would have been inconvenient to have the chief conspirator there to deny what Stanton had decided was the truth of the matter. On the 28th of April, for similar reasons, he had issued an order that all prisoners were to have canvas bags fastened over their heads, for better security against conversation with them. They were to have a hole to breathe and eat through, but no holes for their eyes. Payne was to be secured to prevent self-destruction. Security was his passion, and to maintain security, one must have a plot against it. He wanted no one to deny that plot. He had the prisoners transferred to the Old Capitol Prison, from the various cells in which, until now, he had secluded them.

A curious man, Mr. Stanton, in appearance, since he was so short, rather like a devil doll turned schoolteacher. People said he was completely disinterested, since graft meant nothing to him. Unfortunately power meant a great deal. He did not bother to go home any more at night. He slept on a cot in the War Department instead. He could not bear to be away from the source of power. He was a bully with a low pitched, silky voice. The more of a bully he became, the better modulated and the softer the voice. He was also a coward. He did not like to see his victims. Though he had set up the Old Capitol Prison as an *oubliette*, he never went there. The lowest he descended into his own sewers, was to have his informers brought upstairs to see him.

The best of these was Mrs. Surratt's lodger, Weichmann. He did not stoop to giving Weichmann instructions as to what to say, for he had a horror of known perjury. But he made it plain to the poor, snivelling, self-seeking creature what would happen to him if he didn't say the right things. Weichmann would do as he was told. As for suborning him,

177

there was nothing wrong with that. That was an act in the public interest. It would promote security. So Stanton, one of the new men, those selfless figures who want nothing for themselves but the prerogatives of their office, in which, soft shelled themselves and weak, they lurk like cuttlefish, ready to grasp anything that comes by to nourish their enormous self-importance.

He was not concerned with good and evil. He was concerned with maintaining order in the State; that was his duty, and no one could maintain that so well as he. Thus he was glad Booth was dead. There was no telling what these spies and conspirators might know, and there were some things Stanton did not wish to have known. At times it had been necessary for him to intrigue against and to deceive Lincoln, just as he would have to do against Johnson, for the good of the State and of the War Department. Now the man was dead and deified already, anything blurted out about that would do no good, only harm. Besides, he was a coward.

His power sprang from that system of arbitrary arrest which resulted from the suspension of the writ of habeas corpus. To such powers as he derived from that illegality, he had added his own secret service and complete control over public communications. As he had once told the British Ambassador, he could arrest anyone, and no power on earth, except that of the President, could release them. Could the Queen of England, he had asked the Ambassador, do so much?

Not that he did not have a sense of humour. Three times a week he did his own marketing. It was one of his few pleasures to bumble through the produce stalls, with a servant behind him to carry the basket. When a Confederate sympathizer tried to cheat him on lettuces, he playfully threatened the man with the Old Capitol Prison. Old Madison, his Negro, did the same. That made vegetables much cheaper and shopping much faster. The Old Capitol Prison settled everything.

Perhaps every good man has a bad man to do his dirty work, for since corruption is the price of order, how should a good man keep himself unsullied, otherwise? Every Lincoln has a Stanton. But Lincoln had been shrewd enough to control the man. Now Lincoln was gone. Stanton missed the tug of war between them, but apart from that these days he scarcely gave Lincoln a thought. He had no time. He was too busy with the coming trial. He was anxious about procedure. He even accepted advice, a thing he seldom did, though with a petulant expression. His great soft womanly eyes, behind his spectacles, were full of reproach when he was contradicted, but still, he did listen.

He was always reluctant to let go anybody who had fallen into his prisons, but on advice, he let some of them go. Dr. Stewart was exonerated by Booth's note; Mrs. Quesenberry was a harmless old woman, and if prosecuted, would attract too much sympathy from the press. Mr. Cox's nigger girl swore herself blue that Mr. Booth had not been there. How otherwise could she swear, for she did not want Massa Cox strung up; but there was no way of shaking her story. The actors had to be let go. There was no point in keeping Ford, the owner of the theatre, on display. But he did not like it. He had too few people left to accuse. And now Baker said he had made a deal with that silly young Confederate cavalry man, Jett. He would have to be let off, too. And there *had* to be a trial. He was left only with Mrs. Surratt, Dr. Mudd, Payne, Atzerodt, Herold, Arnold, Spangler, and O'Laughlin.

Mrs. Surratt did not bother him. That John Surratt, her son, could not be rounded up was infuriating. The woman had a neck. She could hang as well as anybody else. Weichmann said she was guilty. That shrinking fool could now go out and say so in court. Stanton would let the daughter and Miss Fitzpatrick off. That was clemency enough.

He turned his attention to the choice of a military commission to try them. To prove that the murder was the result not of his own carelessness, but of the immensity of the plot, he threw everything into the proceedings, and he would need men who could stomach what they were fed. That the trial would be held before a military court, not a civil, and that therefore, there would be no jury, would be some help, but he chose his men carefully. He had not been a public pro-

179

secutor in his youth for nothing. When he had finished his list of the judges he was satisfied. Soldiers will do as they are told, and as for the civilian members, Burnett and Bingham, they had too wobbly a record to show mercy to others now. The way to show innocence in this world, is to prove some-one else guilty, and they had their orders and would obey them. General Wallace, of course, was honest, but he was also a pious fool, he gave the panel of judges a certain distinction, and could be led by them. As for the others, Holt, the leader, was in his pocket, and the rest were straw men. Stanton was ready. It would be an excellent show, but since he knew how it would end, he was now free to turn, with a little relaxed smile, to more important matters.

XXXIV

In Springfield, the funeral train had arrived a little late, at nine o'clock in the morning. Even in death, there were so many demands upon the President's time, all that long journey of seventeen hundred miles.

The procession at Springfield was unostentatious, for Springfield was where he had come from, but it was splendid enough, for Springfield was also the place where they had known him, and where the Todds lived, a place of a certain clapboard and wooden column elegance, despite its mud.

Over his catafalque, in the State House, were lettered his own words, spoken at Philadelphia in 1861. "Sooner than surrender these principles, I would be assassinated on the spot." No doubt they expressed what the *New York World* meant, when speaking, the day of his death, of the quaint and uncouth nature of his rhetoric. He should, of course, have said "rather". But he had not, and now he was dead.

The lying in state was the same as elsewhere, and yet not quite the same. The crowds filed by, saw that face which, ravaged by the demands made upon him in life, was no less ravaged by being exposed to his admirers so often in death. Minute guns sounded, as though to bring rain. There was a choir and a band, a rendition of "Peace, Troubled Soul", and the coffin was closed for the last time. The party then processed to Oak Ridge Cemetery, where, as at the cities on his route, the Last Inaugural was read, with malice towards none.

The grave was temporary.

The malice was to come.

Part Three

XXXV

Edwin said nothing. He wanted to see no one. But as usual he did his best. Though he had sworn never to enter Washington City again, he went down to consult with Defence Counsel. He was only too eager to help those poor people his brother had led astray. The Defence wished him to say that Wilkes had such power over the minds of others that he had rendered the defendants temporarily insane. Edwin did not believe that, but he agreed to say so, if it would help. Unfortunately a good man is not the same thing as a good witness. The Defence decided not to call him.

That was a relief to Edwin. He could not have borne to see any more accusing eyes. One look at the trial room, empty and waiting, and he had guessed what would happen to these misfortunate people. He went back to New York and Mary Ann. All Mary Ann could talk about was Wilkes. Did she not realize that John Wilkes had caused all this?

No, she did not.

The best he could do was to send a cheque to Mr. Garrett, for the furniture stored in his barn and for the barn itself. His only solace was Edwina. With Sleeper Clarke out of prison and back home torturing Asia, it had been necessary to get Edwina out of Philadelphia. Now she was with him. When he went into the nursery, to tuck her in at night, he would say: "Edwina is Papa's baby. Edwina is his darling." She was like a Reynolds portrait: innocent, but artful. She would reach up her chubby little arms, put them around his neck, pull him off balance, and say sleepily: "Papa is my baby."

Perhaps he was, at that. But he was no one else's. He scarcely dared to leave the house. The streets were too ugly. And yet what did it mean? He was a Shakespearian tragedian. He knew better than to ask such a question. It didn't mean anything. It had just happened.

It was still happening. It would always go on happening. He could never forget it.

For though he did not attend the trial, and refused to discuss it, he read about it in the newspapers, all the newspapers, and when the Government brought out Pitman's unbiased, if censured, transcript of the proceedings, he bought a copy and read that, and understood it, perhaps, too well.

It was something he never recovered from, that trial. Being an actor, he knew every audience for the latent mob it was, a democracy is only an audience which has surged up on the stage, and as for Stanton, as for politicians, who are only puppet masters after all, though they can move their own men, they can do nothing to stop the fury of the mob, once they have aroused it, and would not if they could, for they need the diversion of that public clamour and that audience, for that is what allows them profitably to pull the strings.

But we may all of us at any moment be lifted up by those strings. That was the terror of it. Mrs. Surratt might as well have been Mary Ann; Payne, his brother Junius, and all of them himself. Anyone might be caught at any time, and caught or not, be guilty. Yet it was those poor people down in Washington who had to bear the brunt of that guilt. Wilkes had seen to that. Even if innocent, even if spared mere human malice, they were still caught up in the inexorable malice of events. It was inevitable. He recognized that. It was less a process than a parable. He could only watch. He had plenty of time to do that, for, as Sleeper Clarke had said so bitterly, *he* had not been touched. On the contrary: every moment of the process, as he followed it, tore everything he lived for into shreds.

XXXVI

The trial began on May 10th, which was John Wilkes's birthday, though only Mary Ann, Asia, and Edwin remembered that. It had a curious atmosphere of rehearsal, that courtroom, on the first day. There were pauses.

Yet it was some release to the prisoners, just to come into that courtroom to be condemned. The seven men entered first. Even among the condemned there are social distinctions. Six of the men wore what was called a stiff shackle, two handcuffs connected by an iron bar, so that they had to hold their hands out stiffly before them, or up, in the attitude of begging dogs. Dr. Mudd, however, had been allowed links to connect his handcuffs, so that he could chink his hands restlessly in his lap. All seven men clanked their leg chains as they sat down. The iron had developed the acrid, burnt rubber smell of sweaty metal. To a man, they blinked and shut their eyes.

That was because for two weeks they had sat in solitary confinement, with those canvas bags over their heads. The bags had been removed only for their appearance in court, and would be clapped back over their heads, like candle snuffers, when they were returned to their cells. For two weeks they had seen nothing but the dim glow of daylight through the close weave of the canvas. Now they could see what that light contained. They could see their accusers.

The court reporters and spectators were disappointed. Two weeks seemed to have changed the men's appearance very little.

The prisoners sat down to the right of the door. Among them only Dr. Mudd looked worth hanging and only Payne uncowed. That puzzled baby face had a certain physical dignity. He had been given a new black jumper. It spread tight across his enormous chest, and only the stretch of the

187

cloth, as he breathed, showed whether or not he was moved by what he saw and heard.

His appearance was inconvenient. He towered over the others. He, at least, had tried to kill a man. He was a giant. No one was averse to seeing a giant in chains, yet in some manner he dominated that room. Try as you would, your eyes came back to him whenever the prosecution had scored a point against the defence. And despite their elaborate and well pressed uniforms, he made the judges seem somehow puny. But mostly he dominated that room because he was uncowed. The court could not get around the impression that he was in some way scornfully amused by all this pretence of legality, and they did not like that. There is little satisfaction to be gotten from the hanging of a public statue. They would rather have smashed it instead. But that they were forbidden to do. There was the press to be thought of. Besides, how could he seem so amused? He had been examined by War Department doctors. They said he had not the intelligence to betray such an attitude.

The press was staring at the one remaining empty chair, the one to the left of the door into the prisoners' dock. That was Mrs. Surratt's chair.

The door opened and she entered.

There was no one who did not look up. About her already there was the air of a martyr. That she should be on trial at all disturbed everyone but Stanton, who had never seen her. Something in a country should be sacrosanct, and so far, in this country, it had been their mothers and the more innocent of their womenfolk. She made them uneasy. She also cheated them by entering veiled. She had been spared the canvas cap, for women, too, as well as gentlemen, have their prerogatives. She had also been spared handcuffs. Day after day she was to sit there, behind her veil. She raised it only once, in order to be identified. Her face at that moment had had no expression, but veiled, she unnerved them. They tried not to look at her.

For her, too, to be released from solitary confinement and so see people again, if only from a distance, while they condemned her, was a sort of freedom. She sat there in a ram-

188

rod posture. They would not even let her see a priest. She had no one to advise her. Dignity she associated with immobility, and with not being stared at. Hence the veil. Besides, behind the veil she could allow herself to show her fear. She did not understand. What had exposed her to this horrible thing?

For it had been horrible.

It was true she was not entirely innocent. She knew that John, her son, had been up to something. He had, and she knew that, too, though she had never quizzed him, been a runner for the Confederates. But that was just the high spirits of youth, and there had been no harm in it. At least she had been aware of none.

She had not seen her fellow conspirators before. From where she sat, she could see only their profiles. But she recognized three of them. John had brought Payne, under another name, she realized now, which made her angry, Atzerodt, and Herold to the house; and Mr. Booth had been there, of course. To bring such people to the house had been very wicked of John. She looked down at her crocheted black mittens.

John was irresponsible. She had always known that, even though she had refused to admit it, even to herself. And she was deeply hurt that he had not managed to smuggle some word to her in prison. Hurt, but not surprised. He had none of the character of his older brother.

She was not unduly worried for herself. But what had happened to John, Annie, and poor Honora Fitzpatrick, her boarder, who certainly had nothing to do with this mummery? For herself, she had been told that she had merely to sit through this trial. That was her punishment, but that would be the end of it. No matter what the judges might say, no man would hang a woman. When the furore had died down, she would be quietly paroled.

Such was Stanton's way of keeping her quiet. He wanted no one to speak out, which was why he allowed the prisoners to speak to counsel only in court, and he had bought her silence with a rumour. She believed that rumour. There was

189

no reason why she should not, for it was only what Stanton did that was novel. His promises were as conventional as any man's, and so far he had not told even the judges what it was he meant to have them do.

Yet she was bewildered. She had been put in a solitary cell with damp walls and very little light. Only the Superintendent of the prison, a Mr. Wood, had been so much as civil to her.

One day, during her constitutional, she ran into Annie and Honora. Honora had a newspaper with her. In it Mrs. Surratt could read a denunciation of herself and of everyone she knew. It shocked her. There was no trick her captors did not stoop to. No doubt the newspaper was another one. She read the account and said, "I suppose I shall have to bear it."

And so she bore it. It was not, however, so easy to endure.

On Thursday, May 11th, the prisoners were allowed to consult their attorneys, whom they had never seen, for the first time. Court adjourned for the day to make that possible. But what can one say about a matter of life or death in one day?

On the 12th, the legal jockeying over with, the indictment began. It lasted for days, alternating with the general testimony, so that as soon as Counsel defended client against one charge, up rose another. The indictment shook her. It was monstrous what she was accused of.

It was monstrous what they were all accused of. Only Payne seemed to take those accusations calmly. He knew perfectly well how much justice the world contains. That was what had made him willing to commit murder for a friend.

She was guilty of the plot to capture Lincoln. She was the intimate tool of Jefferson Davis. She was in the conspiracy to destroy naval vessels and buildings in the Capital. She was responsible for the City Point Explosion. She would share in the million dollars a Mr. Gayle, a mad lawyer from Selma, Alabama, had demanded as the price of assassinating everyone in the Northern cabinet. He had put an advertisement in the papers in order to make his bid public. She had never even heard of Selma, Alabama. Nor had anyone else in the courtroom. But there was the newspaper clipping of

Mr. Gayle's advertisement, entered as a government exhibit against them.

She and the others had conspired to raid Buffalo, Detroit, and New York. She had aided in the starvation of Union prisoners, she who had fed Yankee soldiers at Surrattsville for nothing, because she was sorry for the boys, whatever side they were on, when their own commissariat failed and they were hungry. She was guilty of Andersonville. She had helped to mine Libby Prison, she who did not even know what a torpedo was. And a wretched shirtmaker's jobber from London, England, reported that one Dr. Blackburn, a Freemason, had promised him 100,000 dollars, if only he would sell shirts infected with plague, and so spread pestilence in Washington City. A Mr. Brenner, of Washington City, even said that the shirts had been sold to him.

In some way the prisoners were responsible for that, too, right down to Dr. Mudd, who, being a doctor, must surely be fully conscious of the mischief planned.

The web of the assassination plot was outlined while she listened. She was caught in its strands. What did she, or anyone else there, know of shirts sold by an anonymous Englishman? He might just as well have been selling Jesus' cloak, for all the sense that shirt selling made. Indeed, he might better have been.

He was a little man who stood in the dock on tiptoe. He had perjurer written all over him. Or perhaps he believed what he said. Perhaps they all believed it. It was patent: everyone but the Defence was doing as he had been told. And for that matter, who could believe in the probity of the Defence? Who could believe in anything?

191

XXXVII

The accusations were the worst. The Defence, before the fury of those, sounded almost meaningless. Even the judges showed their boredom: there was nothing novel about a man's defence. The accusations, at least, had a certain interest, for they were levelled by such disparate people.

The courtroom was forty-five feet long and thirty feet wide. It had four badly placed windows. The judges sat against one wall, the reporters and the Defence Counsel against the wall opposite. The witness stand was in the middle. The prisoners sat on a raised dais at one end of the room, so they could see and be seen. The room had new furniture and was freshly painted. It had been fitted up for the trial. But after a few days it smelled dingy and discouraged enough.

Atzerodt, Arnold, Spangler, Herold, and O'Laughlin were only small fry. Not much was to be said either about them, or in their defence. Along that far wall, only Mrs. Surratt and Dr. Mudd were worth the catching, only that insensate giant Payne worth the pulling down.

The small fry did not see the trial in that way. As far as Herold was concerned, the longer he was talked about the better he liked it. The testimony lengthened his life. At least to have people talking about him was better than silence. He did not like to be ignored.

He sat there with the absurd quavering self-importance of the mentally retarded and did not much care for what the witnesses had to say. He saw no reason why he should be condemned. He had run away when Payne did that wicked thing. And as for going along with Booth, what choice had he had? Surely he was not to be blamed for doing that.

He looked curiously at people he had once known.

James Nokes was up there in the witness box. Old Mr. Nokes was the Herolds' nextdoor neighbour, and an old friend. He tried to wave to Mr. Nokes, but being shackled that way, he couldn't. Mr. Nokes would get him out of this.

Mr. Nokes said that Herold was a light and trifling boy, and that very little reliability was to be placed in him.

Herold did not think that fair. Mr. Booth had relied on him. And of course he lied. After all, nobody wanted to be caught out. He felt hurt. He had always liked Mr. Nokes. He didn't understand why Mr. Nokes had to talk about him that way.

Now it was Dr. Charles W. Davis, who agreed that Herold was a trifler. What was that supposed to mean? What was wrong with trifles? Davis also said he was easily led. Well, if that had anything to do with Mr. Booth, he had liked Mr. Booth. He never followed anybody he didn't like.

"He was more a boy than a man," said Davis, and stepped down. Herold didn't like it. On the other hand, they wouldn't hang a mere boy, would they? A boy didn't mean any harm.

Dr. Samuel McKim testified next. Dr. McKim had never liked him. Again there was that line about his being a very light, trivial, unreliable boy. "So much so that I would never let him put up a prescription of mine if I could prevent it, feeling confident he would tamper with it if he thought he could play a joke on anybody. In mind, I consider him about eleven years of age."

Well, what was wrong with a joke once in a while? You had to get some fun out of life. Herold waited to see what the next witness would have to say.

There wasn't one. This was supposed to be his defence, and yet there wasn't one.

It was the turn of the prosecution. A Mr. Doherty was telling the court what Herold had said when they tied him to that tree. He'd forgotten, but they said he'd said: "Let me go. I will not go away. Who is that who has been shot in there in the barn? I did not know that it was Booth."

He'd been pretty sharp to think of saying that, but what he had said did not seem to help. Nobody ever believed you. Even when he'd said he'd met Booth by accident, seven miles out of Washington City, at midnight, they hadn't believed him. Well, he *had* met Mr. Booth by accident. He

193

had never wanted to see Mr. Booth again. All he'd been doing was lighting out for the swamps until things blew over. He always felt safer in the swamps than he did at home.

And now they wouldn't even let him go home. It wasn't his fault Mr. Booth had made him guide him through the swamps. He'd been scared. He hadn't known what to do, and at least Mr. Booth had been somebody to be with. Didn't they understand that?

No, they didn't.

XXXVIII

It was Edward Spangler's turn to stand accused.

At least Spangler knew why he was here. He sat unshaven in the dock, blinking only because he had *tic douloureux*. He was here because for once in his life, he had done something decent, and he was not ashamed of it.

Spangler had no doubts about what he was. He was a drunk. Life hadn't gone right for him ever, and it had been a lot worse since his wife had died a couple of years ago. She was buried in Baltimore. That was why he always called Baltimore home, even though he worked in Washington City and slept at Ford's Theatre. Why shouldn't he sleep there? That way he saved money.

He knew what the world thinks of a drunk, and what it can do to a man who can't defend himself. He'd had forty years to find out. But because a man's a bum doesn't mean he's stupid, and since he hadn't been able to get any booze in prison, his head was pretty clear. He could follow what was going on, all right.

He hadn't given a damn about President Lincoln, and he had a pretty good hunch that these men didn't either, except perhaps some of the Counsel for the Defence and General Lew Wallace, on the judges' side. General Lew Wallace sometimes had the bamboozled look of a soft-shell liberal who doesn't quite believe that what he is doing for the public good is necessarily justified. Wallace was a gentleman, all right, but the other judges were politicians, and a gentleman among politicians is the easiest dupe in the world. He has about as much chance of survival as a piece of ice on a hot stove.

Alone of the conspirators, Spangler wasn't guilty of anything, apart from having given Booth a head start. That meant he could see the trial for the farce it was.

195

Through some accident, at the beginning of the trial four of the conspirators had entered with those canvas snuffers on. The snuffers were something Stanton insisted they wear, but not something he wanted seen. The accident did not happen again. One gasp from the spectators abolished the snuffers. But Edward Spangler had been one of those four.

He did not like to be stared at. It was quite true, as the witnesses said: he had no self-respect. But he did not like people to observe that for themselves.

He could neither see nor talk to his fellow prisoners, most of whom were strangers to him. He had met Herold and Payne casually, the others he did not even recognize by name. What he could see was the court, the spectators, and the Counsel for the Defence.

Of Defence Counsel he did not think much. Only two of the men seemed worth bothering about: former Provost Marshal William E. Doster, because he seemed to know his business, and Reverdy Johnson, because everyone knew who he was. Not that Johnson wasn't an over-bloated gas-bag. He had a mouth modified by too much sucking at the public tit, and the result was an angry and petulant expression. On the one hand, he posed as a person of probity. On the other, he wanted more. You could tell just by looking at him that he was not happy to be here. He had chosen the wrong lost cause. To get a reputation as a fearless champion of lost causes, you must be canny to choose only that lost cause which people secretly long to find again. One look at the judges, and Johnson knew that he was in the wrong room. He was chief counsel for Mrs. Surratt's defence.

General Hunter, the presiding officer for the prosecution, rose to read a statement by General T. M. Harris, one of the judges. No one could ever be quite sure of what Reverdy Johnson might do, but if he wanted out as much as his appearance indicated he did, Stanton was prepared to give him a pretext.

In 1864 Reverdy Johnson had advised the members of the Maryland Convention to take the oath demanded of them, even though at the same time telling them that the Convention had no right to impose it. Therefore, said Hunter, reading patiently, Johnson did not appear to believe in the validity of sworn oaths, and so was not competent to stand attorney in this court.

Johnson's face turned the colour of boiled beef. It was an out, of course, but he was so infuriated to have his integrity impugned, that he launched into a defence of himself which soon turned, as most of his nobler speeches did, into a denunciation of everybody else. Who gave the court jurisdiction to decide the moral character of the attorneys appearing before them, he demanded. What had his own moral standing to do with the case in hand? Besides, he was a member of the United States Senate, and who was responsible for the legality of this court, if not the Senate?

The court had to back down. Its leaders had misjudged Johnson.

But Johnson had misjudged himself. He backtracked. Having been offered an out, he took it. His honour was impugned. He would not appear before this court again. He withdrew, and left Mrs. Surratt to the mercies of his colleagues, two bright young men competent enough to toddle through a straightforward case in a court of law, given a judge to guide them, but not old enough to stand up against an unjust magistrate. Lost causes were one thing. Being trapped on the losing side was quite another. Johnson had his career to think of. As a parting shot, he filed an argument on the jurisdiction of the Military Court. It was futile, of course. One cannot sway a group of generals by means of a legal quibble. But it would look well in the newspapers.

The court had no difficulty in turning down his argument. That wily creature, the Honourable John A. Bingham, the Assistant Judge Advocate, knew his business. He said that no Court had the power to declare its own authority null and void. "Is it possible," he asked, "that any body of men, constituted as a tribunal, can sit in judgment upon the proposition that they are not a court? Why not crown the absurdity by asking the members to determine that they are not men?" That silenced the argument on jurisdiction, and Johnson slipped gratefully out from under.

The absurdity remained. Edward Spangler watched the

Honourable John A. Bingham, who had the hard face of a Longfellow who had gone into banking. In that face Spangler could see that their lives had already been bought and sold. Bingham was only there to supervise the transaction. He knew Stanton and had a seat in Congress to keep.

Spangler began to sweat. The courtroom was sultry, and he suffered from prickly heat. But he went on watching. As for the evidence itself, he could make nothing of it. Ford was on the stand. Booth, he said, was a peculiarly fascinating man. He had known how to control the lower class of people better than an ordinary man would have done.

That's me, thought Spangler. I'm the lower class of people, all right. But he was grateful to Ford. Ford was doing his best for him, and under the circumstances, that was not only damn decent, but showed courage. It was more than most of the witnesses were trying to do.

He began to see quite easily how a man could be hanged for trying to help a friend. He didn't see that was his fault. You don't usually ask a friend if he's done anything criminal, before you help him.

Now they were talking about whether he wore a moustache. He didn't bother to listen. He'd never worn a moustache in his life.

That was what would save his life.

XXXIX

The first thing which made Mrs. Surratt panic was the withdrawal of Reverdy Johnson. He was an older man. She had always trusted older men. Clampitt and Aiken, her other lawyers, were only children. She sent a message to Stone, who represented Herold and Dr. Mudd. Of all that crowd clustered beyond the dock in their defence, only he seemed to have enough character to stand up to the court. But there was nothing Stone could do for her. He had double work already. There was nothing anyone could do.

Yet there was always a rustle of attention whenever witnesses appeared for or against her. There were more women in the courtroom on those days. She had seen the faces of such women before, as they chattered away amiably about the downfall of a friend. She knew all about that snakelike false sympathy. She had once or twice been guilty of it herself.

Honora Fitzpatrick was on the stand. She was an innocent girl, but Stanton had given her the privilege of seeing the inside of a prison, all the same. She appeared as a witness, though not a willing one, for the prosecution, and was forced to admit that she had gone to Ford's Theatre one evening in March, accompanied by John Surratt and by Payne. Poor girl, that was as close to conspiracy as the detectives had been able to draw her.

By the time the Defence recalled her, at the end of May, Honora had become hollow eyed. No doubt she did not like to be so close to death. For the defence she said that Mrs. Surratt's eyesight was defective.

It was a fault one usually did one's best to conceal. Now her life seemed to depend upon it. It was because she had said she had not recognized Payne in the hall, that night of her arrest. One detective said the hall had been purposely dimmed, another that it had been as purposely brilliantly lit. Whether purposely or not, she remembered it had been dim. Why did the first detective seem so nervous about telling what was merely the truth?

She found it strange to see her former boarders in the witness box. They were only boarders but, a lonely woman, she had tried to make friends out of them, as she did of everyone she met. Perhaps that had been her mistake. There must be some moral reason why she was here.

Now they had her brother on the stand. He, too, had been flung in jail. There seemed no end to the capacity of that prison. It was to her brother that Stanton had relayed that rumour about her own eventual release, if only she would say nothing. So she said nothing. But she began to tremble.

Poor Jenkins had always been a prickly man. During the war he had had a hard time with the Federals. But there was nothing wrong with his courage. He tried to speak up for her. Judge Advocate Bingham would not allow that. It amazed her that a man so well-bred should be so venal and so vile. Sometimes she thought she sat in this dock only for having been so short sighted, for yes, she was short sighted, as to take the world at its own best behaviour. That was the result not so much of optimism, as of wistfulness, but the cause did not matter. The error had landed her here.

Bingham harried Jenkins about Kallenbach. Kallenbach, a country neighbour at Surrattsville, was a witness for the prosecution. He was a worthless man. Everyone round Surrattsville knew that. But no one seemed to wish to know it here.

"All I said," said Jenkins, "to Kallenbach was that my sister had fed his family, but I did not say that if Kallenbach or anyone else testified against my sister, that I would send him to hell or see that they were put out of the way, nor did I use any threats against him in case he appeared as a witness against Mrs. Surratt. What I did say was, that I understood he was a strong witness against my sister, which he ought to be, seeing that she had raised his family for him."

Bingham pounced on that.

"When I said that Mr. Kallenbach ought to be a strong witness against my sister, on account of her bringing up his children, I spoke ironically," explained Jenkins, speaking ironically. "I am under arrest, but I do not know for what. The Commissioners of our County offered 2,000 dollars for any information that could be given leading to the arrest of any person connected with the assassination. Mr. Cottingham asked me to get him that money, since he had arrested my sister's tenant, John M. Lloyd. I suppose that is why I am here."

It did him no good.

She understood Kallenbach well enough. But she would never understand why fear should lead to such conduct. It was true, she had fed his children. Perhaps her error had been in not feeding him as well. Nor had she realized that justice hinged so circumstantially upon its own rewards, or that a criminal could be so easily created out of the sum offered for his apprehension.

Her brother was asked to step down, and John T. Holahan took his place. Mrs. Holahan had testified earlier. "I cannot say that I was intimate with Mrs. Surratt," she had said. "I liked her very much; she was a very kind lady to board with; but I was more intimate with her daughter." Yes, Mrs. Holahan had taken a shine to Annie. She was a well-meaning woman.

Mr. Holahan described himself as a tombstone salesman. That was his whimsy. He was Irish, and so he had his whimsies. But since his arrest the whimsy had been drained out of him. By actual profession, and in fourteen years in America he had had a good many, he was a bounty broker. When some man too busy to go off to die at the front wished to buy a substitute to go in his stead, it was Mr. Holahan who found the man and fixed the price. Who paid the commission, or whether both men did, Mrs. Surratt did not know, but Holahan seemed prosperous, and that was why he described himself as a tombstone salesman. The Holahans had occupied the second floor front bedroom.

It was evident Mr. Holahan wanted no trouble; being Shanty Irish, that was the phrase he would have used; and

201

yet he had a certain integrity. She could see that he did not want to cause her any trouble, either. The prosecution put a stop to that. They got out of him the admission that he had once seen John Surratt help Mrs. Slater into the boarding-house.from her carriage. Mrs. Slater, as everyone knew, was a Southern spy.

Turn where she would, it all came back to what John had done.

When next she looked at the stand, it was her own daughter, Annie, who stood there.

Mrs. Surratt could have wept. Poor Annie was only seven-teen, but she looked thirty. She had a pallid skin anyhow, and neither prison nor a black dress suited her. Mrs. Surratt had always tried to shield her from the world. She had wanted her daughter to have a better life than she had had. And now it had come to this.

At least the Judges Advocate had not had the devilry to call her for the prosecution. Mrs. Surratt was proud of her. She scarcely trembled in that witness box at all. But neither would she ever seem seventeen again. They would have to re-lease her, but in the meantime they had taken away her youth.

It was Weichmann who had brought Atzerodt to the house, Annie said. That was true, but no one else had said so, and Mrs. Surratt had herself forgotten it. It was Weich-mann, also, who had brought Payne there under the name of Wood. Weichmann was always running John's errands.

"Ma was in the dining-room. She said she did not under-stand why strange persons should call there, but she sup-posed their object was to see my brother, and she would treat them politely, as she was in the habit of treating every-one." The prosecution cut her off. She was dismissed from the court, but not from the jail. Mrs. Surratt was so worried for her, that she scarcely heard the testimony of Colonel Wood.

Colonel Wood was in charge of the Old Capitol Prison, where she had been first confined. His appearance for the defence was his own idea. He was the only man in Washing-ton City who was not afraid of Stanton. More than that, Stanton was afraid of him. No one knew why. He believed

Mrs. Surratt innocent. He had himself had word from Stanton that she should be let go, but he had seen the course the trial was taking, and he knew Stanton. Therefore he was here.

His appearance created a sensation. But there was nothing he could do for her. Though he knew her innocent, he had no evidence. He had only seen her in her cell. She was grateful to him, he was a decent man, but he was soon gone.

The worst witness so far had been Lloyd.

As he raised his hand to take the oath, she could see that his arm was wobbling. It would have wobbled at any time. He was a helpless drunk.

He had done his best to wriggle out from under all this, but had been arrested. When that happened, he had thrown his arms round his wife's neck. "I am to be shot," he had moaned. "I am to be shot. Bring me my prayer book." She gave him his prayer book, his legs went out from under him, and the detectives had to support him to the carriage. He had been flung into Carroll Prison. That terrified him. He was willing to say all he knew to get out again. But the detectives who examined him about that vile woman told him that unless he could remember more than he had so far, he would be hanged. So he had remembered more. Stanton had thought that perhaps he might. His statement got fuller and longer.

At first he had tried to tell the truth. He had tried not to lie about Mrs. Surratt. But it seemed that Mrs. Surratt was the one they were trying to nail down, it was his neck or hers, so he had to go along with them. His life had always been like that. Every coward can find a bully somewhere.

For a drunk he did remarkably well on the stand. Her attorneys cross-questioned him. He got shifty, but he would not shift his story. He had been got at. He was desperate to live. She could only wait for Weichmann to contradict him.

Weichmann was her last hope. It was admitted in evidence that she had treated him like a son. She could not believe that he would lie about her. Weichmann was a well educated man. He had been a divinity student. He had taught at a college. He was a fellow Catholic. She put her faith in him.

The room was sultry. At first reporters had been barred

from the trial, but after the clamour in the newspapers about that, even Stanton had to give way and admit them. They had been on duty since May 13th, which was the first day of Weichmann's testimony, and they had brought the stench of stale cigars along with them. Much was expected of Weichmann, by everybody. Nor did he fail them.

Despite the heat of the day, he looked sleek and dapper. He was neatly dressed, his tie was immaculately tied, his little feet were firmly encased in highly polished Congress gaiters, and his trousers were hand tailored and appropriately concertinaed. No creases to prove that they were ready made showed to disgrace him. That little violet face looked resolute. He radiated honesty, but there was nothing warm about him. He spoke in his light, self-consciously manly, self-consciously well-educated voice. He was honest, impartial, full of humanity, and quite cheerful, though in a subdued way appropriate to the occasion. He could be trusted.

He was also a coward.

He had been arrested on April 15th, and was one of the few prisoners Stanton had deigned to see in person, if only for the pleasure of telling him that he had as much of the President's blood on his hands as Booth had. Then the Secret Service report was shown him. That proved quite enough to assure the government of his services at the trial.

Stanton had recognized his man. Weichmann was a clerk at the War Department. One had merely to give him a a government job. If he talked afterwards, he would lose the job. He wondered how much Weichmann would sell out for.

It turned out to be for very little. The overweaning ambitions of small men do not, after all, amount to much, and are easily taken care of. They have not the vision to ask for more. Stanton was relieved. The man had been a spy, and the government cannot admit to harbouring spies in its own departments. He had been a spy for both sides. He was guilty as hell. He had attended Charles College, at Pikesville, with Booth and Arnold. He was friendly with Payne. He knew Atzerodt. He had let Surratt into the War Department after hours, to copy documents and send them south to Richmond. He had been the last person Surratt had seen, before leaving Washington City on April 3rd. He had probably been in the abduction plot which preceded the assassination. He could not have known so much about it, if he had not been. And most important of all, he wished to live. Stanton was satisfied. He would be impressive in the witness box.

The detectives were ordered to write out a list of things for Weichmann to say in court. It covered all those points in the evidence where a little discreet invention would do wonders. Weichmann took the hint. He had an ingenious mind. He turned out to be very good at saying things which could not be disproved, and which tallied with what could not be shaken.

He began by giving Mrs. Surratt an excellent character. He saw no harm in that. He was there to help hang the woman, not to impugn her character. Besides, it would make a good impression.

Mrs. Surratt relaxed. Her faith in Weichmann had not been misplaced. At least there were some honest men in the world.

Indeed there were. But there was no weak point in the prosecution that Weichmann did not bolster.

The trip to Surrattsville loomed large in his evidence. He corroborated John Lloyd, as he had been told to do. He implicated Dr. Mudd. He implicated everyone.

Mrs. Surratt could only hopelessly watch. That man was lying. He was lying deliberately, and with malice aforethought, and there was no way to stop him.

He testified that when the detectives who had come to search the house at two in the morning, after the assassination, had left, Annie had said, "Oh, Ma. Just think of that man's being here an hour before the assassination." It was a lie. Could he not at least leave Annie alone? It was all a lie. But she understood now. There was to be no mercy. The trial was rigged. The trial was a mockery. Fear had made men liars. She could only thank God for the small gratitude of casual acquaintances, whose good will had tried to save her, even if they could not, from the concentrated spleen of those she had been so foolish as to trust.

XL

It was perhaps worst for Annie. She had finally been released from prison. There was nothing to hold her for, once she had testified. Burnett told her that if she came to Secretary Stanton's office she could get the key to the house.

Annie refused to do so. She was only seventeen, but she had spunk. She said they could deliver the key up to her themselves. She did not intend to beg for it.

Like most bullies, Stanton always backed down if challenged. Had he been challenged sooner, perhaps the trial would not have gone as it did. The key was a little thing. She received her key.

Holding it in her hand, she felt reluctant to go back to that house. Yet she had nowhere else to go. Looking at it from the street, she found it terrible. It was empty. Even the Negroes had gone, and though Eliza Hawkins would come back to care for her, it was too late in the day to send for Eliza, who had gone to Surrattsville.

Annie let herself in. The hall was cold and dark. The living room was disarrayed. No one had tidied it since the detectives had searched it. Over the mantelpiece was a spot of discoloured wallpaper. *Morning, Noon, and Night* had hung there. It was now an exhibit at the trial.

She pushed the shutters open, but not much light came in. Then she went upstairs to her own room. In the hall she passed the mirror, its surface dusty. The glimpse she caught of herself was unrecognizable. She could see her mother's features, poking out through her own young flesh.

She did not even have a change of clothes. The government had impounded all movables. She had to petition the Assistant Judge Advocate to get them back. The house disturbed her. It was full of shadows. If all those who had once lived there had not been alive, in the Old Penitentiary Prison, she would have called those shadows ghosts.

She supposed she owned the house now, but though she had it back, she did not know what to do with it. Mrs. Holahan came to stay with her. She was a merciful woman. She did her best. Annie was grateful to her. It was more than Honora had offered to do. Annie had not seen Honora since the trial. But what could Mrs. Holahan do?

Annie could not bear the thought of her mother alone in jail. She got a court order to see her. They were allowed to talk to each other for an hour and a half, in the courtyard. But there was nothing for them to say. Ma looked awful. She said they must hope for reprieve. The prison yard was not agreeable. Their meeting was supervised by Rath, the common hangman. He seemed a decent man but everyone knew he was the executioner. He was not agreeable company, whether he loathed his work or not.

What reprieve could there be from this terrible place? Annie did not understand how her mother could seem so stoical and so calm.

Neither did Mrs. Surratt. After Rath took her daughter home, she fainted.

XLI

It was a farce. But the farce went on. Doster decided to do something extreme. He subpoenaed President Johnson, in order to prove that Johnson had been at Kirkwood House for Atzerodt to kill, which would make Atzerodt's refusal to do so the more valid proof of innocence. Johnson refused to appear, and sent a man called Farwell instead. Farwell, the Governor of Wisconsin, had been in the room with him at the time, he said. Johnson was not a wily politician for nothing. He had enemies, he knew who they were, Stanton was among them, and he refused to be dragged into this thing. Subpoena or not, Johnson was President. Doster had to make do with Farwell.

But Farwell also had his enemies. Farwell's testimony sank Atzerodt's defence. Not that the man was worth saving from the gallows, for Atzerodt was impossible to deal with. He seemed to think that because Mrs. Surratt had flung him out of her boarding-house, his innocence was proved. He had run away and refused to kill anybody. He had been afraid then, and he was afraid now. But fear would not help him here. Had he had the courage to speak out at the time, things might have gone differently, but the Atzerodts of this world never speak out, at any time. They would rather cringe and run. One could not even make him understand why he was guilty, or of what. He seemed to rely on his family to save him, but his family was insupportable. They turned and twisted even more than Atzerodt did. Irresolution seemed their only principle. Let George look out for himself.

With Payne it was a different matter. Payne puzzled Doster.

That giant of a man was the only one of the conspirators

208

with sufficient dignity to seem contrite. He also seemed to be in some kind of despair that had nothing to do with the trial. He had made up his mind to die, he said, and the trial was a waste of time. Doster could not tell whether his attitude sprang from lunacy, unparalleled stupidity, or fear of prejudicing his own cause. Yet he could be saved, if there was to be even a shred of legality about these proceedings. The most that could be charged against him was assault and battery, with Seward as plaintiff.

He would say nothing. Yet of all the prisoners, he seemed the most alert. Alone of them, he had some expression in his face, half-way between scorn and grief, that had nothing to do with the anxiety about their own necks which dominated the others. He held himself well. Doster admired a man who could hold himself well. Perhaps that was because, unlike the others, he did not sit there waiting to be condemned. He had already condemned himself.

Doster could only marvel at the ramifications of what are at first glance illiterate and inarticulate minds. A detected criminal is usually the last person to assume responsibility for his own acts. And that Payne did, Doster supposed, made him in some backwoods but valid way a gentleman, whereas the tergiversations of Dr. Mudd proved that gentleman merely a stupidly wily fool.

What was bothering Payne anyway? There must be some reason why he would not talk.

XLII

Indeed there was. What was bothering Payne was Herold. If it had not been for Herold, Cap would not be dead now. Or at any rate, the two of them would have fared better in those swamps together than ever Cap did with Herold.

It was Herold who had thought up the idea of getting into Seward's house by means of a medical prescription. It was the sort of feather-brained idea Herold would have had. But Booth had told Herold to hold Payne's horse until Payne came out of the house, and instead Herold had run off and left him. That was Herold all over. It was like the prosecution said. He was a light and trivial boy. For running off like that, he deserved to hang, for he had let Cap down. But Cap had caught up with him and forced him to behave himself, not having Payne there to take care of him, and needing somebody to help. And then Herold had bungled the whole damn escape. Cap was dead as a result. Herold deserved to die. He had never been worth keeping alive, anyhow.

Payne had never been able to understand why Cap kept people like Herold, Weichmann, and Atzerodt around him. O'Laughlin and Arnold were a little better, but you could see there wasn't any good in them either. As for Surratt, Surratt might be okay, but he didn't see him here. Surratt was slippery. Payne didn't blame him for that. He did blame him for Mrs. Surratt's being here. He also blamed himself. Mrs. Surratt upset him badly.

While Weichmann was testifying, Payne could almost see Mrs. Surratt's boarding-house. He'd only been there three or four days, all told, and yet he could remember everything about the place, because it was the first real house he'd been in for years. Mrs. Surratt had been real kind to him. She was a nice lady. He didn't like to see her here.

He hadn't exactly enjoyed sleeping in that tree and wandering round Washington City, not knowing where to find Cap or what had happened to him. He'd only gone to Mrs. Surratt's to find out about Cap. Then the door had opened, and he'd seen the glitter of spurs and uniforms, in the dim hallway, and made up that story about coming to see about the gutter, and they'd brought her in to identify him.

All this malarky about her being able to see or not was nothing but lies. She hadn't recognized him at all. But he had recognized her. Her face had been puzzled and wan. He'd wanted to get right out of there before he got her into any more trouble, but the officers hadn't let him. So far as he was concerned, he was responsible for her arrest. It never would have happened so bad for her otherwise, if he hadn't turned up just then.

He'd been taken down to General Augur's headquarters, and Mrs. Surratt had recognized him there, all right. He'd never forget the hopeless look on her face when she did. She'd read the newspapers. She must have known how the net was tightening around her.

Something had to be done. Payne sent for Doster.

For a wonder, Doster was allowed to come. There wasn't room for both of them in Payne's cell, in fact there wasn't even room for Payne, because the ceiling was so low. But at least in the cells they didn't have to wear that damned hood. Doster said it was a little late for Payne to want to talk, but that he'd do his best.

Payne couldn't understand it. There must be something somebody could do. She was an innocent woman. You could tell that just by the look of her. Doster agreed, but saw no point in telling Payne that no one in court wanted to look. About all he'd learned from Payne's wish to talk was that the boy's real name was Lewis Thornton Powell, that he was the son of a Baptist minister, and that he had a heart.

XLIII

As for Dr. Mudd's attitude, nobody could make anything out of it, least of all Mr. Frederick Stone, his counsel. Dr. Mudd seemed determined to hang himself. His prevarications were painful. He had given his whole case away by trusting neither his counsel, his neighbours, his family, nor his kinsfolk. It was a terrible thing to try to extricate him from the web he had woven about himself. Yet Stone was his attorney, and had to try.

Mudd denied what was true, and claimed to be true what was patently not. Half his coloured people lied for him, the other half against. Either way, Negroes were not good liars. They could be tripped up. But Mudd's brother Jeremiah was as bad, and so were George and William Mudd. The whole clan was given to a taciturn mendacity.

It was exasperating. The defence called character witnesses until Dr. Mudd had no virtues left to discuss. Dr. Mudd merely sat there in the dock, with his high bald forehead, compressed lips, and astute little blue eyes, and showed nothing. His attitude seemed to be that the Court had no right to arrest a Mudd. That was ridiculous. This was no time to stand on one's high horse. But stand on it he did. Stone told him he would hang himself, if he persisted in misrepresenting the facts to his own attorney. Mudd thought that over and reluctantly emitted a little, a very little, truth. It did no good to ask him an outright question. Professional ethics forebade a direct answer about anything. Unfortunately he was applying those ethics to the wrong profession. Yet the man had to be defended. Stone cursed and did his best.

Ewing, who had Arnold to defend, and Cox, who was saddled with O'Laughlin, had an even worse problem. It was

212

that their clients were obviously innocent. Neither man had anything to do with the assassination. Not even the prosecution had been able to establish that they had. Arnold had repudiated the abduction plot which preceded it, and O'Laughlin had been dropped by Booth as useless. There was scarcely a reason for their presence in the court. O'Laughlin was harmless. The worst that could be said of Arnold was that Booth had once sent him fifty dollars. One might make of that what one would. Booth's relations with young men were in some ways anomalous. But to be given money was not a hanging offence. True, he had been in the Confederate Army at one time, but supposedly that was not a hanging offence either.

In some curious way, Arnold and O'Laughlin went together in everybody's mind. It was not so much that they seemed twins, as that they both seemed to be slightly different versions of the same thing. So O'Laughlin's case was treated as summarily as Arnold's had been. The best defence for Arnold and O'Laughlin seemed to be to ignore them.

Meanwhile the Defence tried to prove that Payne was morally insane. It was a strange thing to do to the son of a Baptist minister, who was probably as sane as anyone in that room, but he had to be defended in some way, and Doster could think of no other. Unfortunately his doctor bucked and quibbled, and had not been allowed to examine Payne anyway, so that Doster could present him only with a hypothetical case.

The prosecution's surgeons had been allowed to examine the accused at length, and had pronounced him sane.

Payne could have told them that himself. He had been costive for three weeks, which had nearly driven him mad, but the question was one of sanity. The test used by the Government surgeons was called the Shakespearian Test. Barnes, the Surgeon General, considered it an infallible test of moral and mental sanity. The Shakespearian Test consisted of seeing whether or not the subject could tell the same story the same way twice. Sanity, then, consisted of no more than consistency, an idea not exposited by Shakespeare in his plays, but the test was no doubt more reliable than its name.

As an added safeguard, the surgeons had asked Payne if he believed in God. He had said that he did, and that He was a just God. That settled the problem of God. As for Payne's statement that he thought private assassination upon an enemy in a public war justifiable, Dr. Hall, Barnes's colleague, said that he could readily conceive that there were persons whose minds and morals were such that they would believe a crime similar to that committed by Payne to be justifiable and proper, even a duty. The question of the sanity of such persons was not gone into. Dr. Hall had heard of monomaniacs, he said, but never met one. The insanity plea was dropped.

By then the trial was almost over. The last testimony was heard on the 16th of June. The proceedings had lasted for thirty-seven humid days. It was now time for the summing up, and for the arguments of the Defence; and then the verdict and sentences would be delivered.

Now that the preliminary ordeal was over with, Mrs. Surratt was moved to more comfortable quarters on the third floor of the prison. Annie was allowed to visit her. General Hartranft, the Provost Marshal in charge of the prisoners, sent her food from his own table. It was what was usually done for condemned prisoners, but everyone pretended not to notice that. General Hartranft was thought most kind.

The male prisoners were also treated better now. Stanton was worried about their health. Dr. John T. Gray had informed him that the men had nothing to sit on in their cells but a hair pillow. That was shocking. Why had he not been told before? Stanton authorized the governor of the prison to give them a box or stool apiece, and suggested that Mrs. Surratt might be allowed a chair. Such changes or additions to her furniture as might add to her comfort were also authorized.

Her exoneration was not.

XLIV

The Defence did its best. Mr. Ewing tried to establish the illegality of the court. He knew he could not expect to explain law to a courtroom of military men still under orders, but such was his duty as he saw it.

"I should like an answer to my question, if it is to be given: How many distinct crimes are my clients charged with and being tried for? I cannot tell."

It was Assistant Judge Advocate Bingham who answered him. He was the ablest of the judges, and had the least compunction about what he did of any man Ewing had ever seen.

"We have told you, it is all one transaction," he said. And so it was. Ewing tried again. He pointed out that in a crime of treason, the accused had legally to have a copy of the indictment, a list of the jury, and of the witnesses to be brought against them, which they were to receive three days before they were to be tried. Nor were they to be kept in the dock in chains. Yet the prisoners were chained, and they had received the indictment only the night before their arraignment. What of it? It would never have been allowed in a civil court. But this was not a civil court. It was not a court at all. It was merely a self-constituted viewing stand. Further, the charge against the accused stated that they had maliciously, unlawfully, and traitorously conspired. So stated, the charge was meaningless, said Ewing, under any known rules of war, coming only under the head of what the Judge Advocate called, "The common law of war". What was this law of war? It was a term unknown, a *quiddity*, and incapable of definition.

The Judges Advocate let him talk on. When he had finished, Bingham informed the lawyers for the Defence that they might proceed with their arguments. Ewing had accomplished nothing. But then he had not expected to do so.

215

To state the truth in that room was futile. No one could expect justice there. Justice does not sit in so low ceilinged or so squalid a room. At the most, they could hope for mercy or reprieve. But of what use was mercy? What use was reprieve? The soul has no reprieve. The best one can hope for there is an extended sentence.

Yet the arguments had to be made. The first man to rise was Frederick Stone, in defence of Herold. Stone had dignity, common sense, and humanity. He faced the court. The judges sat before him, bored, a little uncertain, but with their minds made up like a picnic lunch, awaiting only a delayed departure, after one last errand was done, and they had delivered a prepared verdict and so were free to leave. Did they not realize that none of them would ever leave the memory of this sweat soaked room and this injustice?

Herold sat between his two guards, motionless, and yet quivering, with his look of a shabby porcupine too heavy to amble off. He must have had that look sometimes in the parlour, peering into a stereopticon. To him, now, life, punishment, and the nature of his crime must be as real, as close, as flat, and as endlessly far away as that. So was the court.

The ceiling was too low for the dimensions of the room and the acoustics were bad. Stone spoke, for what seemed a very long time, of the legalities of the case. Herold stirred. It was his life that was being discussed out there, but it did not sound like his life. His life was a matter of salt marshes and indistinguishable plump hounds who came when you called them, with a pheasant in their mouths. He was beyond thought, being simple minded, but he could not help but look indignant.

"Who is this Herold?" asked Stone. "And what does the testimony disclose him to be? A weakly, cowardly, foolish, miserable boy. Dr. McKim, who probably knew him best, declared that his mind was that of a boy of eleven years of age, although his age was actually about twenty-two."

Herold did not know what his lawyer was talking about. Murder and treason, he had not been guilty of that. Booth had been guilty of that, but what had that to do with him?

"I beg leave to conclude this defence with a quotation
216

from *Benet on Military Law and Courts-Marshal*," said Stone. "The Mandate of the Constitution must be strictly kept in view, and the benign influence of a mandate from a still higher law ought not to be ignored, that justice should be tempered with mercy."

Well, it would not be. Stone knew that. He sat down, and let Thomas Ewing rise to the defence of Edward Spangler, who was so innocent of any crime, there was nothing to say in his defence. Mrs. Surratt stirred uneasily. They had come to her now. Her small clothes were foul. Under her dress, she could feel the sleezy dirt of her muslin pantalettes and chemise. She had always been fastidious. It was torture for her, as she sat there, a demurely clad pyramid, to feel what might or might not be lice crawling beneath her clothes. How could they hang her? There was mercy in this world, if nothing else.

That was what Frederick Aiken, her counsel, asked for, but he misjudged his tone. He was a young man, scarcely out of Howard College. He had not yet had the experience to learn that those things which we must learn in order to qualify for a profession have little or nothing to do with the business of practising it successfully. The schools teach us how to behave in the world as it should be. Confronted with the world as it was, Aiken made the mistake of an appeal to reason.

He referred to Reverdy Johnson, as the great panjandrum of the legal profession who had already, so said Aiken, defined the illegality of the proceedings. And so he had, which was why Johnson was not here. He said the accused should be acquitted when there was reasonable doubt of his or her guilt. The faces of the judges did not change expression. He hit at all Weichmann's insinuations and perjuries. Unfortunately, Weichmann had spoken for the government, which had itself spoken to them.

And yet she was a woman. That made them restive. They had no objection to doing as they were told. They were military men of the second class. Initiative was not part of their responsibility. But they did not like to be asked to consider whether or not what they were told to do was justified.

217

Aiken finished his argument and swept into his oratory, which was florid, but hopeless.

"A daughter of the South, her life associations confirming her natal predilections, her individual preferences inclined, without logic or question, to the Southern people, but with no consciousness nor intent of *disloyalty* to her *Government*, and causing no exclusion from her friendship and active favours of the people of the loyal North, nor repugnance in the distribution among our Union soldiery of all needed comforts within her command, and on all occasions. . . ."

That was true.

"A strong but guileless hearted woman, her maternal solicitude would have been the first denouncer, even abrupt betrayer, of a plotted crime in which one companion of her son could have been implicated, had such cognizance reached her."

She no longer knew whether that was true or not. She could not understand why John had not found some way to get in touch with her. And yet she did. The irresponsible are always cruel to save their own skins. But surely a message would have gotten him in no danger?

Perhaps it had been intercepted.

"In our country, where reason and moderation so easily quench the fires of insane hate, and where *La Vendetta* is so easily overcome by the sublime grace of forgiveness, no woman . . ."

She did not listen. She had once thought the country so herself. In the past few weeks she had learned much of those fires, and the judges, so far as she could tell, very little.

"Since the days when Christian tuition first elevated womanhood to her present free, refined, and refining position, man's power and honouring regard have been the palladium of her sex. Let no stain of injustice, eager for a sacrifice to revenge, rest upon the reputation of the men of our country and time. Let not this first State tribunal in our country's history which involves a woman's name, be blazoned before the world in the harsh tints of intolerance."

Such was her only hope. She admitted it. There was no one here with the will to exonerate the innocent. Innocence

218

did not matter here. But there remained the plea to mercy. There remained only that.

Now it was the others' turn. Doster turned to his defence of Payne.

"The question of his identity and the question of his sanity are settled, and among the things of the past. The sole question that remains is how far shall his convictions serve to mitigate his punishment."

They sure were, but Payne did not want his punishment mitigated. He had told Doster that.

"Let us pause a moment in this narrative, and consider what, in the eyes of this Florida boy, was the meaning of war, and what the thoughts that drove him from a pleasant home to the field of arms."

What pleasant home? War had no meaning. It was an environment, not an idea. It might mean something to those who lost it, and to those who won it, but all it meant to those who fought it was a sea of mud, kill or be killed, pain, boredom, and a crap game on Saturday night.

Doster knew that. He was a military man himself, young enough to remember what war was like, and unlike the judges, out of uniform.

"These two years of carnage and suffering, from sixteen to eighteen, when the character is mobile and pliable, and which he would have naturally spent at college among poets and mythologies and tutors [that was a laugh] are spent on picket, with fierce veterans, in drunken quarrels, with cards, with oaths, in delirious charges, amid shot and shell, amid moaning wounded and stinking dead [that wasn't], until, at eighteen, he has the experience of a Cambronne, the ferocity of an Attila, and the cruelty of a Tartar."

Payne didn't know who all those fancy people were, but he had never been cruel. Like his judges, he had merely followed orders, until he could follow them no more and had deserted.

Military judges have no sympathy with a deserter. They forget the man in the offence, and few of these had seen a battle any closer than the nearest hill. They were career men,

219

in a few years they would retire on pension. They had never wished to desert. Why should the ranks under them? They had served their country and their country had paid them well. No, they did not approve of deserters.

Doster began to tell them what war was. "This, gentlemen, is the horrible demoralization of civil war. It makes loyalty a farce, justifies perjury, dignifies murder, instills ferocity, scorns religion, and enjoins assassination as a duty. And whose fault is it that he was so demoralized, and so educated in public vices, on the field of war? Was it our forefathers who sowed the seed of discord in the charter of the Union? Was it Lee and Jackson and Hill? Then punish them, and spare their pupil."

That was never done. From time to time the world enjoys its holiday, and reverts to its natural condition, and is shamefaced only afterwards. There will always be wars. Now if Doster had just mentioned the destruction of private property attendant upon a conflict, he might have sobered his judges' military exhilaration. All men own some property. But no other restraint would govern the outbreak of that hilarious charade, a war. Men do not like to die. But from time to time, given they do not have to knot the rope themselves, they like the kill.

Doster was a man of action. He admired vigour. He had a fine eye for a good horse. And something about Payne moved him, as he had once been moved by a good horse who went wild and had to be shot. One hates to see the proud beast go.

It was Booth who had gotten the boy here, just as that horse had been savaged by having the wrong owner. Booth, whom the boy called Cap, was dead. Given an easy rider, the boy would behave well enough. Yet the case was hopeless. He knew that.

"What then has he done that every rebel soldier has not tried to do? Only this: he has ventured more; he has shown a higher courage, a bitterer hate, and a more ready sacrifice."

It was true. He had only attacked Seward because Cap had asked him to.

"As Arnold Winkelried was braver than all the combined

220

legions of Switzerland, as Leonidas, as Mucius Scaevola, as Harmodius and Aristogeiton, as Gerard of the Netherlands, Revaillac, Jacques Clément, Orsini, Byron, Garibaldi, Kossuth, Hofer, and Washington . . ." Doster had gotten carried away. From there it was only a step to Shakespeare. "So Brutus said in the market place: *As I slew my best lover for the good of Rome, I have the same dagger for myself when it shall please my country to need my death.*"

The boy was determined to die. And all because of that white skinned wretch Booth, and Mrs. Surratt, perhaps. The boy, at least, was capable of grief, compunction, and atonement. Who else in this courtroom, prisoners, judges, and counsel, reporters and sensation mongers, even himself, could say as much?

Doster realized he had gone too far. He doubled back to call the late President the great *salvator*, and then dived into Shakespeare again. In Shakespeare he knew where he was.

> "*Why, man, he doth bestride the narrow world*
> *Like a Colossus, and we petty men*
> *Walk under his huge legs, and peep about*
> *To find ourselves dishonourable graves.*"

That was how Payne must have seen Lincoln and Seward.

Payne had not seen them at all. It was Cap who had done the seeing. He didn't understand what Doster was talking about. Rogeri and Catherine de Medici, Orloff and Catherine of Russia, Richard III, Tiberius, Philip II, Mary Queen of Scots, Louis XI, the Sand of Kotzebue, Corday, Murat, Count Ankarström, Gustavus III: who were all these people? Then there was Shakespeare again.

> "*For, let the gods so speed me, as I love*
> *The name of honour more than I fear death* . . ."

That was true enough. But why did they have to have poetry? Why couldn't they just hang him?

That is what they meant to do.

When Doster had finished, the court adjourned for lunch.

There he was twitted on his oration. It had been a fine speech. It had also been useless. As one of the Military Commission said, over his boiled beef, "Payne seems to want to be hung, so I guess we may as well hang him." There was no difficulty there.

It was a better than average lunch. Afterwards the judges filed back to their table, and the arguments in defence of Mudd, Arnold, and O'Laughlin were heard. The room was as sultry as ever. Under the bench the Wellingtons of the Military Judges creaked, as they tried to stretch their legs, and the hot weather brought up the stench of well-polished morocco.

On the 27th and the 28th of June, Assistant Judge Advocate Bingham got up to deliver the rebuttal. It was only four months since Lincoln had given his Second Inaugural Address, with its last sentence about "malice towards none; charity for all; and firmness in the right." But the Inaugural had been delivered on a rainy day and few people had listened to those last sentences. They had been more concerned about their dinners. And it was unlikely that anyone in the courtroom remembered them now.

Since he was a Congressman, the Honourable John A. Bingham was a strong winded and drafty speaker, but he made short work of Mrs. Surratt's case. He reshaped the evidence with all the professional agility of a hatter blocking a hat. Since he was supposed to present an unbiased review of the case, for the benefit of the Military Commission, he did so. He said she was guilty. That Payne had gone to her house proved that.

As for the legality of the court, Lincoln, in his proclamation of 24th September 1862, had taken care of that by establishing martial law. If he had done nothing else, the late President had at least constituted a competent authority.

So Lincoln was mentioned at last. A martyr of vision, he had long ago established the conditions under which his assassins should be tried. It was an astute point, and justified everything. On the 29th, the Commission adjourned to deliberate its verdict. There was nothing more for the Defence to do.

XLV

Stanton was furious. He was the ruler of the country, not that treacherous booby, Johnson. Whatever happened, he did not mean to let loose his grip upon the reins of government. But he had made an error of judgment. Martial law had not yet been repealed, but the war was over. It was no longer possible entirely to disregard public opinion. He had made a mistake.

It was because of the theatre manager, Ford. Ford had the gall to announce the reopening of his theatre. Stanton could not allow a crowd of sensation mongers in there, so he seized the theatre in the name of the Government. If forty days in Old Capitol Prison had not taught Ford a lesson, this would.

But it was no longer possible to stifle the press. Someone called Orville Brown, a hired columnist, wrote Ford was helpless, without means of defending himself, in a *free* country. Of course it was a free country. What was that man Brown jabbering about?

But there was also criticism of himself, and Stanton was sensitive to personal criticism. An Edward Bates said publicly that if Stanton could seize a theatre, he could go so far as to transfer estates from one man to another, or to dissolve the marriage ties.

Whatever else he had done, Stanton had never touched private property, except when necessary. Bates' statement was a canard. But this was no time to have questions raised in Congress. Johnson, he knew, would take any excuse to deprive him of office. So Stanton agreed to buy the theatre. He hated to expend the money, for Congress begrudged him every penny, so that it was already necessary to pad the budget with imaginary expenses, in order to pay his secret police, but there was nothing else he could do. At least the theatre would remain closed.

And now, just when he had thought the Conspiracy Trial over and done with, Holt, who as Judge Advocate should never have permitted such a thing, had arrived to tell him that five out of nine members of the Commission, though agreeing on Mrs. Surratt's guilt, had written out a clemency plea to be laid before President Johnson.

It was too much. The woman had to hang. Where was justice, if females were allowed to do what they pleased, while their husbands and sons could be restrained only by fear of reprisal? Half the Southern spies had been women. That had not saved them. Why should it save her? Besides, her son was still at large. What right had she to clemency, when her son evaded arrest?

The plea could not very well be torn up. In small matters Stanton practised an exact legality. But there were other ways of dealing with it.

Johnson wanted no trouble. That was clear from his behaviour, for he seemed unwilling to go out of the White House until the trial was over with, and saw few visitors. The clemency plea would have to be presented to him, of course. But that did not mean that he had to see it.

One had merely to slip the plea inside the end of the record, out of order, and begin the death warrant immediately after the last signature on the report of the proceedings of the Commission. Instead of continuing the death warrant from top to bottom on the obverse, begin it from bottom to top, so that, having to turn the papers over to see where to add his signature, Johnson would be even less likely to riffle through the endless pages of the report, and so find the plea. Holt had not thought of such a device. Stanton had. That was why he was still Secretary of War.

Holt delivered the papers to the White House. When they came back, there was Johnson's signature all right, on the reverse of the last page. As for the clemency plea, that could now be taken out and buried in the official files.

The execution was scheduled for the 7th of July, between noon and two in the afternoon. As an added precaution,

224

Stanton suggested that the Commission need not read the verdict to the accused until the afternoon of the 6th.

There was a leak, somewhere, to the press. Damn the press. The Defence Counsel sat in their offices. No one expected the hanging of Mrs. Surratt, least of all themselves. But the sentence was certainly long delayed. At noon Aiken heard newsboys crying in the street, and opened the window. Both he and Clampitt leaned out. Reverdy Johnson, needless to say, was not with them. He was off somewhere denouncing President Johnson one moment, and intriguing, successfully it turned out, to be appointed by him Minister to England the next.

"Execution of Mrs. Surratt," shouted the newsboys. "Execution of Mrs. Surratt."

The two men did not bother to go down for a paper. There was too much to be done in too short a time. Yet they hardly knew how to proceed. The law is not adjusted to haste, and yet it was now five o'clock in the afternoon.

They tried to reach the President, without success. Then they wired Reverdy Johnson. Johnson wired back telling them to get a writ of habeas corpus. His answer was delayed until midnight. None the less, they called on Judge Wylie at two in the morning. After telling them he would probably land in the Old Capitol before the day was out if he did so, he issued them a writ, which they left off at the United States Marshal's office at four, with instructions that it be served on Hancock, the Governor of the Prison. At ten, President Johnson informed Hancock that since the writ of habeas corpus had been suspended by Lincoln, and had not been restored, he hereby especially condemned the writ. The execution was to proceed.

Annie Surratt went to the White House. All she wanted was three days' stay of execution, so that her mother might prepare for death. It was useless. The President would see no one.

Even Wood tried to intervene. He went to the White House, and, being turned away from the portico, tried the rear entrance instead. He found Lafayette Baker waiting for

225

him there, on Stanton's orders. Of all people, said Stanton, Wood specifically was to be prevented from seeing the President. That took care of Wood.

But then Stanton found that he had Father Walter to deal with.

XLVI

When the prisoners' religious advisers asked for a stay of execution, so that the condemned might prepare for death, the Commission answered that the prisoners had had the whole period of the trial to prepare for death. And so they had. But death was not the same as being confronted with a death sentence.

At noon on the 6th of July the Military Commission appeared at the prison. They made a spot of colour in that grey gloom. Methodically they moved from cell to cell. Stopping before the door of Mrs. Surratt's, they informed her, drily, that she was guilty of the specification. She was to hang. She was not, however, guilty of harbouring Arnold and O'Laughlin.

She burst into tears. Before the doctors calmed her with valerian, she had time to request that she be allowed to see Annie and her spiritual adviser, Father Walter. She had asked for him before, though without success, but surely now he would be allowed to come. She was a Catholic. They had no right to condemn her to die unshriven.

The Commission made note of her request, and then moved on to the other cells.

Herold was to die.

Atzerodt was to die.

Payne was to die.

It was what Payne wanted, but even he was shaken by the haste with which he was to be shuffled off. He sent for Captain Rath. He wanted to attest to Mrs. Surratt's innocence again. The woman must not be hanged. That was all he cared about any more.

The Commission stopped before Spangler's cell. He was virtually exonerated. Someone had testified to having seen two men conspiring in front of Ford's Theatre, the one

Booth, the other a man with a moustache who resembled Spangler. But Spangler had never worn a moustache. Not even the prosecution could prove that he had. So he was innocent. He would not hang. He had only to serve at hard labour for six years.

Dr. Mudd received hard labour for life. So did Arnold and O'Laughlin. The Commission had shown its clemency in the case of Spangler. That was enough.

It was not enough, however, for Stanton. Johnson had foolishly assigned the men to Albany Penitentiary, in New York State, where anyone might speak to them, and who was to know what they might say? New York State had been disloyal during the war. Its Governor had defied Stanton himself. Let them therefore be transferred to the Dry Tortugas.

He forced Johnson to sign the transfer. Perhaps they would catch the yellow fever there, and so die. The Dry Tortugas were notorious. They were dry only in the sense that they were not under water, and Fort Jackson was the toughest, and least healthy of all the Federal prisons. A red brick fort, surrounded by a moat, it sat in the bright shark infested sea off Florida, unvisited and ominous. No one had ever escaped from there. No news came from there. If a prisoner tried to escape, the sharks would get him, even if the guards did not.

Mudd quailed when he heard the news. As he told his jailers, he was a gentleman. He could not survive in such a place.

Stanton heartily hoped he would not. Meanwhile there was this meddlesome fool, Walter, to be dealt with. Mrs. Surratt had sent for him. He was a priest. He would have to be bottled.

Stanton bottled him. A Protestant himself, he was at least the equal to a Catholic priest.

Mrs. Surratt did not know Father Walter, except by repute. She had first sent for him on the 23rd of April, before the trial had begun. He had not been allowed to attend her then. He did not intend to be prevented from seeing her now.

228

He was an absurd looking person. He had a flat white face, an enormous nose, wore his hair long, and beamed at the world from behind chunky spectacles. He looked more like Hans Christian Andersen than a real person. But though people often found him tedious, no one had ever called him dishonest. He was not a political priest. He was not a famous orator. In fact, he could scarcely deliver a sermon at all. But he did believe in his vocation. He scarcely knew who Mrs. Surratt was, but since she had called for his help, he would not let her go to the scaffold unshriven. As soon as he had received her request, he asked the War Department for a pass, so he might visit her. A messenger brought him one. He told the messenger he believed her innocent, and prepared to go to the prison.

He did not get there. An hour later Hardie, one of Stanton's men, called on him to say that the pass was invalid unless countersigned by Stanton.

Father Walter did not understand.

Hardie explained. Walter must promise to say no more about Mrs. Surratt's innocence. Only then might he receive the necessary pass.

Walter was indignant. What right had the Government to deny Mrs. Surratt the rights of her religion? He told Hardie he would say what he believed to be true.

Hardie looked embarrassed. He said that as yet there were no charges lodged against Walter at the War Department.

Walter lost his temper. He said he would proclaim the woman's innocence, and the War Department could hang him if it thought proper. Hardie turned to leave. There was an overweaning cringe about the man Walter did not care for, but he could not allow him to leave. Scruples or no, it was his duty to give the woman what comfort he could. He said he would agree to the conditions.

Even so, he was not allowed into the prison until the morning of Mrs. Surratt's execution. In the meantime, one of Stanton's men was sent to Bishop Spaulding of Baltimore, to urge that silence be enjoined upon Walter. Spaulding had to agree. He also believed Mrs. Surratt to be innocent, but like Walter, he did not see why, on that account, she should be denied extreme unction and the solace of confession. He wrote to Walter, as Stanton directed, but he refused to make his advice an order. He made the condition a suggestion and a request, nothing more.

Stanton did not care about that. He had bottled Walter. Walter did not care either. It was his duty to save the woman's soul, and that he had succeeded in doing. As for damning the Government, that could wait.

XLVII

The morning of the execution indicated a hot, windless, and suffocating day. It was scarcely dawn, the prisoners were not to be killed until one, and yet the crowd was already assembling outside the prison walls, and, for those privileged actually to gain admittance to the spectacle, inside. After all, in the history of the country so far this was to be a unique event.

Payne was still trying to exonerate Mrs. Surratt. He had sent his statement to General Hartranft, the Provost Marshal in charge of the execution, who believed him, soothed him, but could do nothing.

Herold was surrounded by his sisters. He had wept ever since his sentence had been read to him. Now his sisters wept. In their best dresses, black, and with long trailing skirts, they clustered around him, all seven of them. Rath, the executioner, found the sight an affecting one. They wept, but they did not seem to have much to say. What was there to say?

Atzerodt and Payne had no visitors.

Atzerodt's conduct was disgusting. Since he did not believe in God, he had no one to appeal to, so prayer meant nothing to him. He could only kneel, as though at a block, and shriek, "Oh, oh, oh." It was a demeaning sight.

Payne was, as usual, stolid.

As for Mrs. Surratt, she was three-fourths dead, and drugged with valerian. She asked a Mr. Brophy, a friend of the family who had managed to get in to see her, to try, at some future time, when the passions of the war were cooled, to clear her name. He promised to do so.

The interview with Annie was worse. What can one say, when one will never be able to speak again? Once Annie had gone, Mrs. Surratt wrote a note to Mrs. Holahan to ask that good woman to stay with Annie during the execution. Poor Annie, what would she do now?

Then she sent for Father Walter. It was time for her confession. She had been moved down to a condemned cell. Father Walter found her on a pallet on the floor. He heard her confession, and found her innocent as a babe unborn, or so he said. Later he was to put the matter even more strongly: there was not enough evidence against her to hang a cat.

But you do not need evidence to hang a cat.

Atzerodt asked to know if there was no hope.

At eleven twenty-five Rath filled a bag with shot to test the efficacy of the drops. He did not like what he was doing. He was so sure Mrs. Surratt would get a last minute reprieve, that he had tied only five knots in her noose, instead of the customary six. And yet the reprieve did not come.

It was noon. The crowd was restless. It did not like to be kept waiting for its death.

A chair was placed outside Mrs. Surratt's cell, on which she sat. Neither was it kind to keep the prisoners waiting for theirs.

At fifteen minutes after one the procession formed. Mrs. Surratt, in black, walked between her priests. The last time she had seen this yard was when she had walked in it with Annie. It had been deserted then. Now its red brick wall was lined with Union soldiers, their fatigue caps at jaunty angles. She could not see their faces, but their bodies were lean and negligent. Three men on the left end of the wall sat with their legs over the parapet. As she entered the yard they scrambled to their feet. Except for a trivial accident of birth, John might have stood among them.

The yard was rank with grass. Summer had turned it yellow. Against the wall one or two ladders lay on their sides. A guard of soldiers faced the scaffold. The scaffold itself was raw yellow pine, oozing at the pores. More than anything else, it resembled a hall settle with the cane back removed, so one might see the ropes.

To the left stood an annex to the main prison, green shuttered, but with some of its windows open to the scaffold.

232

The spectators huddled under that, some in black frock coats and some in white, with white dusters and white caps on their heads. A few carried bumbershoots, because of the heat. The bumbershoots were made of black silk. These were privileged people, or at the least, members of the press, and impatient with her for being late.

She was herself privileged. Being a woman, she too had her umbrella.

The walk to the scaffold was brief. As she approached, the soldiers gave way. Atzerodt and Herold went snivelling ahead of her. Apparently the prison doctor had omitted to give them a sedative. Overhead the sky was taut enough to crack or splinter. In colour it was a porcellaneous blue. Payne also went ahead of her. That giant did not walk. He processed. From time to time he would halt to look around at the spectators. He was a proud man, and pride steadies the nerves. He seemed calm. It was a shame that, except for his guards, he should have to walk alone.

Though half the spectators had come here for thrills, that did not mean that they were willing to watch. They fidgeted. The condemned reached the bottom of the scaffold and began to mount. The thick boards of the platform were unplaned and unevenly laid, and rattled beneath their feet. There were two chairs to the left, and two to the right. You could see the join of the drop, where its boards did not quite match those of the flooring. From above, the spectators looked trivial, anxious, and silly. It was not how she would have chosen to see the last of the world. She looked at the blank, uncurtained windows of the prison and scarcely noticed them.

Someone held her umbrella over her head. General Hartranft read the death warrant. A door opened at the bottom of the yard, and General Hancock appeared. He had give up all hope of reprieve. It was one thirty. He ordered the executioner to proceed.

"Her too?" asked Rath.

Hancock frowned and said she could not be saved.

Rath looked at the tie beam. She was not a heavy woman. Five knots should hold her.

233

His assistants began to bind her dress around her, so it would not billow immodestly as she dropped, and so she would not struggle. She asked Father Walter if she might not once more state her innocence. Father Walter said no. The world and all that was in it had now receded forever. It would do no good to protest, and it might disturb her serenity. She did not ask what serenity, but what else could he say? The white cloth covering was put over her head. Her chair was drawn back. Her umbrella was clicked down. The soldiers beneath the scaffold knocked out the beams supporting the trap.

The bodies dropped. The ropes gave an ugly twang. Payne, being the heaviest, died first. His own strength snapped his neck. For the others, death took a moment longer. One can think of a great deal in a moment.

At sixteen minutes before two the prison doctor pronounced them dead. Ten minutes later they were cut down, put in packing boxes, and buried a few feet south of the scaffold, near the prison wall. The earth over them made a fresh, wet wound. The spectators drifted away.

For Mrs. Surratt it was over.

Part Four

XLVIII

For Edwin it was not. On 3rd January 1866, he returned to the stage.

It was too soon. He still wanted to hide. But he had no choice, he needed money, and only by acting could he provide for Edwina, Mary Ann, and Rosalie. So he faced up to it. That took courage, for not even his friends had foreseen the assaults levelled against him by the gutter press. "Is the Assassination of Caesar to be Performed?" raved the *New York World*, needlessly, since the bill was to be *Hamlet*. "Will Edwin Booth appear as the Assassin of Caesar? That would be, perhaps, the most suitable character." Other newspapers took up his defence. "The Winter Garden will be thronged tonight as it has rarely been," they promised.

And so it was.

He tried not to think of the crowd out there. He thought of his performance instead. There were more police in the audience than usual. A riot was expected, for the audience was less an assembly than a mob. And yet Edwin did not feel nervous. Once on a stage, and he knew what to do. It was only off it that he felt at a loss.

Hamlet was his play. In it he was dark, mysterious, afflicted, melancholy, or so the critics said. Perhaps. He had played it in the Gold Fields of California, as a promise to his father. He had played it for a hundred nights in New York, closing less than a month before the death of the President. As Wilkes had said, he was Hamlet, melancholy and all.

Wilkes's boast had been, *I am myself alone*, and the whole world now knew what that had led to. But Edwin had not wanted to be himself alone. He had wanted some part in the world. He had wanted company in this busy loneliness of life. His efforts had come to nothing. His family existed only on a stage. Turn where he would, eventually he had to climb back into that gaslit parable. It was true. He *was* Hamlet. And whatever we may think of Hamlet, he is not a clubbable man. He is not someone we would ask to dinner. So Edwin was the first to establish that Hamlet should always wear black. In a suit of sables, having lost spontaneous laughter, like Hamlet himself, he could at least be jesting gay.

Yet now he shrank from his customary staging of the piece. He would not be himself alone. He wanted to be sheltered in some family, since he could no longer take shelter in his own, even if it be only the stage family of Elsinore.

The curtain went up on the first scene. Marcellus, Bernardo, Horatio, and the Ghost. "*Thou art a scholar; speak to it, Horatio.*" "*It started like a guilty thing upon a fearful summons.*" "*Let us impart what we have seen tonight unto young Hamlet.*" And, "*I this morning know where we shall find him most conveniently.*"

The curtain dropped. The audience was restless. Perhaps it was as nervous as Edwin, for it too had its part to play to-tonight, and perhaps had not yet decided upon the interpretation.

He had. It had been forced upon him willynilly. One learns from what one does. A parable shows one what one is. It is inevitable, but each time we experience it, the times have changed, we have changed, and so also changes the meaning of the parable itself. Such is the malice of events. The whole world is a parable. To act it out, is only to play it for one's self. Old age releases one from parts of which one is tired. From Romeo one progresses to Richelieu. But *Hamlet* has no age. One has to play it forever. One has to play it to the grave, *a little little grave, an obscure grave.* When one has played it enough, no doubt that is all one any longer wants.

And yet he was excited. What would the audience do to him?

He walked from his dressing-room. The actors made way for him with a curiously disconcerted silence, as though he were not a fellow actor, but some priest on his way to the altar, to offer up the rites. That was not their usual be-

238

haviour. Usually they jabbered until it was time for them to play their parts.

He took his seat. For an instant they looked at the heavy back of the curtain, as though not knowing what was on the other side of it. It was a world that was about to be unveiled for them, out there, and perhaps they did not want to see its expression. The audience was ominously quiet.

The guy ropes tugged and grew taut. So did the actors. The King turned to mime a conversation with the Queen, the others fell into their familiar supporting attitudes, and the curtain rose.

There was no applause. Out of the corners of their eyes, they could see that shapeless heaving mass of black and blobs of coloured dresses, beyond the footlights, waiting. There was nothing to do but go on.

Usually in this scene they walked on after the curtain was up, or at least while it was rising. They did not like the new stage business of being imprisoned in their chairs. And they missed, too, that usual flourish of trumpets which broke the silence and sent them on their way.

The King began:

> *"Though yet of Hamlet our dear brother's death*
> *The memory be green, and that it us befitted*
> *To bear our hearts in grief and our whole kingdom*
> *To be contracted in one brow of woe,*
> *Yet so far hath discretion fought with nature,"*

he said to that void out there, and could not help but stumble. He might as well have been speaking of Lincoln. Why was it so quiet out there? What was the audience doing?

The audience had been taken by surprise. They were used to a Hamlet who posed decoratively upstage, in front of the rest of the company. At first they could not find him. The players were brilliantly dressed. Then they saw Edwin, black amid all that dazzle, sitting in a heavily carved curule chair, his small figure and wasted calves huddled there, waiting. In the utter silence of that face only the eyes burned.

Again the King faltered. The players had seen that figure, too.

The audience did not move. And then something happened. The players could feel it in the instant before it came, and glanced quickly at each other. The audience rose, almost in unison, and began to cheer. From gallery to pit the house was white with waving handkerchiefs.

"Three groans for *The New York World*," somebody shouted. Three hollow boos went echoing through the house, but even while they booed, they went on clapping. That tidal noise swept over the stage in waves.

Edwin began to tremble. His head dropped on to his breast. He could not help it. The tears welled down his cheeks. Slowly he rose and walked upstage, towards the audience, until he was alone. And then, looking out over that sea of hands, he made his bow.

The audience sat down. The play went on. Ophelia died. Laertes died. The Queen and King died. And then it was Hamlet's turn to die.

There's a special providence in the fall of a sparrow. If it be now, 'tis not to come; if it be not to come, it will be now; if it be not now, yet it will come: the readiness is all.

They were Edwin's favourite lines. They were his philosophy and his Hamlet too. Hamlet died. The empty world was left to Fortinbras, who though he went through the proper forms, was not loath to claim it. Do what we will, in the end it is all the same. The world belongs to Fortinbras.

But the audience would not soon forget the expression in those anguished eyes.

He was back. He was the glory of their stage. They told him so. Yet somehow it was not the same Edwin who was back. In '57, in the Gold Fields, he had been vivacious. And now, it was hard to define, but as one of his fellow actors said, what a change. Somehow he had become uncomfortably moving.

On 22nd January 1867, a year after his return, the stage scenery was sent up to the flies, a dining-room table was moved in, the stage became a drawing-room, and a committee presented him with a Tiffany Gold Medal for the hundred nights of his first great *Hamlet*. They had meant to do that before, but the assassination had intervened. However, that was over with now, and they were proud of him, those businessmen who gave him the medal. He was the palladium of the American arts, those arts they had no time for, and regarded with suspicion. But Edwin was an exception. Not only was he admired by the best critics, he made forty or fifty thousand dollars a year. The arts might degenerate below the level of a trade, as he said, but no tradesman makes that much money. Therefore what he did must be art. Besides, he moved them. There was something gentle in Edwin, and at the same time something enormously strong, which made him acceptable. Perhaps it was dignity. Or perhaps it was that he was a sort of talisman, that he had to live with something that they knew they should remember, and yet, being human and every day, quite sensibly forgot. He was a tragedian. He did their suffering for them. And since he kept quiet about it while he did so, they loved him none the less for that.

And yet, he was changed.

XLIX

So was the country. The Civil War had made it an Imperium. Perhaps even Lincoln could not have checked that monstrous growth, but though the country, which had once seemed so spacious, now merely seemed complex, there was no longer any place in it, as far as Edwin could see, for anything he believed in, and as time went on, others, no doubt, would also find less and less. The movement to Europe had begun. The young, when they had something to do or say, went there. That did not make them any the less American, but somehow it made America the less. He even went himself, twice to England, and once to Germany. He felt lost everywhere. He was no political thinker, but he could not help but notice things. People now said servants, where formerly they had been content to chatter away with the hired help. And it seemed to him that everything had been taken away from him. That was why he was so afraid for Edwina. Because he had nothing else left to lose, he had an irrational terror that she might be taken, too.

Yet alone of that family, he was afflicted with self-control. Nothing of what he felt showed outwardly. It was just that he became very quiet, and that his burning eyes watched everything, for no matter what we become, we still look out at the world from the snug corner of what we once were. He wanted only to be left in peace, and to forget.

Mary Ann would not let him. Life had addled her. She was sixty-five. Wilkes had been her favourite son. If she could not have him, she could at least have his body. The assassination meant nothing to her, Wilkes everything. Edwin was no substitute for Wilkes, but he always saw to things. Would he see if he could get the body back?

He sighed, but he did so. He always did what she asked, if only because they had nothing in common. He wrote to

Stanton, got no answer, wrote to Grant, failed again, and at last appealed to President Johnson.

Johnson was going out of office, wished to leave a good record, had never approved of Stanton's tactics, and was pleased, as one of his last official acts, to affront the man. Besides, there had been another trial, of John Surratt this time, who had finally been apprehended. The trial proved Lloyd a liar, Weichmann a complacent perjuror, the Government venal, Surratt an irresponsible fool, Stanton a megalomaniac, Mrs. Surratt falsely hanged, and what was even worse, it brought the suppressed clemency plea to light. Johnson would not be tarred with that brush. He sacked both Holt and Stanton.

Stanton refused to leave. He barricaded himself in the War Department, intrigued with Congress, got his position back, and to keep it, tried to have Johnson impeached. The effort failed. Johnson was not a politician for nothing, and he could outmanœuvre Stanton any day. There was nothing for Stanton to do but leave. He could not see that he had done anything wrong, and if others said so, they lied. He was a good Christian and a good hater. Lincoln, perhaps, he had hated most of all. But he had enjoyed to fight him, for Lincoln had been an opponent worth the tricking, since he was hard to trick. But what did it all matter? He was out of office. There was nothing to do but die.

Johnson pardoned the conspirators. O'Laughlin had died of yellow fever at the Dry Tortugas, but the others went free. And he released Wilkes' body, and his theatrical trunk, which the War Department had taken from the National Hotel and impounded. He made only one condition. The man's grave must go unmarked. He would not have that man commemorated.

Neither would Edwin. Asia had just published a memoir of their father. It was an untruthful little idyll. She concealed the elder Booth's drunkenness, his madness, and his bigamy. Their grandfather she presented as a picturesque old gentle-man, tall, slender, dressed in knee breeches, and with snow-white hair braided in a queue. She made no mention of his stalking them at night, with naked feet, his long toenails clacking on the deal floors. Wilkes she referred to as "his well-beloved—his bright boy Absalom". How could she believe such nonsense? Why did she have to bank these fires? Why couldn't she let them go out? She wrote from England, where Sleeper Clarke had taken her. But he was here.

And now there was the painful mummery of the funeral to live through. The body was exhumed and taken to an undertaking parlour in Baltimore. It had been wrapped in an old army blanket. The body was well preserved, but began to fall away as soon as air hit it. Mary Ann had her look. She had seen death often enough before, and then of course, what she saw and what she wanted to remember having seen were two different things. Still, when a Miss Chapman, an actress who was there, asked for a lock of the glossy black hair, Mary Ann gave her a radiantly grateful smile. Edwin was so stern.

The body was buried in Greenmount Cemetery on 26th June. The day was gloomy. There were a few friends, and the casket, an expensive one, was borne by some actors, perhaps more as a favour to Edwin than anything else. A clergyman said what he could. And then it was over with, at least Edwin hoped so. He wanted it all dead, buried, or destroyed. If he could do that himself, he would.

But it was 1873 before he could bring himself to burn Wilkes's theatrical trunk. One by one he stuffed the costumes into a fire in the basement furnace, a Hamlet hauberk, Mark Antony's toga, a robe of Indian shawls, used in *Othello*, all initialled JWB, but there was no costume for that last role. That costume had been buried with him.

The last clothing to come out of the trunk was a purple velvet tunic. Edwin sat down on the edge of the trunk and wept. He could not help it. His father had worn it in Boston, the first night Edwin had appeared with him on a public stage.

The boy with him asked if he shouldn't keep it.

"No," said Edwin. "Put it in with the others." The light

244

was getting stronger. It must be almost dawn. Edwin told the boy to chop up the trunk, and then watched it burn.

"That's all," he said, "we'll go now," in that still, throbbing, quiet voice of his. In the face of any personal emotion, Edwin always froze like a hunted hare.

But of course it was not all. It went on and on.

He made a grand tour of the South. He was a curiosity down there: he was John Wilkes's brother. In Mobile he received a request for free tickets from a man named Boston Corbett, Sergeant Boston Corbett.

"I am sure," Corbett wrote, "that you will not refuse, when I tell you that I am the United States soldier who shot and killed your brother."

Edwin sent the tickets. What else could he do? He was not an actor down there, but a raree-show. He moved on. Asia wanted him to come to London. Her husband, she said, would not even speak to her. "It is marvellous how he hates me, the mother of his babies, but I am a *Booth*, that is sufficient. I call myself the secret ladder that he mounted by." She did not want to live. "I shall bless God when my hour comes to relieve me from the thralldom."

He had always been fond of Asia, but England was not possible just yet. He went to Chicago instead. He played *Richard II* there. That was one of Wilkes's old roles, but Edwin played it differently, for he understood it better. He sat in a chair, in his cell at Pomfret, to recite the last great speech of the play:

> "*I have been studying how I may compare
> This prison where I live unto the world;
> And for because the world is populous,
> And here is not a creature but myself,
> I cannot do it.*"

The stage was dark, except for one calcium flare on Edwin. Always he played this scene in the same habitual posture. But it was true. He could not do it. There was not a creature but himself. He shifted his position.

A young man stood up in the audience and shot at him.

He was a demented dry goods clerk named Mark Gray.

245

The shot meant nothing. But the newspapers hauled the whole sorry story of the Booths and John Wilkes up again. In London, Clarke was furious, wrote Asia. Edwin was safe. "He dwells upon that. Not *touched*, not *hurt*, as if it was a great pity to have escaped. The Booths got all the notoriety without *suffering*!! Look at me! I was *dragged* to jail by the neck. Literally *dragged* to prison, and Edwin goes scot free —gets all the fame, sympathy. Who thinks of what *I* endured?"

"Without *suffering*," read Edwin. They had all played together as children, Sleepy Clarke, Asia, himself, before he had been put out at fourteen to work his life away. And now it came to this.

Irony is as good a substitute for laughter as any other. He had the bullet dug out of the scenery and mounted on a gold cartridge cap for his watch chain, with an inscription: From Mark Gray to Edwin Booth. And he made up his quarrel with his old friend Barrett, though it was Barrett's quarrel, not his. Barrett was someone from the past. It was agreeable to know a few old friends from the past. Then he went to England, taking Edwina with him.

There he had Christmas dinner with the Clarkes. Edwin did not take everything Asia reported about Clarke's private vendetta seriously. He enjoyed himself. Yet it could not be denied that Clarke occupied rooms in that house deliberately separate from those of his wife and children, to which he pointedly and publicly retired, once the social civilities were over with. It seemed impossible to believe that he had ever excelled in low comedy. He was a theatre manager now. That was good for his pride, no doubt, but Edwin rather missed Toodles.

One night, as he was leaving the stage door of the theatre where he was playing, and had just settled in his carriage, gazing at the pea soup fog outside, a face loomed up at the window, young, black haired, with black eyes, and mouthing at him.

Edwin leaned forward to roll down the window. "Wilkes," he called. "For God's sake, Wilkes." By the time he had got the window down, the face had disappeared. He leaned back in the cushions and let the fog pour over him. He closed his eyes. The horse jogged on into the mist. But it took him a while to get over that apparition. It was enough to have to live with ghosts, without having to see them as well.

The apparition was a Lieutenant William C. Allen, who had always been thought a ringer for Wilkes. Allen and some friends had gone to see Edwin perform, and had enjoyed the performance so much that they had decided to play a little trick on him afterwards, out of pure animal high spirits. Edwin was not such an animal. He covered his face with his hands.

There had to be an end to it somewhere.

But when Garfield was assassinated, the whole matter came out once more. For solace he went to Shakespeare. He had to go somewhere.

> *Nor I, nor any man that but man is,*
> *With nothing shall be pleas'd, till he be eas'd*
> *With being nothing.*

What other ease was there? Mary Ann had died at last. He went to Germany, with Edwina, their last trip together, before her marriage.

The tour was a triumph. At home, this horrible business would never be buried, but in Germany it was different. They remembered not his family, there, for once, but him. He acted in English, the other members of the cast in German. That made it difficult for him to pick up his cues. The Germans like loud and declamatory noises. His own manner, as the years had gone by, had become more and more quiet, until now he acted most intensely when he was most intensely still. The audience was also still. How could they make anything of it, if they could not understand what he was saying?

They could not understand the words, but they understood what he was saying well enough. What he was saying had nothing to do with words. He spoke through them, for the talents of a virtuoso exist neither in himself nor in his medium. They exist in what the world has done to him, that he should be able so selflessly to show what this which has

247

been done means. The play was *Hamlet*. Who cares for the slings and arrows of outrageous fortune, if they have no meaning? But for him they had a meaning. It was a concerto his audience was listening to, for voice. Sometimes that solo instrument rose above the accompaniment, and sometimes it sank below it, but always the solo instrument performed the invisible in the visible rite, and so transubstantiated the word.

"You can understand him perfectly, even though you may not know a single word of what he utters," said the *Tägliche Berliner Rundschau.*

It was true enough. Germans understand such things. When he had done, they wept. "This Hamlet was not played, but *lived*," said the *Berliner Fremdenblatt.* And so it was. The Germans love what makes an American or an Englishman uneasy, which is to say, a scapegoat. They pulled his carriage in triumph through the streets. They are a devout people. They can never have enough of such a mass.

But Shakespeare would have us individual and human, too.

At a reception in Hamburg the women in the audience formed a double line on the stage. He had to kiss hands. He did not care for that. He swayed mechanically towards the last extended, bent over, and pursed his lips.

"I am an American," she said.

And hearing that fresh voice, he said, "Oh, I beg your pardon, and thank you so very much."

He meant it. Though his Hamlet might be lived, it was not the role in life he would have chosen to play. He had had enough of tragedy.

And then he lost Edwina, not by death, as he had always feared, but marriage. He did not know what he would do without her, but he was glad to see her happy. To see her happy was the only purpose his life any longer had. "You must think of me as not at all lonesome," he wrote her.

But he was lonesome. The house at 29 Chestnut Street, in

Boston, seemed endlessly empty. It was an old house, with purple panes in the windows to prove it. Sometimes he was allowed to visit Edwina. He knew she loved him. But she had a husband, a life, and children of her own. He could not visit them all the time.

At the house at Newport he had built for Edwina years ago and given her on her marriage, he had had a little Norman tower built on the shore. When he was out sailing his yacht, late in the afternoon, Edwina would mount the tower and put out a lantern to guide him home. That was over with now. He sold the yacht.

His only family now was what his family had always been, the stage. But life had worn him out. He could not go on acting much longer. So he founded the Players Club, in Gramercy Park, and retired there, to the third floor of it.

"I used to enjoy acting comedy," he told a man who had come to interview him. "Especially farce. Oh, I went through it all. I went through it all."

Indeed he had. It had been time to retire.

One day at the club, Richard Harding Davis, a new member, tactless and brash, but you could not blame him for that, said he had an interesting relic he would like to present to the club, a playbill used at Ford's Theatre, in Washington, on the night Lincoln was . . .

Well, these things could not be avoided. Booth went up to his rooms on the third floor. When he went, he saw Barrett's death mask staring at him, from the centre table. The man had only died a few days before, and the messenger had left it there by mistake, instead of in the library downstairs. Edwin did not like the look of it. He had it removed. But with Barrett gone, and Edwina married, he was lonelier than ever, even in his own club. That's why he left Barrett's aeolian harp in place.

Sometimes he went for a short stroll around the square. He always dined downstairs in the restaurant. He talked with the members. Edwina came to see him. But mostly he sat in his room. The club was stuffed with memorabilia, from the Sargent portrait over the mantelpiece of the main room, to old costumes in cases along the walls. If he cared to

249

look up, he could see himself in all roles and at all ages. But he did not often care to do so. There were pictures of his brothers, and of his father, too. But none of Wilkes.

The picture of Wilkes was upstairs, in his own rooms.

Epilogue

He sat there now, a frail old man with a long face, a sensitive mouth, balding straggly hair, strong hands, and those firm eyes. The harp was silent, but from downstairs he could hear the click of balls, from time to time, in the billiard room. The sound raised a faint memory, but he did not know of what. Some dream, perhaps.

He would die soon, he supposed, but that did not much bother him. What did bother him was the manuscript of that play by Miss Althea Lathrop Lee, *The Judges of the Secret Court*. He would have to tell her something, but what?

He had gone through life with this sense of guilt, but now he saw that it was not guilt after all. For what did life mean? What had the assassination meant? Both were meaningless, to Wilkes, at any rate; for it is the bystander who has to live with the crime, not the criminal. When criminals are caught, they die. It is the rest of us who have to go on living with what they have done, with what life has done, with what the world does, with what has been done to us.

No, there was no guilt in this world, yet somehow life makes us culpable. That is the meaning of the Judges of the Secret Court. No matter what we do, they are always there. And though one is seldom apprehended, one does not get off so easily, in this world which runs after Fortinbras, and so belongs to him. Why be Hamlet, when the whole world runs after Fortinbras? He had outlived his time.

On the wall beside his bed hung a portrait of Johnny. It always had. "*I am myself alone.*" "*Why I can smile, and murder whiles I smile, and cry 'Content!' to that which grieves my heart, and frame my face to all occasions.*" "*Conscience avaunt! Richard's himself again.*" But that was Cibber, not Shakespeare. And Johnny would never be himself again. Nor would any of them be.

253

Yet we defy augury. He preferred his own lines. Even as a child, he had felt their definition, though he had not then known why. Shakespeare turned a better jest than ever Dante and Byron knew.

If it be now, 'tis not to come; if it be not to come, it will be now; if it be not now, yet it will come: the readiness is all.

And so it was. Yet what special providence was there in Wilkes, who had snared them all? What providence in Asia, Sleeper Clarke, Mrs. Surratt, Mary Ann, Dr. Mudd, himself; in Mary Todd, that other Mary, his first wife, who had died so soon, or in Lincoln? What providence was there in Johnson, Stanton, Spangler, Arnold, Payne, or John Surratt? All of them, and so many deaths. He could see none. They had merely been caught before their time. Hence the Judges of the Secret Court. He began to perceive that he owed Miss Althea Lathrop Lee a good deal. Her play might be twaddle, but she had given him his explication.

And yet, before him, somehow, he seemed to see Mr. Lincoln's slow, sad, warm, and understanding smile. Death, too, had made him a judge, and yet he smiled.

So Edwin smiled, too. Everybody knows Tom Fool.

It was Julia Ward Howe who once asked Charles Sumner if he had heard of young Booth yet.

"Why no, Madam," said Sumner. "I long since ceased to take any interest in individuals."

"You have made great progress, sir," Julia told him. "God has not yet gone so far—at least according to the last accounts."

Tucson
November 1959*–April* 1960

OTHER NEW YORK REVIEW CLASSICS*

J.R. ACKERLEY My Dog Tulip
J.R. ACKERLEY We Think the World of You
HENRY ADAMS The Jeffersonian Transformation
WILLIAM ATTAWAY Blood on the Forge
W.H. AUDEN (EDITOR) The Living Thoughts of Kierkegaard
W.H. AUDEN W.H. Auden's Book of Light Verse
ERICH AUERBACH Dante: Poet of the Secular World
DOROTHY BAKER Cassandra at the Wedding
J.A. BAKER The Peregrine
HONORÉ DE BALZAC The Unknown Masterpiece *and* Gambara
STEPHEN BENATAR Wish Her Safe at Home
FRANS G. BENGTSSON The Long Ships
ALEXANDER BERKMAN Prison Memoirs of an Anarchist
ADOLFO BIOY CASARES The Invention of Morel
CAROLINE BLACKWOOD Corrigan
NICOLAS BOUVIER The Way of the World
MALCOLM BRALY On the Yard
MILLEN BRAND The Outward Room
JOHN HORNE BURNS The Gallery
ROBERT BURTON The Anatomy of Melancholy
CAMARA LAYE The Radiance of the King
DON CARPENTER Hard Rain Falling
J.L. CARR A Month in the Country
EILEEN CHANG Love in a Fallen City
UPAMANYU CHATTERJEE English, August: An Indian Story
ANTON CHEKHOV Peasants and Other Stories
RICHARD COBB Paris and Elsewhere
COLETTE The Pure and the Impure
JOHN COLLIER Fancies and Goodnights
CARLO COLLODI The Adventures of Pinocchio
IVY COMPTON-BURNETT A House and Its Head
IVY COMPTON-BURNETT Manservant and Maidservant
BARBARA COMYNS The Vet's Daughter
EVAN S. CONNELL The Diary of a Rapist
ALBERT COSSERY The Jokers
HAROLD CRUSE The Crisis of the Negro Intellectual
ASTOLPHE DE CUSTINE Letters from Russia
LORENZO DA PONTE Memoirs
ELIZABETH DAVID A Book of Mediterranean Food
ELIZABETH DAVID Summer Cooking
L.J. DAVIS A Meaningful Life
VIVANT DENON No Tomorrow/Point de lendemain
TIBOR DÉRY Niki: The Story of a Dog
ARTHUR CONAN DOYLE The Exploits and Adventures of Brigadier Gerard
CHARLES DUFF A Handbook on Hanging
BRUCE DUFFY The World As I Found It
DAPHNE DU MAURIER Don't Look Now: Stories
ELAINE DUNDY The Dud Avocado
ELAINE DUNDY The Old Man and Me

* *For a complete list of titles, visit www.nyrb.com or write to:*
Catalog Requests, NYRB, 435 Hudson Street, New York, NY 10014